In the beginning, in his first minutes of being held captive by the damned machine, Lars Kanakuru had cursed its metallic guts for keeping him alive. The damned berserker machine ignored his curses, though he was sure it heard them, even as it had seemed to ignore the missile he had launched at it from his small oneseater spacecraft. Lars never saw what happened to the missile. But he had seen on his instruments how the damned berserker had extended forcefield arms, reaching out many kilometers for his little ship, and he saw and felt how it pulled him into the embrace of death.

BY

☆ POUL ANDERSON ☆ EDWARD BRYANT ☆
☆ STEPHEN R. DONALDSON ☆
☆ LARRY NIVEN ☆ FRED SABERHAGEN ☆
☆ CONNIE WILLIS ☆ ROGER ZELAZNY ☆

A TOM DOHERTY ASSOCIATES BOOK

This is a work of fiction. All the characters and events portrayed in this book are fictional, and any resemblance to real people or incidents is purely coincidental.

BERSERKER BASE

A TOR Book

Published by Tom Doherty Associates
8-10 West 36 Street
New York, N.Y. 10018

First TOR printing: March 1985

ISBN: 0-812-55316-0
CAN. ED.: 0-812-55317-9

Printed in the United States of America

BERSERKER
BASE

CONTENTS

Prisoners' Base

In the beginning, in his first minutes of being held captive by the damned machine, Lars Kanakuru had cursed its metallic guts for keeping him alive. The damned berserker machine ignored his curses, though he was sure it heard them, even as it had seemed to ignore the missile he had launched at it from his small oneseater spacecraft. Lars never saw what happened to the missile. But he had seen on his instruments how the damned berserker had extended forcefield arms, reaching out many kilometers for his little ship, and he saw and felt how it pulled him into the embrace of death.

Not to quick death. He was not going to be that lucky. Suicide attacks by fanatical humans were perhaps not unknown in this berserker machine's experience, but they must be at least sufficiently rare for it to find their perpetrators interesting. It had evidently decided that he ought to be studied.

Lars had no sidearm with him in the tiny cabin of his

oneseater, nothing that he could use to quickly kill himself. And before he could use the materials on hand to improvise a way to do the job, some kind of gas was being injected into the cabin of his fighter, hissing into his breathing air, and he lost consciousness . . .

When his senses returned to him he was no longer inside his fighter ship. Now, with his head aching, he was stretched out on a hard, unfamiliar deck, enclosed in a small, windowless, and apparently doorless cell. Light, faint and reddish, came from somewhere above, and warmed air hissed faintly around him.

He sat up. Gravity, doubtless artificial, held him with standard, Earth-normal strength. There wouldn't be quite room in the cell to stand erect. Nor room to walk, or crawl, more than a couple of meters in any direction.

Lars did not rejoice to find himself still alive. It was certain now that he was not going to be killed quickly. He was going to be studied.

At the same time, he found that the idea of suicide no longer attracted him. It had been a basically alien thought for him anyway.

So, he had been captured by a berserker machine. Others had survived the experience and had returned to human worlds to tell about it—a few others, benefiting from rare miracles of one kind or another. A very few others, a very few miracles, in all the millions of cubic light years, in all the centuries, across which the human race had had to fight its war against berserkers.

As a veteran space traveler, Lars could tell almost from the moment of his awakening that he was now in flightspace. There were certain subtle indications of motion, alterations in gravity, inward twinges to go with them. The machine that held him captive was outpacing light through realms of mathematical reality, bearing him across some section of the Galaxy, in what direction he had no way of guessing.

The human body was never really totally at home in the inhuman world of flightspace. But it had long been a familiar world to Lars Kanakuru, and to find himself in it now was, oddly, almost reassuring. There had been no prospect of help for him in the particular sector of normal space in which he had been captured. That little fragment of the Galaxy, Lars was certain, belonged to the berserkers now, along with the few planets that it held. One of which had been his home . . .

His immediate physical surroundings were such as to allow him to stay alive, no more. He took stock again, more carefully. His spacesuit had been removed, along with all the contents of his pockets. He was still dressed in the coverall and light boots he had been wearing under the spacesuit, standard combat gear of the service to which he belonged.

Lars was surrounded by dim reddish light, bound in by cramping metal or ceramic—he was not sure which—walls and floor and ceiling. There was air, of course, of breathable content and pressure, through which from time to time there passed a wave of some exotic, inorganic stench. There was, he soon discovered, a supply of water. Almost icy cold, it gushed on demand from a wall nozzle over a small hole in the deck that served as plumbing.

He thought back over the space battle, the combat mission, that had landed him in this cell. Next time he would do better. He found that he was telling himself that over and over. He couldn't seem to make himself realize that there would be no next time, not for him.

Then he thought ahead, or tried to. As a rule, berserkers killed quickly; human suffering had no intrinsic value for machines. What berserker machines were programmed to want was human nonexistence. But in his case the time for quick killing had already passed.

Then Lars tried not to think ahead, because none of the things that were known to happen to berserker prisoners were better than being quickly killed. In fact all of the other things—except, of course, the occasional miraculous rescue—were, in his opinion, considerably worse.

Think about the present, then. Lars Kanakuru decided that it was quite likely that he was the only living thing within many light years. But then it almost immediately occurred to him that that could not be exactly true. There would be a horde of microorganisms within his body, as in that of every other living human. He carried a population of a sort along. The idea gave him an odd kind of comfort.

His mental state, he supposed, was already becoming rather odd.

There was no way for him in his cruel simple cell to keep track of time. But in time—it might have been hours, or it might have been a day—he slept again, and dreamed.

In his dream Lars saw a ship's control panel before him, covered with electronic gages, and in the way of dreams he understood that this was the control panel of some new kind of fighter craft. He was happy to see this, because it meant he had escaped from the berserker. But his troubles were not over. One of the gages on the panel was a very strange one, for it seemed to be displaying pairs of rhyming words, and it was very important that Lars understand what this meant, and he could not.

The dream was not really frightening, but still it was incredibly vivid and forceful, and Lars awoke from it sweating, his hands scraping the warm smooth deck. A very odd dream.

He lay there feeling groggy and apathetic. He drank water, and would have eaten, had any food been provided. Well, he wasn't starving yet. The berserker would feed him when necessary. If it had wanted him dead, he'd be that way already. He dozed again, and awakened.

And then there came the realization that the machine that bore him was in flightspace no longer.

Presently, faintly perceptible though the masses of metal that surrounded him, came sounds and vibrations that suggested a heavy docking. He decided that the berserker that had captured him had reached its base. And that meant that soon he should know exactly what was going to happen to him.

Shortly after he felt the docking, one wall of Lars's cell opened, and a machine came in to get him. The metallic-ceramic body of the mobile unit was shaped rather like the body of an ant, and it was half as large as Lars himself. It said nothing to him, and he offered it no resistance. It brought with it a spacesuit, not his own, but one that would fit him and looked to be of human make. Doubtless the suit had been captured too, sometime, somewhere, and doubtless the man or woman who had worn it was now dead. It bore some faded-looking insignia, but in the faint red light the symbols were hard to read.

The berserker tossed the suit at his feet. Obviously it wanted him to wear the suit, not puzzle out its provenance. He could have played dumb, tried to give his captor a hard time, but he discovered that he was no longer at all anxious to find death. He put on the suit and sealed himself into it. Its air supply was full, and sweet-smelling.

Then the machine conducted him away, into airless regions outside his cell. It was not a very long journey, only a few hundred meters, but one of many twists and turnings, along pathways not designed for human travel. Most of this journey took place in reduced gravity, and Lars felt this gravity was natural. There were subtleties you could sense when you had enough experience.

At about the halfway point, his guide brought him out of the great space-going berserker that had captured him, to stand under an airless sky of stars, upon a rocky surface streaked with long shadows from a blue-white sun, and Lars saw that his feeling about the gravity had been right. He was now standing on the surface of a planet. It was all cracked rock, as far as he could see out to the near horizon, and populated by marching ghost-forms of dust, shapes raised by drifting electrical charges and not wind. Lars had seen shapes similar to those once before, on another dead world. This world was evidently a small one, to judge by the near horizon, the gravity only a fraction of Earth-standard normal, and the lack of atmosphere. The place was certainly lifeless now, and had probably been utterly devoid of life even before berserkers had arrived on it.

It looked like they had come here to stay. There was a lot of berserker construction about, towers and mineheads and nameless shapes, extending across most of what Lars could see of the lifeless landscape.

The fabrication wasn't hard to identify as to its origin, or its purpose either. What did berserkers ever build? Titanic shipyard facilities, in which to construct more of their own kind, and repair docks for the units that had suffered in battle. Lars got a good look—when he thought about it later, it seemed to him that matters were arranged deliberately by the machine so that he would be able to catch a very good look—at the power and infernal majesty surrounding him.

And then he was conducted underground, into a narrow tunnel, the faceplate of his suit freed of that blue-white solar glare.

A door closed behind him, and then another door, sealing

him into a small chamber of half-smoothed rock. Air hissed around him, and then another door ahead of him slid open. Air and sound, and a moment of realization. He was no longer alone. There were other prisoners here, his fellow humans. At the moment of realization Lars was intensely surprised, though later he was not sure why.

Human voices reached him from just ahead. Human figures, all dressed in space coveralls as he was, looked up. Gathered in a small group were four Earth-descended humans, two women and two men.

The chamber where they gathered was perhaps ten meters square, and high enough to stand in, not much more. It was barren of furnishings, and the four people were sitting on the stone floor. Three other doors, each in a different wall, led out of it. Two of the other doors were open, one was closed.

Three of the people got to their feet as Lars approached. One of the women remained sitting on the floor, in an attitude that suggested she was indifferent to anything that happened.

Lars introduced himself: "Flight Officer Lars Kanakuru, Eight Worlds Combined Forces."

"Captain Absalom Naxos, New Hebrides Strategic Defense Corps." The captain spoke quickly, as if he might be conveying urgently needed information. He was a hungry-looking, intense man, with jet black eyebrows looking almost artificial on a pallid face, and a thin black stubble of beard that appeared to be struggling to establish itself with only moderate success.

Lars said: "Glad to meet you. Wish it could be under different conditions . . ."

"Don't we all. There's no goodlife here."

The woman who had got to her feet, younger and better-looking than the other, moved a half step forward. "Pat Sandomierz. I'm just a civilian."

"Hello." Lars took the hand that she extended. In the background, coming always through the rock, was a noise of machinery, sometimes louder, sometimes faint. Lars assumed that it was coming from the berserkers' mining and manufacturing operations somewhere nearby.

Pat had truly beautiful gray-blue eyes. She said she had been taken off a passenger liner by an attacking berserker. She was sure that the crew and all the other passengers were dead.

"I'm Nicholas Opava." The second man in the group gave an immediate overall impression of softness. A naturally dark skin kept him from showing a prison pallor. He radiated hopelessness, Lars thought. Opava said he had been the sole human manning a lonely scientific outpost, from which a berserker had picked him up.

The remaining woman, Dorothy Totonac, was somewhat older than the other people, and looked withdrawn. It was Pat who gave Lars Dorothy's name; Dorothy had finally gotten to her feet, but seemed disinclined to do more than nod.

Lars asked how long the others had been here. The answer seemed to be no more than a matter of days, for any of them. A mild argument over timekeeping methods had just started, when Lars was distracted by a glance through one of the open doorways. In the adjoining room, about the same size as the one where Lars was standing, there were other living beings gathered, eight or ten of them. But they were not Earth-descended humans.

Lars reached to take Nicholas Opava by the arm. Lowering his voice automatically, he asked: "Aren't those Carmpan?" For all his spacefaring, Lars had never seen the like before. But still he recognized those squarish, leathery Carmpan bodies at first glance; almost any educated human, of any world, would do so. Pictures of the Carmpan were somewhat rare, but everyone had seen them.

Opava only nodded wearily.

"We've gotten on quite well with them," Captain Naxos put in, in his businesslike way. "Conditions being what they are, all of us locked up together, they're disposed to be comparatively sociable."

Lars stood staring at the Carmpan. He saw that something he had heard about them was correct: the shape of their bulky, angular bodies did suggest machinery. But he had never heard the Carmpan mind described as in the least mechanical.

Besides mental skills that were bizarre by Earthly standards, and sometimes awesome, the Carmpan were famed also for a general tendency to avoid contact with Earth-descended humans. But now one of the Carmpan was coming out of their room, proceeding toward them. The Carmpan's pace was a slow, rolling but not awkward walk.

"Coming to greet the newcomer, I'll bet," said Pat Sandomierz.

She was right. The thick-bodied being (two arms, two legs, and was the outer surface all scaly modified skin, or in part tight clothing? Lars couldn't tell) was heading straight for Lars. The other two men, and the two women, retreated minimally.

"It is not possible to welcome here." The voice, to Lars, sounded surprisingly clear and Earthly, though the mouth and throat that produced it were obviously from somewhere else. "But it is possible to wish you well, and that I and my fellow Carmpan do."

"Thank you. The same to you." What to say to an alien? "How were you captured?"

An armlike appendage gestured. The wide unearthly mouth shaped Earthly words with uncanny precision. "Unhappily, my friend. Unhappily." With that the Carmpan turned its back on them slowly, and got under way again, retreating to rejoin its fellows. Male or female? Lars couldn't tell. He had heard that the Carmpan themselves rarely became interested in the distinction.

"I thought they never talked to us that freely," Lars muttered, watching the retreating back.

Pat repeated in effect what Captain Naxos had already said: that the Carmpan, constrained by necessity, could be and were being good companions. And yet even the berserker had known enough to provide two rooms, realizing the necessity for a psychological separation between its two kinds of biological specimens.

Lars was ravenously hungry, and there was food of a sort available, the pink-and-green cakes that some of the rare survivors of berserker imprisonment had described. He could see the Carmpan in their room munching cakes of other colors. After Lars had eaten, his fellow prisoners pointed out to him an individual cell that he could use for sleeping, or for such privacy as was attainable. It much resembled his cell on the berserker craft, except that this one was dug out of rock, and its open doorway had no door. Each prisoner had a similar retreat, with one spare cell still remaining unoccupied. The individual cells used by the Earth-descended prisoners were all located down a little side hall from their common room.

Utterly tired, stretching out alone on the provided blanket, letting his eyes close, he felt locked somehow to the other people he had just met. It was as if he could still feel them around him even as he slept.

He dreamt again. And again encountered the mysterious control panel, and the gage, displaying rhyming words, whose meaning he could not decipher.

At the moment he awoke, Lars turned his head to one side on impulse. His line of vision passed out the open doorway of his cell and down the short hallway at an angle, into the common room. There was another doorway beyond that, the door to the Carmpan room, through which one of the Carmpan was looking at him. After a moment of eye contact, the being turned away.

Well, one of the things known about the Carmpan was their mental powers; there were the Prophets of Probability among them. There was also the demonstrated fact of extremely long-distance (though largely useless, it seemed) telepathic ability possessed by at least some Carmpan individuals, such as the Third Historian, who had also been famed for his communications with Earth. Lars would not have been astonished to learn that his vivid dream had been caused by some exercise of Carmpan mental powers. But he could think of no reason why the Carmpan should care what he dreamed, or if he dreamed at all.

Had it been some attempt to convey a message, through telepathic contact? Of course the gage-dream had first come to Lars days ago, before he arrived at this base, and before he had known that the Carmpan here existed. But that might not be an argument against true telepathy, as Lars understood what little was known by Earth-descended humans of the subject. Time, he thought, might not always be an effective barrier.

So, the dream might be a way to convey a secret message of some kind, a communication beyond the berserkers' power to intercept. On that chance, Lars decided that he would not mention the dream aloud.

The four other ED humans were all awake when Lars rejoined them in the common room. One was eating, two talking, one—Opava, this time—lounging about lethargically. Dorothy Totonac still looked sad, but this time she said hello. Lars ate some more pink-and-green cake, meanwhile exchanging a few words with his fellow prisoners.

No one else said anything to him about odd dreams. No one remarked that the berserker brain that ran this base was sure to be listening somehow to everything that they were saying, watching everything they did, but Lars was sure that everyone understood that fact. It gave him some minimal sense of power, to be able to withhold even so little as a dream from the enemy.

The conversation had not proceeded far when the same door opened through which Lars had been brought into the prisoners' complex. Several of the ant-shaped escort machines entered. None of them were carrying spacesuits. The conversation among the humans broke off, and as if at a signal all stood and faced the enemy.

There was a moment of silence. Then the door in the third wall, the door that since Lars's arrival had remained closed, slid open, revealing a red-lit passageway beyond.

Captain Naxos stirred uneasily. "Something new. They've never opened that door since I've been here." The captain was, by some hours at least, the senior prisoner.

The half-dozen ant-shaped machines were pointing, gesturing the prisoners toward the newly opened door.

"Looks like we march," Pat Sandomierz muttered.

Lars could think of no way to argue for even a momentary delay, and no real reason to try. With his fellow prisoners he moved, under the guidance of the small machines, through an air-filled passage, with atmosphere and gravity held at Earth-standard normal all along the way.

Dorothy, brightening as if perhaps the novelty of the new passage pleased her, commented: "The Carmpan tolerate our native conditions well. It doesn't work that well in the reverse, or so I've been told."

No one else felt like making conversation. The passage was no more than thirty meters long. At its far end it branched into a complex of several more chambers cut from rock, each much larger than the sleeping cells, but smaller than the common room. Each chamber was largely filled with exotic-looking machinery. The humans looked at each other blankly; whatever the gear was, none of them could recognize it.

Lars heard a sound and looked back. Five of the Carmpan were also being brought along through the passage by the small berserker guides, into this complex of chambers full of sophisticated machines.

Live bodies and mechanical ones milled around. Now each ED human prisoner was paired off—whether at random or not, Lars could not tell—with one of the Carmpan. Lars and his new partner were taken into one of the chambers containing machinery. There were two couches visible. First Lars had to watch as the Carmpan was put on one couch, and there connected into the complex of equipment, by means of wires and other things more subtle. Then Lars himself was taken to the other couch and made to lie down. The small ant-shaped berserkers attached restraints to his limbs, and things to his head.

At once strange thoughts moved through his mind, as if projected from outside. Visual pictures came, outlandish and indecipherable, though clear.

Presumably, adjustments were made. Coherence soon evolved. At last there were some clear, plain words:

I am Carmpan. Do not be more frightened than you can

help. I do not believe the berserker intends at this moment to do us permanent harm.

The message came through clearly, but whether it was coming somehow directly from the Carmpan's mind, or from that mind through the medium of the machinery, Lars could not tell. He opened his eyes, but the relative positioning of the two couches kept him from looking at his Carmpan partner. The rock chamber that held his body seemed, if anything, less real than the new world of strange communication within his skull.

It seeks to use our minds, yours and mine, together. We are so different in our modes of thought, yet with this subtle machinery our thoughts can be made in a sense compatible. Together, doing much more than either could do alone. It seeks to use our thoughts to probe the far places where—

Something in the subtle machinery operated silently, and the contact was broken off. Still, it had provided Lars with understanding of a sort, or at least a theory. It would make sense, or it might, that the huge berserker computer that dominated and ran this whole base was using their two diverse biological minds to try to do what neither mind alone, nor the berserker's machinery alone, could do: to probe whatever section of space had been targeted by the latest sortie of its attacking units.

That first session was all probing and testing, and it went on for long, exhausting hours. Lars experienced glimpses of life and activity on several worlds, and on ships in space. He had little comprehension of what he was seeing and experiencing, and not the least choice about it. He supposed that the Carmpan had no choice either. The berserker was using them, like so much animated radio equipment . . .

No radio signal could carry information faster than light through space. The signals of the mind—if that was the right word for those ethereal transactions—were evidently another matter.

Knowledge of another kind trickled into Lars's awareness, brought perhaps by the cold probe of the berserker itself, coming to drain the man's consciousness of knowledge, being forced by some law to leave something in exchange. Lars understood that ten or more huge berserker craft had been launched from this base some time ago, and the object of the current exercise was to see how well those machines were doing, at a distance impossible or impractical for other types of communication.

The telepathic session was interrupted. The Carmpan who had been hooked up in tandem with Lars was disconnected and taken out by the guide machines, and another Carmpan brought in. Lars understood that different pairings of live minds were being tried, always one ED and one Carmpan, hooked somehow in . . . series? Parallel? Did it make sense to look for an electronic equivalent? The Carmpan and ED minds, Lars realized, must complement each other in some way that the berserkers expected to be able to turn to their advantage.

When the subtle machinery was turned on, Lars got the impression that the enforced contact was much more unpleasant for the Carmpan than it was for him.

At last he was unwired, and released from his couch. He had no idea how long the session had lasted. As exhausted as if he had been running or fighting for hours, he was allowed to return to the cell complex, the other prisoners straggling wearily with him.

They were allowed a brief interlude for rest and food.

Then they were marched back through the passage, where the testing and probing began again. This time some of the

ED prisoners showed mental confusion afterward. Exhaustion became the normal state. But so far the side effects were bearable.

Repeated sessions went on for what must certainly have been several days. All these sessions at the machines were devoted, as Lars thought, to testing and in some sense training. At last, when the most compatible partners had been determined, they were put to work together.

Only then did the first of the real working telepathic sessions take place.

Lars, hooked up again with one of the Carmpan (he still had no certain way of telling them apart) experienced blasts of mental noise, confusion, gibberish . . . the touch of the living Carmpan mind alternated with the cold mental probing from the berserker's circuits.

Time warped away. Future and past were blurred in the realm where dwelt the speeding Carmpan mind, and the hurtling thought of Lars Kanakuru. Now again clear images began to come through, from other minds. They were fragmentary, practically unintelligible. They came and went through the Carmpan mind before Lars could do more than glimpse them.

A fragment was seized, then tossed aside. Not by Lars. Toward him.

Hide this, my Earth-descended ally, partner. This must be hidden at all costs. Do not let the berserker perceive this . . .

Lars tried to answer the Carmpan, though at the moment he hardly felt capable of generating a coherent independent thought.

And yet again, another speeding fragment: *Hide this.*

And then the mental landscape was lighted, seared, frozen, all in one instant, as if by lightning. And immediately after that, just as suddenly, the world went dark.

Presently Lars, drifting in some dreamland, realized that the Carmpan now sharing the machine with him was dead. Lars thought that perhaps he knew the fact even before the berserker did, or just as soon.

Sudden death in harness, presumably accomplished by the berserker. As Lars read the situation, the berserker considered that the guilty, unreliable badlife had done something treacherous, some telepathic trick. But it did not know exactly what the badlife had done, or that anything of value had been kept from it by being passed on to Lars. Otherwise it would already be trying to turn the mind of Lars Kanakuru inside out . . .

. . . two fragments, that the Carmpan had said must be concealed.

The Remora program. That was one of them. A mere name. That of a computer program? Or perhaps a program of rearmament, somewhere, the effort of some world getting ready to defend itself against berserkers? As to what the Remora program really was, where it was, or why it had to be kept secret, Lars had no clue.

He thought the other fragment was, if anything, even more meaningless: *qwib-qwib*. Not even a real word, at least not in any language that Lars had ever known or heard.

His general impression from the telepathic visions he had experienced so far was that at least three of the ten or more dispatched berserkers were proceeding about their business satisfactorily. In other cases the berserkers were having . . . certain difficulties. Life in its many modes could be amazingly tough and stubborn.

Another brief rest was allowed the telepathic life-units. Then another session began. And now, through the alien filter of a new (and perhaps more malleable?) Carmpan mind,

Lars began to perceive another segment of the lives of incredibly distant humans.

And this information, this vision, he had no choice but to pass on . . .

WHAT MAKES US HUMAN

Aster's Hope stood more than a hundred meters tall—a perfect sphere bristling with vanes, antennae, and scanners, punctuated with laser ports, viewscreens, and receptors. She left her orbit around her homeworld like a steel ball out of a slingshot, her sides bright in the pure sunlight of the solar system. Accelerating toward her traveling speed of .85c, she moved past the outer planets—first Philomel with its gigantic streaks of raw, cold hydrogen, then lonely Periwinkle glimmering at the edge of the spectrum—on her way into the black and luminous beyond. She was the best her people had ever made, the best they knew how to make. She had to be: she wasn't coming back for centuries.

There were exactly three hundred ninety-two people aboard.

They, too, were the best Aster had to offer. Diplomats and meditechs, linguists, theoretical biologists, physicists, scholars, even librarians for the vast banks of knowledge *Aster's Hope* carried: all of them had been trained to the teeth especially for this mission. And they included the absolute cream of Aster's young Service, the so-called "puters" and "nicians" who knew how to make *Aster's Hope* sail the fine-grained winds of the galaxy. Three hundred ninety-two people in all, culled and tested and prepared from the whole population of the planet to share in the culmination of Aster's history.

Three hundred ninety of them were asleep.

The other two were supposed to be taking care of the ship. But they weren't. They were running naked down a mid-shell corridor between the clean, impersonal chambers where the cryogenic capsules hugged their occupants. Temple was giggling because she knew Gracias was never going to catch her unless she let him. He still had some of the ice cream she'd spilled on him trickling through the hair on his chest, but if she didn't slow down he wasn't going to be able to do anything about it. Maybe she wasn't smarter or stronger than he was, better-trained or higher-ranking—but she was certainly faster.

This was their duty shift, the week they would spend out of their capsules every half-year until they died. *Aster's Hope* carried twenty-five shifts from the Service, and they were the suicide personnel of this mission: aging at the rate of one week twice every year, none of them were expected to live long enough to see the ship's return home. Everyone else could be spared until *Aster's Hope* reached its destination; asleep for the whole trip, they would arrive only a bit more mature than they were when they left. But the Service had to maintain the ship. And so the planners of the mission had been forced to a difficult decision: either fill *Aster's Hope* entirely with puters and nicians and pray that they would be able to do the work of diplomats, theoretical physicists and linguists; or sacrifice a certain number of Service personnel to make room for people who could be explicitly trained for the mission. The planners decided that the ability to take *Aster's Hope* apart chip by chip and seal after seal and then put her all back together again was enough experience to ask of any individual man or woman. Therefore the mission itself would have to be entrusted to other experts.

And therefore *Aster's Hope* would be unable to carry enough puters and nicians to bring the mission home again.

Faced with this dilemma, the Service personnel were naturally expected to spend a significant period of each duty shift trying to reproduce. If they had children, they could pass on their knowledge and skill. And if the children were born soon enough, they would be old enough to take *Aster's Hope* home when she needed them.

Temple and Gracias weren't particularly interested in having children. But they took every other aspect of reproduction very seriously.

She slowed down for a few seconds, just to tantalize him. Then she put on a burst of speed. He tended to be just a bit dull in his love-making—and even in his conversation—unless she made a special effort to get his heart pounding. On some days, a slow, comfortable, and just-a-bit-dull lover was exactly what she wanted. But not today. Today she was full of energy from the tips of her toes to the ends of her hair, and she wanted Gracias at his best.

But when she tossed a laughing look back over her shoulder to see how he was doing, he wasn't behind her anymore.

Where—? Well, good. He was trying to take control of the race. Win by tricking her because he couldn't do it with speed. Temple laughed out loud while she paused to catch her breath and think. Obviously, he had ducked into one of the rooms or passages off this corridor, looking for a way to shortcut ahead of her—or maybe to lure her into ambush. And she hadn't heard the automatic door open and close because she'd been running and breathing too hard. Very good! This was the Gracias she wanted.

But where had he turned off? Not the auxiliary compcom: that room didn't have any other exit. How about the nearest capsule chamber? Form there, he'd have to shaft down to inner-shell and come back up. That would be dicey: he'd have to guess how far and fast, and in what direction, she was moving. Which gave her a chance to turn the tables on him.

With a grin, she went for the door to the next capsule chamber. Sensing her approach, it opened with a nearly silent whoosh, then closed behind her. Familiar with the look of the cryogenic capsules huddled in the grasp of their triple-redundant support machinery, each one independently supplied and run so that no system-wide failure could wipe out the mission, she hardly glanced around her as she headed toward the shaft.

Its indicators showed that it wasn't in use. So Gracias wasn't on his way up here. Perfect. She'd take the shaft up to outer-shell and elude him there, just to whet his appetite. Turn his own gambit against him. Pleased with herself, she approached the door of the shaft.

But when she impinged on the shaft's sensor, it didn't react to her. None of the lights came on: the elevator stayed where it was. Surprised, she put her whole body in front of the sensor. Nothing. She jumped up and down, waved her arms. Still nothing.

That was strange. When Gracias ran his diagnostics this morning, the only malfunction anywhere was in an obscure circuit of foodsup's beer synthesizer. And she'd already helped him fix it. Why wasn't the shaft operating?

Thinking she ought to go to the next room and try another shaft, find out how serious the problem was, Temple trotted back to the capsule chamber door.

This time, it didn't open for her.

That was so unexpected that she ran into the door—which startled more than hurt her. In her nearly thirty years, she had never seen an automatic door fail. All doors opened except locked doors; and locked doors had an exterior status light no one could miss. Yet the indicators for this door showed open and normal.

She tried again.

The door didn't open.

That wasn't just strange. It was serious. A severe malfunction. Which didn't show up on diagnostics? Or had it just now happened? Either way, it was time to stop playing. *Aster's Hope* needed help. Frowning, Temple looked for the nearest speaker so she could call Gracias and tell him what was going on.

It was opposite her, on the wall beside the shaft. She started toward it.

Before she got there, the door to the chamber slid open.

A nonchalant look on his dark face, a tuneless whistle puckering his mouth, Gracias came into the room. He was carrying a light sleeping pallet over one shoulder. The door closed behind him normally.

"Going somewhere?" he asked in a tone of casual curiosity.

Temple knew that look, that tone. In spite of herself, she gave him a wide grin. "Damn you all to pieces," she remarked. "How did you do that?"

He shrugged, trying to hide the sparkle in his eyes. "Nothing to it. Auxcompcom's right over there." He nodded in the direction of the comp command room she had passed. "Ship motion sensors knew where you were. Saw you come in here. Did a temporary repro. Told the comp not to react to any body mass smaller than mine. You're stuck in here for another hour."

"You ought to be ashamed." She couldn't stop grinning. His ploy delighted her. "That's the most irresponsible thing I've ever heard. If the other puters spend their time doing repros, the comp won't be good for alphabet soup by the time we get where we're going."

He didn't quite meet her happy gaze. "Too late now." Still pretending he was nonchalant—in spite of some obvious evidence to the contrary—he put the pallet on the floor in front of him. "Stuck here for another hour." Then he did look at her, his black eyes smoldering. "Don't want to waste it."

She made an effort to sound exasperated. "Idiot." But she practically jumped into his arms when he gave her the chance.

They were still doing their duty when the ship's brapper sounded and the comp snapped *Aster's Hope* onto emergency alert.

Temple and Gracias were, respectively, the nician and puter of their duty shift. The Service had trained them for their jobs almost from birth. They had access, both by education and through the comp, to the best knowledge Aster had evolved, the best resources her planners and builders had been able to cram into *Aster's Hope*. In some ways, they were the pinnacle of Aster's long climb toward the future: they represented, more surely than any of the diplomats or librarians, what the Asterins had been striving toward for three thousand years.

But the terms themselves, "nician" and "puter," were atavisms, pieces of words left over from before the Crash—sounds which had become at once magic and nonsense during the period of inevitable barbarism that had followed the Crash. Surviving legends spoke of the puters and nicians who had piloted the great colonization ship *Aster* across the galactic void from Earth, lightyears measured in hundreds or thousands from the homeworld of the human race. In *Aster*, as in all the great ships which Earth had sent out to preserve humankind from some now-forgotten crisis, most of the people had slept through the centuries of space-normal travel while the nicians and puters had spent their lives and died, generation after generation, to keep the ship safe and alive as the comp and its scanners hunted the heavens for some world where *Aster*'s sleepers could live.

It was a long and heroic task, that measureless vigil of the men and women who ran the ship. In one sense, they succeeded; for when *Aster* came to her last resting place it was on the surface of a planet rich in compatible atmosphere and vegetation but almost devoid of competitive fauna. The planet's sun was only a few degrees hotter than Sol: its gravity, only a fraction heavier. The people who found their way out of sleep onto the soil and hope of the new world had reason to count themselves fortunate.

But in another sense the nicians and puters failed. While most of her occupants slept, *Aster* had been working for hundreds or thousands of years—and entropy was immutable. Parts of the ship broke down. The puters and nicians made repairs. Other parts broke down and were fixed. And then *Aster* began to run low on supplies and equipment. The parts that broke down were fixed at the expense of other parts. The nicians and puters kept their ship alive by nothing more in the end than sheer ingenuity and courage. But they couldn't keep her from crashing.

The Crash upset everything the people of Earth had planned for the people of *Aster*. The comp was wrecked, its memory banks irretrievable, useless. Fires destroyed what physical books the ship carried. The pieces of equipment which survived tended to be ones which couldn't be kept running without access to an ion generator and couldn't be repaired without the ability to manufacture microchips. *Aster*'s engines had flared out under the strain of bringing her bulk down through the atmosphere and were cold forever.

Nearly nine hundred men and women survived the Crash, but they had nothing to keep themselves alive with except the knowledge and determination they carried in their own heads.

That the descendants of those pioneers survived to name their planet Aster—to make it yield up first a life and then a future—to dream of the stars and space flight and Earth—was a tribute more to their determination than to their knowledge. A significant portion of what they knew was of no conceivable value. The descendants of the original puters and nicians knew how to run *Aster*; but the theoretical questions involved in how she had run were scantly understood. And none of those personnel had been trained to live in what was essentially a jungle. As for the sleepers: according to legend, a full ten percent of them had been politicians. And another twenty percent had been people the politicians deemed essential—secretaries, press officers, security guards, even cosmeticians. That left barely six hundred individuals who were accustomed to living in some sort of contact with reality.

And yet they found a way to live.

First they survived: by experimentation (some of it fatal), they learned to distinguish edible from inedible vegetation; they remembered enough about the importance of fire to procure some from *Aster*'s remains before the wreckage burned itself out; they organized themselves enough to assign responsibilities.

Later they persisted: they found rocks and chipped them sharp in order to work with the vegetation; they made clothing out of leaves and the skins of small animals; they taught themselves how to weave shelter; they kept their population going.

Next they struggled. After all, what good did it do them to have a world if they couldn't fight over it?

And eventually they began to reinvent the knowledge they had lost.

The inhabitants of Aster considered all this a slow process. From their point of view, it seemed to take an exceptionally long time. But judged by the way planetary civilizations usually evolved, Asterin history moved with considerable celerity. A thousand years after the Crash, Aster's people had remembered the wheel. (Some theorists argued that the wheel had never actually been forgotten. But to be useful it needed someplace to roll—and Aster was a jungle. For several centuries, no wheel could compare in value with a good axe. Old memories of the wheel failed to take hold until after the Asterins had cleared enough ground to make its value apparent.) A thousand years after the wheel, the printing press came back into existence. (One of the major problems the Asterins had throughout their history to this point was what to do with all the dead lumber they created by making enough open space for their towns, fields, and roads. The reappearance of paper offered only a trivial solution until the printing press came along.) And a thousand years after the printing press, *Aster's Hope* was ready for her mission. Although they didn't know it, the people of Aster had beaten Earth's time for the same development by several thousand years.

Determination had a lot to do with it. People who came so far from Earth in order to procure the endurance of the human race didn't look kindly on anything that was less than what they wanted. But determination required an object: people had to know what they wanted. The alternative was a history full of wars, since determined people who didn't know what they wanted tended to be unnecessarily aggressive.

That object—the dream which shaped Asterin life and

civilization from the earliest generations, the inborn sense of common purpose and yearning which kept the wars short, caused people to share what they knew, and inspired progress—was provided by the legends of Earth and *Aster*.

Within two generations after the Crash, no one knew even vaguely where Earth was: the knowledge as well as the tools of astrogation had been lost. Two generations after that, it was no longer clear what Earth had been like. And after two more generations, the reality of space flight had begun to pass out of the collective Asterin imagination.

But the *ideas* endured.

Earth.

Aster.

Nicians and puters.

Sleep.

On Aster perhaps more than anywhere else in the Galaxy, dreams provided the stuff of purpose. On Aster evolved a civilization driven by legends. Communally and individually, the images and passions which fired the mind during physical sleep became the goals which shaped the mind while it was awake.

To rediscover Earth.

And go back.

For centuries, of course, this looked like nonsense. If it had been a conscious choice rather than a planetary dream, it would have been discarded long ago. But since it was a dream, barely articulate except in poetry and painting and the secret silence of the heart, it held on until its people were ready for it.

Until, that is, the Asterins had reinvented radio telescopes and other receiving gear of sufficient sophistication to begin interpreting the signals they heard from the heavens.

Some of those signals sounded like they came from Earth.

This was a remarkable achievement. After all, the transmissions the Asterins were looking at hadn't been intended for Aster. (Indeed, they may not have been intended for anybody at all. It was far more likely that these signals were random emissions—the detritus, perhaps, of a world talking to itself and its planets.) They had been traveling for so long, had passed through so many different gravity wells on the way, and were so diffuse, that not even the wildest optimist in Aster's observatories could argue these signals were messages. In fact, they were scarcely more than whispers in the ether, sighs compared to which some of the more distant stars were shouting.

And yet, impelled by an almost unacknowledged dream, the Asterins had developed equipment which enabled them not only to hear those whispers, sort them out of the cosmic radio cacophony, and make some surprisingly acute deductions about what (or who) caused them, but also to identify a possible source on the star charts.

The effect on Aster was galvanic. In simple terms, the communal dream came leaping suddenly out of the unconscious.

Earth. EARTH.

After that, it was only a matter of minutes before somebody said, "We ought to try to go there."

Which was exactly—a hundred years and an enormous expenditure of global resources, time, knowledge, and determination later—what *Aster's Hope* was doing.

Naturally enough—people being what they were—there were quite a few men and women on Aster who didn't believe in the mission. And there was also a large number who did believe who still had enough common sense or native pessimism to be cautious. As a result, there was a large planet-wide debate while *Aster's Hope* was being planned and built. Some people insisted on saying things like, "What if it isn't Earth at all? What if it's some alien planet where they don't know humanity from bat-dung and don't care?"

Or, "At this distance, your figures aren't accurate within ten parsecs. How do you propose to compensate for that?"

Or, "What if the ship encounters someone else along the way? Finding intelligent life might be even more important than finding Earth. Or they might not like having our ship wander into their space. They might blow *Aster's Hope* to pieces—and then come looking for us."

Or, of course, "What if the ship gets all the way out there and doesn't find anything at all?"

Well, even the most avid proponent of the mission was able to admit that it would be unfortunate if *Aster's Hope* were to run a thousand lightyears across the galaxy and then fail. So the planning and preparation spent on designing the ship and selecting and training the crew was prodigious. But the Asterins didn't actually start to build their ship until they found an answer to what they considered the most fundamental question about the mission.

On perhaps any other inhabited planet in the Galaxy, that question would have been the question of speed. A thousand lightyears was too far away. Some way of traveling faster than the speed of light was necessary. But the Asterins had a blind spot. They knew from legend that their ancestors had *slept* during a centuries-long, space-normal voyage; and they were simply unable to think realistically about traveling in any other way. They learned, as Earth had millennia ago, that c was a theoretical absolute limit: they believed it and turned their attention in other directions.

No, the question which troubled them was safety. They wanted to be able to send out *Aster's Hope* certain that no passing hostile, meteor shower, or accident of diplomacy would be able to destroy her.

So she wasn't built until a poorly-paid instructor at an obscure university suddenly managed to make sense out of a field of research that people had been laughing at for years: C-vector.

For people who hadn't done their homework in theoretical mathematics or abstract physics, "c-vector" was defined as "at right angles to the speed of light." Which made no sense to anyone—but that didn't stop the Asterins from having fun with it. Before long, they discovered that they could build a generator to project a c-vector field.

If that field were projected around an object, it formed an impenetrable shield—a screen against which bullets and laser cannon and hydrogen torpedoes had no effect. (Any projectile or force which hit the shield bounced away "at right angles to the speed of light" and ceased to exist in material space. When this was discovered, several scientists spent several years wondering if a c-vector field could somehow be used as a faster-than-light drive for a spaceship. But no one was able to figure out just what direction "at right angles to the speed of light" was.) This appeared to have an obvious use as a weapon—project a field at an object, watch the object disappear—until the researchers learned that the field couldn't be projected either at or around any object unless the object and the field generator were stationary in relation to each other. But fortunately the c-vector field had an even more obvious application for the men and women who were planning *Aster's Hope*.

If the ship were equipped with c-vector shields, she would be safe from any disaster short of direct collision with a star. And if the ship were equipped with a c-vector self-destruct,

Aster would be safe from any disaster which might happen to—or be caused by—the crew of *Aster's Hope*.

Construction on the ship commenced almost immediately.

And eventually it was finished. The linguists and biologists and physicists were trained. The meditechs and librarians were equipped. The diplomats were instructed. Each of the nician and puter teams knew how to take *Aster's Hope* down to her microchips and rebuild (not to mention repro) her from spare parts.

Leaving orbit, setting course, building up speed, the ship arced past Philomel and Periwinkle on her way into the galactic void of the future. For the Asterins, it was as if legends had come back to life—as if a dream crouching in the human psyche since before the Crash had stood up and become real.

But six months later, roughly .4 lightyears from Aster, Temple and Gracias weren't thinking about legends. They didn't see themselves as protectors of a dream. When the emergency brapper went off, they did what any dedicated, well-trained, and quick-thinking Service personnel would have done: they panicked.

But while they panicked they ran naked as children in the direction of the nearest auxcompcom.

In crude terms, the difference between nician and puter was the difference between hardware and software—although there was quite a bit of overlap, of course. Temple made equipment work: Gracias told it what to do. It would've taken her hours to figure out how to do what he'd done to the door sensors. But when they heard the brapper and rolled off the pallet with her ahead of him and headed out of the capsule chamber, and the door didn't open, he was the one who froze.

"Damn," he muttered. "That repro won't cancel for another twenty minutes."

He looked like he was thinking something abusive about himself, so she snapped at him, "Hold it open for me, idiot."

He thudded a palm against his forehead. "Right."

Practically jumping into range of the sensor, he got the door open; and she passed him on his way out into the corridor. But she had to wait for him again at the auxcompcom door. "Come on. Come *on*," she fretted. "Whatever that brapper means, it isn't good."

"I know." Leftover sweat made his face slick, gave him a look of too much fear. Grimly, he pushed through the sensor field into the auxcompcom room and headed for his chair at the main com console.

Temple followed, jumped into her seat in front of her hardware controls. But for a few seconds neither of them looked at their buttons and readouts. They were fixed on the main screen above the consoles.

The ship's automatic scanners were showing a blip against the deep background of the stars. Even at this distance, Temple and Gracias didn't need the comp to tell them the dot of light on the phosphors of the screen was moving. They could see it by watching the stars recede as the scanners focused in on the blip.

It was coming toward them.

It was coming fast.

"An asteroid?" Temple asked, mostly to hear somebody say something. The comp was supposed to put *Aster's Hope* on emergency alert whenever it sensed a danger of collision with any object large enough to be significant.

"Oh, sure." Gracias poked his blunt fingers around his board, punching readouts up onto the other auxcompcom screens. Numbers and schematics flashed. "If asteroids change course."

"Change—?"

"Just did an adjustment," he confirmed. "Coming right at us. Also"—he pointed at a screen to her left—"decelerating."

She stared at the screen, watched the numbers jump. Numbers were his department; he was faster at them than she was. But she knew what words meant. "Then it's a ship."

Gracias acted like he hadn't heard her. He was watching the screens as if he were close to apoplexy.

"That doesn't make sense," she went on. "If there are ships this close to Aster, why haven't we heard from them? We should've picked up their transmissions. They should've heard us. God knows we've been broadcasting enough noise for the past couple of centuries. Are we hailing it?"

"We're hailing," he said. "No answer." He paused for a second, then announced, "Estimated about three times our size." He sounded stunned. Carefully, he said, "The comp estimates it's decelerating from above the speed of light."

She couldn't help herself. "That's impossible," she snapped. "Your eyes are tricking you. Check it again."

He hit some more buttons, and the numbers on the screen twisted themselves into an extrapolation graph. Whatever it was, the oncoming ship was still moving faster than *Aster's Hope*—and it was still decelerating.

For a second, she put her hands over her face, squeezed the heels of her palms against her temples. Her pulse felt like she was going into adrenaline overload. But this was what she'd been trained for. Abruptly, she dropped her arms and looked at the screens again. The blip was still coming, but the graph hadn't changed.

From above the speed of light. Even though the best Asterin scientists had always said that was impossible.

Oh, well, she muttered to herself. One more law of nature down the tubes. Easy come, easy go.

"Why don't they contact us?" she asked. "If we're aware of them, they must know we're here."

"Don't need to," Gracias replied through his concentration. "Been scanning us since they hit space normal speed. The comp reports scanner probes everywhere. Strong enough to take your blood pressure." Then he stiffened, sat up straighter, spat a curse. "Probes are trying to break into the comp."

Temple gripped the arms of her seat. This was his department; she was helpless. "Can they do it? Can you stop them?"

"Encryption's holding them out." He studied his readouts, flicked his eyes past the screens. "Won't last. Take com."

Without waiting for an answer, he keyed his console to hers and got out of his seat. Quickly, he went to the other main console in the room, the comp repro board.

Feeling clumsy now as she never did when she was working with tools or hardware, she accepted com and began trying to monitor the readouts. But the numbers swam, and the prompts didn't seem to make sense. Operating in emergency mode, the comp kept asking her to ask it questions; but she couldn't think of any for it. Instead, she asked Gracias, "What're you doing?"

His hands stabbed up and down the console. He was still sweating. "Changing the encryption," he said. "Whole series of changes. Putting them on a loop." When he was done, he took a minute to doublecheck his repro. Then he gave a grunt of satisfaction and came back to his com seat. While he keyed his controls away from Temple, he said, "This way, the comp can't be broken by knowing the present code. Have to know what code's coming up next. That loop changes often enough to keep us safe for a while."

She permitted herself a sigh of relief—and a soft snarl of anger at the oncoming ship. She didn't like feeling helpless. "If those bastards can't break the comp, do you think they'll try to contact us?"

He shrugged, glanced at his board. "Channels are open. They talk, we'll hear." For a second, he chewed his lower lip. Then he leaned back in his seat and swung around to face her. His eyes were dark with fear.

"Don't like this," he said distinctly. "Don't like it at all. A faster-than-light ship coming straight for us. Straight for Aster. And they don't talk. Instead, they try to break the comp."

She knew his fear. She was afraid herself. But when he looked like he needed her, she put her own feelings aside. "Would you say," she said, drawling so she would sound sardonic and calm, "that we're being approached by somebody hostile?"

He nodded dumbly.

"Well, we're safe enough. Maybe the speed of light isn't unbreakable, but a c-vector shield is. So what we have to worry about is Aster. If that ship gets past us, we'll never catch up with it. How far away is it now?"

Gracias turned back to his console, called up some numbers. "Five minutes." His face didn't show it, but she could hear in his voice that he was grateful for her show of steadiness.

"I don't think we should wait to see what happens," she said. "We should send a message home now."

"Right." He went to work immediately, composing data on the screens, calling up the scant history of *Aster's Hope*'s contact with the approaching ship. "Continuous broadcast," he murmured as he piped information to the transmitters. "Constant update. Let Aster know everything we can."

Temple nodded her approval, then gaped in astonishment

as the screens broke up into electronic garbage. A sound like frying circuitry spat from all the speakers at once—from the hailing channels as well as from intraship. She almost let out a shout of surprise; but training and recognition bit it back. She knew what that was.

"Jammer," Gracias said. "We're being jammed."

"From this distance?" she demanded. "From *this distance*? That kind of signal should take"—she checked her readout—"three and some fraction minutes to get here. How do they do that?"

He didn't reply for a few seconds: he was busy restoring order to the screens. Then he said, "They've got faster-than-light drive. Scanners make ours look like toys. Why not better radio?"

"Or maybe," she put in harshly, "they started broadcasting their jammer as soon as they picked us up." In spite of her determination to be calm, she was breathing hard, sucking uncertainty and anger through her teeth. "Can you break through?"

He tried, then shook his head. "Too thick."

"Damn! Gracias, what're we going to do? If we can't warn Aster, then it's up to us. If that ship is hostile, we've got to fight it somehow."

"Not built for it," he commented. "*Aster's Hope*. About as maneuverable as a rock."

She knew. Everything about the ship had been planned with defense rather than offense in mind. She was intended, first, to survive; second, not to give anything away about her homeworld prematurely. In fact as well as in appearance, she wasn't meant as a weapon of war. And one reason for this was that the mission planners had never once considered the idea of encountering an alien (never mind hostile) ship this close to home.

She found herself wishing for different armament, more speed, and a whole lot less mass. But that couldn't be helped now. "We need to get their attention somehow," she said. "Make them cope with us before they go on." An idea struck her. "What've the scanners got on them?"

"Still not much. Size. Velocity." Then, as if by intuition, he seemed to know what she had in mind. "Shields of course. Look like ordinary force-disruption fields."

She almost smiled. "You're kidding. No c-vector?"

"Nope."

"Then maybe—" She thought furiously. "Maybe there's something we can do. If we can slow them down—maybe do them some damage—and they can't hurt us at all—maybe they won't go on to Aster.

"Gracias, are we on a collision course with that thing?"

He glanced at her. "Not quite. Going to miss by a kilometer."

As if she were in command of *Aster's Hope*, she said, "Put us in the way."

A grin flashed through his concentration. "Yes, sir, Temple, ma'am, sir. Good idea."

At once, he started keying instructions into his com board.

While he set up the comp to adjust *Aster's Hope*'s course—and then to adjust it continuously to keep the ship as squarely as possible in the oncoming vessel's path—Temple secured herself in her momentum restraints. Less than three minutes, she thought. Three minutes to impact. For a moment, she thought Gracias was moving too slowly. But before she could say anything, he took his hands off the board and started strapping his own restraints. "Twenty seconds," he said.

She braced herself. "Are we going to feel it?"

"Inertial shift? Of course."

"No, idiot. Are we going to feel the impact?"

He shrugged. ''If we hit. Nobody's ever hit a c-vector shield that hard with something that big.''

Then Temple's stomach turned on its side, and the whole auxcompcom felt like it was starting into a spin.

The course adjustment was over almost immediately: at the speeds *Aster's Hope* and the alien were traveling, one kilometer was a subtle shift.

Less than two and a half minutes. If we hit. She couldn't sit there and wait for it in silence. ''Are the scanners doing any better? We ought to be able to count their teeth from this range.''

''Checking,'' he said. With a few buttons, he called a new display up onto the main screen—

—and stared at it without saying anything. His mouth hung open; his whole face was blank with astonishment.

''Gracias?'' She looked at the screen for herself. With a mental effort, she tightened down the screws on her brain, forced herself to see the pattern in the numbers. Then she lost control of her voice: it went up like a yell. ''Gracias?''

''Don't believe it,'' he murmured. ''No. Don't believe it.''

According to the scanners, the oncoming ship was crammed to the walls with computers and weaponry, equipment in every size and shape, mechanical and electrical energy of all kinds—and not one single living organism.

''There's nothing—'' She tried to say it, but at first she couldn't. Her throat shut down, and she couldn't unlock it. She had to force a swallow past the rigid muscles. ''There's nothing alive in that ship.''

Abruptly, *Aster's Hope* went into a course shift that felt like it was going to pull her heart out of her chest. The alien was taking evasive action, and *Aster's Hope* was compensating.

One minute.

''That's crazy.'' She was almost shouting. ''It comes in faster than light and starts decelerating right at us and jams our transmissions and shifts course to try to keep us from running into it—and there's nobody *alive* on board? Who do we talk to if we want to surrender?''

''Take it easy,'' Gracias said. ''One thing at a time. Artificial intelligence is feasible. Ship thinks for itself, maybe. Or on automatic. Exploration probe might—''

Another course shift cut him off. A violent inertial kick—too violent. Her head was jerked to the left. Alarms went off like klaxons. *Aster's Hope* was trying to bring herself back toward collision with the other ship, trying—

The screens flashed loud warnings, danger signs as familiar to her as her name. Three of the ship's thrusters were overheating critically. One was tearing itself to pieces under the shift stress. *Aster's Hope* wasn't made for this.

She was the ship's nician: she couldn't let *Aster's Hope* be damaged. ''Break off!'' she shouted through the squall of the alarms. ''We can't do it!''

Gracias slapped a hand at his board, canceled the collision course.

G-stress receded. Lights on Temple's board told her about thrusters damaged, doors jammed because they'd shifted on their mounts, a locker in the meditech section sprung, a handful of cryogenic capsules gone on backup. But the alarms were cut off almost instantly.

For a second, the collision warnings went into a howl. Then they stopped. The sudden silence felt louder than the alarms.

Gracias punched visual up onto the screens. He got a picture in time to see the other ship go by in a blur of metal too fast for the eye to track. From a range the scanners measured in tens of meters, the alien looked the size of a fortress—squat, squarish, enormous.

As it passed, it jabbed a bright red shaft of force at *Aster's Hope* from pointblank range.

All the screens in the auxcompcon went dark.

"God!" Gracias gasped. "Scanners burnt out?"

That was Temple's province. She was still reeling from the shock, the knowledge that *Aster's Hope* had been fired upon; but her hands had been trained until they had a life of their own and knew what to do. Hardly more than a heartbeat after she understood what Gracias said, she sent in a diagnostic on the scanner circuits. The answer trailed across the screen in front of her.

"No damage," she reported.

"Then what?" He sounded flustered, groping for comprehension.

"Did you get any scan on that beam?" she returned. "Enough to analyze?" Then she explained, "Right angles to the speed of light isn't the same direction for every force. Maybe the c-vector sent this one off into some kind of wraparound field."

That was what he needed. "Right." His hands went to work on his board again.

Almost immediately, he had an answer. "Ion beam. Would've reduced us to subatomic particles without the shield. But only visual's lost. Scanners still functioning. Have visual back in a second."

"Good." She doublechecked her own readouts, made sure that *Aster's Hope*'s attempts to maneuver with the alien hadn't done any urgent harm. At the same time, she reassured herself that the force of the ion beam hadn't been felt inside the shield. Then she pulled her attention back to the screens and Gracias.

"What's our friend doing now?"

He grunted, nodded up at the main screen. The comp was plotting another graph, showing the other ship's course in relation to *Aster's Hope*.

She blinked at it. That was impossible. Impossible for a ship that size moving that fast to turn that hard.

But of course, she thought with an odd sensation of craziness, there isn't anything living aboard to feel G-stress.

"Well." She swallowed at the way her voice shook. "At least we got their attention."

Gracias tried to laugh, but it came out like a snarl. "Good for us. Now what?"

"We could try to run," she offered. "Put as much distance as possible between us and home."

He shook his head. "Won't work. They're faster."

"Besides which," she growled, "we've left a particle trail even *we* could follow all the way back to Aster. That and the incessant radio gabble— If that mechanical behemoth wants to find our homeworld, we might as well transmit a map."

He pulled back from his board, swung his seat to face her again. His expression troubled her. His eyes seemed dull, almost glazed, as if under pressure his intelligence were slowly losing its edge. "Got a choice?" he asked.

The thought that he might fail *Aster's Hope* made panic beat in her forehead; but she forced it down. "Sure," she snapped, trying to send him a spark of her own anger. "We can fight."

His eyes didn't focus on her. "Got laser cannon," he said. "Hydrogen torpedoes. Ship like that"—he nodded toward the screen—"won't have shields we can hurt. How can we fight?"

"You said they're ordinary force-disruption fields. We can break through that. Any sustained pounding can break through.

That's why they didn't build *Aster's Hope* until they could do better."

He still didn't quite look at her. Enunciating carefully, he said, "I don't believe that ship has shields we can hurt."

Temple pounded the edge of her console. "Damn it, Gracias! We've got to try! We can't just sit here until they get bored and decide to go do something terrible to our homeworld. If you aren't interested—" Abruptly, she leaned back in her seat, took a deep breath and held it to steady herself. Then she said quietly, "Key com over to me. I'll do it myself."

For a minute longer, he remained the way he was, his gaze staring disfocused past her chin. Slowly, he nodded. Moving sluggishly, he turned back to his console.

But instead of keying com over to Temple, he told the comp to begin decelerating *Aster's Hope*. Losing inertia so the ship could maneuver better.

Softly, she let a sigh of relief through her teeth.

While *Aster's Hope* braked, pulling her against her momentum restraints, and the unliving alien ship continued its impossible turn, she unlocked the weaponry controls on her console. A string of lights began to indicate the status of every piece of combative equipment *Aster's Hope* carried.

It wasn't supposed to be like this, she thought to herself. She'd never imagined it like this. When/if the Asterin mission encountered some unexpected form of life, another spacegoing vessel, a planetary intelligence, the whole situation should've been different. A hard-nosed distrust was to be expected: a fear of the unknown; a desire to protect the homeworld; communication problems; wise caution. But not unprovoked assault. Not an immediate pitched battle out in the middle of nowhere, with Aster itself at issue.

Not an alien ship full of nothing but machinery? Was that the crucial point?

All right: what purpose could a ship like that serve? Exploration probe? Then it wouldn't be hostile. A defense mechanism for a theoretically secure sector of space which *Aster's Hope* had somehow violated? But they were at least fifty lightyears from the nearest neighbor to Aster's star; and it was difficult to imagine an intelligence so paranoid that its conception of "territorial space" reached out this far. Some kind of automated weapon? But Aster didn't have any enemies.

None of it made any sense. And as she tried to sort it out, her confusion grew worse. It started her sliding into panic.

Fortunately, Gracias chose that moment to ask gruffly, "Ready? It's hauling up on us fast. Be in range in a minute."

She made an effort to control her breathing, shake the knots of panic out of her mind. "Plot an evasive course," she said, "and key it to my board." Her weapons program had to know where *Aster's Hope* was going in order to use its armament effectively.

"Why?" he asked. "Don't need evasion. Shield'll protect us."

"To keep them guessing." Her tension was plain in her voice. "And show them we can hit them on the run. Do it."

She thought he was moving too slowly. But faster than she could've done it he had a plot up on the main screen, showing the alien's incoming course and the shifts *Aster's Hope* was about to make.

She tried to wipe the sweat from her palms on her bare legs; but it didn't do much good. Snarling at the way her hands felt, she poised them over the weapons com.

Gracias's plot stayed on the main screen; but the display in front of her gave her visual again, and she saw the alien ship approaching like a bright metal projectile the Galaxy had flung to knock *Aster's Hope* out of the heavens. Suddenly frantic, as if she believed the other ship were actually going to crush her, she started firing.

Beams of light shot at the alien from every laser port the comp could bring to bear.

Though the ship was huge, the beams focused on a single section: Temple was trying to maximize their impact. When they hit the force-disruption field, light suddenly blared all across the spectrum, sending up a rainbow of coruscation.

"Negative," Gracias reported as *Aster's Hope* wrenched into her first evasion shift. "No effect."

Her weight rammed against the restraints, the skin of her cheeks pulling, Temple punched the weapons com into continuous fire, then concentrated on holding up her head so that she could watch the visual.

As her lasers turned the alien ship's shields into a fireworks display, another bright red shaft of force came as straight as a spear at *Aster's Hope*.

Again, the screen lost visual.

But this time Gracias was ready. He got scanner plots onto the screen while visual was out of use. Temple could see her laser fire like an equation on a graph connecting *Aster's Hope* and the unliving ship. Every few seconds, a line came back the other way—an ion beam as accurate as if *Aster's Hope* were stationary. "Any effect yet?" she gasped at Gracias as another evasion shift kicked her to the other side of her seat. "We're hitting them hard. It's got to have an effect."

"Negative," he repeated. "That shield disperses force almost as fast as it comes in. Doesn't weaken."

Then the attacker went past. In seconds, it would be out of reach of Temple's laser cannon.

"Cancel evasion," she snapped, keying her com out of continuous fire. "Go after them. As fast as we can. Give me a chance to aim a torpedo."

''Right,'' he responded. And a second later G-stress slammed at her as all the ship's thrusters went on full power, roaring for acceleration.

Aster's Hope steadied on the alien's course and did her best to match its speed.

''Now,'' Temple muttered. ''Now. Before they start to turn.'' Her hands quick on the weapons board, she primed a whole barrage of hydrogen torpedoes. Then she pulled in course coordinates from the comp. ''Go.'' With the flat of her hand on all the launch buttons at once, she fired.

The comp automatically blinked the c-vector shield to let the torpedoes out. Fired from a source moving as fast as *Aster's Hope* was, they attained .95c almost immediately and went after the other ship.

Gracias didn't wait for Temple's instructions. He reversed thrust, decelerating *Aster's Hope* again to stay as far as possible from the blast when the torpedoes hit.

If they hit. The scanner plot on the main screen showed that the alien was starting to turn.

''Come on,'' she breathed. Unconsciously, she pounded her fists on the arms of her seat. ''Come on. Hit that bastard. Hit.''

''Impact,'' he said as all the blips on the scanner came together.

At that instant, visual cleared. They saw a hot white ball explode like a balloon of energy rupturing in all directions at once.

Then both visual and scan went haywire for a few long seconds. The detonation of that many hydrogen torpedoes at once filled all the space around *Aster's Hope* with chaos: energy emissions on every frequency; supercharged particles phasing in and out of existence as they screamed away from the point of explosion.

''Hit him,'' Gracias murmured.

Temple gripped the arms of her seat, stared at the garbage on the screens. ''What do you think? Can they stand up to that?''

He didn't shrug. He looked like he didn't have that much energy left. ''Wouldn't hurt us.''

''Can't you clear the screens? We've got to *see*.''

''The comp's doing it.'' Then, a second later: ''Here it comes.''

The screens wiped themselves clear, and a new scanner plot mapped the phosphors in front of him. It showed the alien turning hard, coming back toward *Aster's Hope*.

The readout was negative. No damage.

''Oh, God,'' she sighed. ''I don't believe it.'' All the strength seemed to run out of her body. She sagged against her restraints. ''Now what do we do?''

He went on staring at the screens for a long moment while the attacking ship completed its turn. Then he said, ''Don't know. Try for collision again?''

When she didn't say anything, he gave the problem to the comp, told it to wait until the last possible instant—considering *Aster's Hope*'s poor maneuverability—and then thrust the ship into the alien's path. After that, he keyed his board onto automatic and leaned back in his restraints. To her surprise, he yawned hugely.

''Need sleep,'' he mumbled thickly. ''Be glad when this shift's over.''

Surprise and fear made her acid. ''You're not thinking very clearly, Gracias.'' She needed him, but he seemed to be getting further and further away. ''Do you think the mission can continue after this? What do you think the chances are that ship's going to give up and let us go on our way? My God, there isn't even anybody *alive* over there! The whole thing is just a machine. It can stay here and pound at us for centuries, and it won't even get bored. Or it can calculate the odds on Aster building a c-vector shield big enough to cover the whole planet—and it can just forget about us, leave us here and go attack our homeworld because there won't be anything we can do to stop it and Aster is *unprotected*. We don't even know what it *wants*. We—''

She might have gone on; but the comp chose that moment to heave *Aster's Hope* in front of the alien. Every thruster screaming, the ship pulled her mass into a terrible acceleration, fighting for a collision her attacker couldn't avoid. Temple felt like she was being cut to pieces by the straps holding her in her seat. She tried to cry out, but she couldn't get any air into her lungs.

Her damage readouts and lights began to put on a show.

But the alien ship skipped aside and went past without being touched.

For a second, *Aster's Hope* pulled around, trying to follow her opponent. Then Gracias forced himself forward and canceled the comp's collision instructions. Instantly, the G-stress eased. The ship settled onto a new heading chosen by her inertia, the alien already turning again to come after her.

''Damn,'' he said softly. ''Damn it.''

Temple let herself rest against her restraints. We can't—she thought dully. Can't even run into that thing. It can't hurt us. But we can't hurt it. *Aster's Hope* wasn't built to be a warship. She wasn't supposed to protect her homeworld by fighting: she was supposed to protect it by being diplomatic and cunning and distant. If the worst came to the very worst, she was supposed to protect Aster by not coming back. But this was a mission of peace, the mission of Aster's dream: the ship was never intended to fight for anything except her own survival.

"For some reason," Temple murmured into the silence of the auxcompcom, "I don't think this is what I had in mind when I joined the Service."

Gracias started to say something. The sound of frying circuitry from the speakers cut him off. It got her attention like a splash of hot oil.

This time, it wasn't a jammer. She saw that in the readouts jumping across the screens. It was another scanner probe, like the one that tried to break into the comp earlier. But now it was tearing into the ship's unprotected communication hardware—the intraship speakers.

After the initial burst of static, the sounds began to change. Frying became whistles and grunts, growls and moans. For a minute, she had the impression she was listening to some inconceivable alien language. But before she could call up the comp's translation programs—or ask Gracias to do it—the interference on the speakers modulated until it became a voice and words.

A voice from every speaker in the auxcompcom at once.

Words Temple and Gracias understood.

The voice sounded like a poorly calibrated vodor, metallic and insensitive. But the words were distinct.

"Surrender, badlife. You will be destroyed."

The scanner probe had turned up the gain on all the speakers. The voice was so loud it seemed to rattle the auxcompcom door on its mounts.

Involuntarily, Temple gasped, "Good God. What in hell is that?"

Gracias replied unnecessarily, "The other ship. Talking to us." He sounded dull, defeated, almost uninterested.

"I *know* that," she snapped. "For God's sake, *wake up*!" Abruptly, she slapped a hand at her board, opened a radio channel. "Who are you?" she demanded into her mike.

"What do you want? We're no threat to you. Our mission is peaceful. Why are you attacking us?"

The scanner plot on the main screen showed that the alien ship had already completed its turn and caught up with *Aster's Hope*. Now it was matching her course and speed, shadowing her at a distance of less than half a kilometer.

"Surrender," the speakers blared again. "You are badlife. You will be destroyed. You must surrender."

Frantic with fear and urgency, and not able to control it, Temple slapped off her mike and swung her seat to rage at Gracias. "Can't you turn that *down*? It's splitting my eardrums!"

Slowly, as if he were half asleep, he tapped a few buttons on his console. Blinking at the readouts, he murmured, "Hardware problem. Scanner probe's stronger than the comp's line voltage. Have to reduce gain manually." Then he widened his eyes at something that managed to surprise him even in his stunned state. "Only speakers affected are in here. This room. Bastard knows exactly where we are. And every circuit around us."

That didn't make sense. It made so little sense that it caught her attention, focused her in spite of her panic. "Wait a minute," she said. "They're only using *these* speakers? The ones in this room? How do they know we're in here? Gracias, there are three hundred ninety-two people aboard. How can they possibly know you and I are the only ones awake?"

"*You must surrender*," the speakers squalled again. "You cannot flee. You have no speed. You cannot fight. Your weapons are puny. When your shields are broken, you will be helpless. Your secrets will be lost. Only surrender can save your lives."

She keyed her mike again. "No. You're making a mistake. We're no threat to you. Who are you? What do you want?"

"Death," the speakers replied. "Death for all life. Death for all worlds. You must surrender."

Gracias closed his eyes. Without looking at what he was doing, he moved his hands on his board, got visual back up on the main screen. The screen showed the alien ship sailing like a skyborne fort an exact distance from *Aster's Hope*. It held its position so precisely that it looked motionless. It seemed so close Temple thought she could have hit it with a rock.

"Maybe," he sighed, "don't know we're the only ones awake."

She didn't understand what he was thinking; but she caught at it as if it were a lifeline. "What do you mean?"

He didn't open his eyes. "Cryogenically frozen," he said. "Vital signs so low the monitors can hardly read them. Capsules are just equipment. And the comp's encrypted. Maybe that scanner probe thinks we're the only life-forms here."

She caught her breath. "If that's ture—" Ideas reeled through her head. "They probably want us to surrender because they can't figure out our shields. And because they want to know what we're doing, just the two of us in this big ship. It might be suicide for them to go on to Aster without knowing the answers to questions like that. And while they're trying to find out how to break down our shields, they'll probably stay right there.

"Gracias," her heart pounding with unreasonable hope, "how long would it take you to repro the comp to project a c-vector field at that ship? We're stationary in relation to each other. We can use our field generator as a weapon."

That got his eyes open. When he rolled his head to the side

to face her, he looked sick. "How long will it take you," he asked, "to rebuild the generator for that kind of projection? And what will we use for shields while you're working?"

He was right: she knew it as soon as he said it. But there had to be something they could do, *had* to be. They couldn't just sail across the galactic void for the next few thousand years while their homeworld was destroyed behind them.

There had to be *something* they could do.

The speakers started trumpeting again. "Badlife, you have been warned. The destruction of your ship will now begin. You must surrender to save your lives."

Badlife, she wondered crazily to herself. What does that mean, badlife? Is that ship some kind of automatic weapon gone berserk, shooting around the Galaxy exterminating what it calls badlife?

How is it going to destroy *Aster's Hope*?

She didn't have to wait long to find out. Almost immediately, she felt a heavy metallic thunk vibrate through the seals that held her seat to the floor. A fraction of an instant later, a small flash of light from somewhere amidships on the attacking vessel showed that a projectile weapon had been fired.

Then alarms began to howl, and the damage readouts on Temple's board began to spit intimations of disaster.

Training took over through her panic. Her hands danced on the console, gleaning data. "We've been hit." Through the shield. "Some kind of projectile." *Through the c-vector shield.* "It's breached the hull." All three layers of the ship's metal skin. "I don't know what it was, but it's punched a hole all the way to the outer-shell wall."

Gracias interrupted her. "How big's the hole?"

"About a meter square." She went back to the discipline of her report. "The comp is closing pressure doors, isolating the breach. Damage is minor—we've lost one heat-exchanger for the climate control. But if they do that again, they might hit something more vital.'' Trusting the c-vector shields, *Aster's Hope*'s builders hadn't tried to make her particularly hard to damage in other ways.

The alien ship did it again. Another tearing thud as the projectile hit. Another small flash of light from the attacker. More alarms. Temple's board began to look like it was monitoring a madhouse.

''The same place,'' she said, fighting a rising desire to scream. ''It's pierced outer-shell. Atmosphere loss is trivial. The comp is closing more pressure doors.'' She tapped commands into the console. ''Extrapolating the path of those shots, I'm closing all the doors along the way.'' Then she called up a damage estimate on the destructive force of the projectiles. ''Two more like that will breach one of the mid-shell cryogenic chambers. We're going to start losing people.''

And if the projectiles went on pounding the same place, deeper and deeper into the ship, they would eventually reach the c-vector generator.

It was true: *Aster's Hope* was going to be destroyed.

''Gracias, what is it? This is supposed to be impossible. How are they doing it to us?''

''Happening too fast to scan.'' In spite of his torpor, he already had all the answers he needed up on his screen. ''Faster-than-light projectile. Flash shows after impact. Vaporize us if we didn't have the shields. C-vector brings it down to space-normal speed. But then it's inside the field. Ship wasn't built for this.''

A faster— For a moment, her brain refused to understand the words. A faster-than-light projectile. And when it hit the shield, just enough of its energy went off at right angles to the speed of light to slow it down. Not enough to stop it.

As if in mockery, the speakers began to blast again. ''Your ship is desired intact. Surrender. Your lives will be spared. You will be granted opportunity to serve as goodlife.''

So exasperated she hardly knew what she was doing, she slapped open a radio channel. ''Shut up!'' she shouted across the black space between *Aster's Hope* and the alien. ''Stop shooting! Give us a chance to think! How can we surrender if you don't give us a chance to think?''

Gulping air, she looked at Gracias. She felt wild and didn't know what to do about it. His eyes were dull, low-lidded: he might've been going to sleep. Sick with fear, she panted at him, ''Do something! You're the ship's puter. You're supposed to take care of her. You're supposed to have ideas. *They can't do this to my ship*!''

Slowly—too slowly—he turned toward her. His neck hardly seemed strong enough to hold his head up. ''Do what? Shield's all we've got. Now it isn't any good. That''—he grimaced—''that thing—has everything. Nothing we can do.''

Furiously, she ripped off her restraints, heaved out of her seat so that she could go to him and shake him. ''There has to be something we can do!'' she shouted into his face. ''We're human! That thing's nothing but a pile of microchips and demented programming. We're more than it is! Don't surrender! *Think*!''

For a moment, he stared at her. Then he let out an empty laugh. ''What good's being human? Doesn't help. Only intelligence and power count. Those machines have intelligence. Maybe more than we do. More advanced than we are. And a lot more powerful.'' Dully, he repeated, ''Nothing we can do.''

In response, she wanted to rage at him, We can refuse to give up! We can keep fighting! We're not beaten as long as we're stubborn enough to keep fighting! But as soon as she thought that she knew she was wrong. There was nothing in life as stubborn as a machine doing what it was told.

"Intelligence and power aren't all that count," she protested, trying urgently to find what she wanted, something she could believe in, something that would pull Gracias out of his defeat. "What about emotion? That ship can't care about anything. What about love?"

When she said that, his expression crumpled. Roughly, he put his hands over his face. His shoulders knotted as he struggled with himself.

"Well, then," she went on, too desperate to pull back, "we can use the self-destruct. Kill *Aster's Hope*"—the bare idea choked her, but she forced it out—"to keep them from finding out how the shield generator works. Altruism. That's something they don't have."

Abruptly, he wrenched his hands down from his face, pulled them into fists, pounded them on the arms of his seat. "Stop it," he whispered. "*Stop* it. Machines are altruistic. Don't care about themselves at all. Only thing they can't do is feel bad when what they want is taken away. Any second now, they're going to start firing again. We're dead, and there's nothing we can do about it, *nothing*. Stop breaking my heart."

His anger and rejection should have hurt her. But he was awake and alive, and his eyes were on fire in the way she loved. Suddenly, she wasn't alone: he'd come back from his dull horror. "Gracias," she said softly. "Gracias." Possibilities were moving in the back of her brain, ideas full of terror and hope, ideas she was afraid to say out loud. "We can wake everybody up. See if anybody else can think of anything. Put it to a vote. Let the mission make its own decisions.

"Or we can—"

What she was thinking scared her out of her mind, but she

told him what it was anyway. Then she let him yell at her until he couldn't think of any more arguments against it.

After all, they had to save Aster.

Her part of the preparations was simple enough. She left him in the auxcompcom and took the nearest shaft down to inner-shell. First she visited a locker to get her tools and a magnetic sled. Then she went to the central command center.

In the cencom, she keyed a radio channel. Hoping the alien was listening, she said, "I'm Temple. My partner is crazy—he wants to fight. I want to surrender. I'll have to kill him. It won't be easy. Give me some time. I'm going to disable the shields."

She took a deep breath, forced herself to sigh. Could a mechanical alien understand a sigh? "Unfortunately, when the shields go down it's going to engage an automatic self-destruct. That I can't disable. So don't try to board the ship. You'll get blown to pieces. I'll come out to you.

"I want to be goodlife, not badlife. To prove my good faith, I'm going to bring with me a portable generator for the c-vector field we use as shields. You can study it, learn how it works. Frankly, you need it." The alien ship could probably hear the stress in her voice, so she made an extra effort to sound sarcastic. "You'd be dead by now if we weren't on a peace mission. We know how to break down your shields—we just don't have the firepower."

There. She clicked off the transmitter. Let them think about that for a while.

From the cencom, she opened one of the access hatches and took her tools and mag-sled down into the core of *Aster's Hope*, where most of the ship's vital equipment operated—the comp banks, the artificial gravity inducer, the primary life-support systems, the c-vector generator.

While she worked, she didn't talk to Gracias. She wanted to know how he was doing; but she already knew the intraship communication lines weren't secure from the alien's scanner probe.

In a relatively short time—she was *Aster's Hope*'s nician and knew what she was doing—she had the ship's self-destruct device detached from its comp links and loaded onto the mag-sled. That device (called "the black box" by the mission planners) was no more than half Temple's size, but it was a fully functional c-vector generator, capable from its own energy cells of sending the entire ship off at right angles to the speed of light, even if the rest of *Aster's Hope* were inoperative. With the comp links disconnected, Gracias couldn't do anything to destroy the ship; but Temple made sure the self-destruct's radio trigger was armed and ready before she steered the mag-sled up out of the core.

This time when she left the cencom she took a shaft up to the mid-shell chamber where she and Gracias had their cryogenic capsules. He wasn't there yet. While she waited for him, she went around the room and disconnected all the speakers. She hoped her movements might make her look from a distance like one furtive life-form preparing an ambush for another.

He was slow in coming. The delay made her fret. Was it possible that he had lapsed back into half somnolent panic? Or had he changed his mind—decided she was crazy? He'd yelled at her as if she were asking him to help her commit suicide. What if he—?

The door whooshed open, and he came into the chamber almost at a run. "Have to hurry," he panted. "Only got fifteen minutes before the shield drops."

His face looked dark and bruised and fierce, as if he'd spent the time she was away from him hitting himself with his fists. For a second, she caught a glimpse of just how terrible what she was asking him to do was.

Ignoring the need for haste, she went to him, put her arms around him, hugged him hard. "Gracias," she breathed, "it's going to work. Don't look at me like that."

He returned her embrace so roughly he made her gasp. But almost immediately he let her go. "Keep your suit radio open," he rasped while he pushed past her and moved to his capsule. "If you go off, the comp will take over. Blow you out of space." Harshly, he pulled himself over the edge into the bed of the capsule. "Two-stage code," he continued. "First say my name." His eyes burned blackly in their sockets, savage with pain and fear. "If that works, say 'Aster.' If it *doesn't* work, say 'Aster.' Whatever happens. Ship doesn't deserve to die in her sleep."

As if he were dismissing her, he reclined in the capsule and folded his arms over his chest.

But when she went to him to say goodbye, he reached out urgently and caught her wrist. "Why?" he asked softly. "Why are we doing it this way?"

Oh, Gracias. His desperation hurt her. "Because this is the only way we can persuade them not to blow up *Aster's Hope*—or come storming aboard—when we let down the shields."

His voice hissing between his clenched teeth, he asked, "Why can't I come with you?"

Tears she couldn't stop ran down her cheeks. "They'll be more likely to trust me if they think I've killed you. And somebody has to stay here. To decide what to do if this all goes wrong. These are the jobs we've been trained for."

For a long moment, he faced her with his dark distress. Then he let go of her arm. "Comp'll wake me up when you give the first code."

She was supposed to be hurrying. She could hardly bear to leave him; but she forced herself to kiss him quickly, then step back and engage the lid of his capsule. Slowly, the lid closed down over him until it sealed. The gas that prepared his body for freezing filled the capsule. But he went on staring out at her, darkly, hotly, until the inside of the lid frosted opaque.

Ignoring the tears that streaked her face, she left him. The sled floating on its magnetic field ahead of her, she went to the shaft and rode up to outer-shell, as close as she could safely get to the point where the faster-than-light projectiles had breached *Aster's Hope*'s hull. From there, she steered the mag-sled into the locker room beside the airlock that gave access to the nearest exterior port.

In the locker room, she put on her suit. Because everything depended on it, she tested the suit's radio unit circuits four times. Then she engaged the suit's pressure seals and took the mag-sled into the airlock.

Monitored automatically by the comp, she cycled the airlock to match the null atmosphere/gravity in the port. After that, she didn't need the mag-sled anymore. With hardly a minute to spare, she nudged the black box out into the high metal cave of the port and keyed the controls to open the port doors.

The doors slid back, leaving her face-to-face with the naked emptiness of space.

At first, she couldn't see the alien ship: everything outside the port was too dark. But *Aster's Hope* was still less than half a lightyear from home; and when Temple's eyes adjusted to the void she found that Aster's sun sent out enough illumination to show the attacking vessel against the background of the stars.

It appeared too big and fatal for her to hurt.

But after the way Gracias had looked at her in farewell she couldn't bear to hesitate. This had to be done. As soon as the alarm went off in the port—and all over *Aster's Hope*—warning the ship that the shields were down, she cleared her throat, forced her taut voice into use.

"All right," she said into the radio. "I've done it. I've killed my partner. I've shut down the shields. I want you to keep your promise. Save my life. I'm coming out. If we're within a hundred kilometers of the ship when the automatic self-destruct goes, we'll go with it.

"I've got the portable field generator with me. I can show you how to use it. I can teach you how to make it. You've got to keep your promise."

She didn't wait for an answer: she didn't expect one. The only answer she'd received earlier was a cessation of the shooting. That was enough. All she had to do was get close to the alien ship.

Grimly, she tightened her grip on one handle of the black box and fired her suit's small thrusters to impell herself and her burden past the heavy doors out into the dark.

Automatically, the comp closed the doors after her, shutting her out.

For an instant, her own smallness almost overwhelmed her. No Asterin had been where she was now: outside her ship half a lightyear from home. All of her training had been in comfortable orbit around Aster, the planet acting as a balance to the immensity of space. And there had been light! Here there were only the gleams and glitters emitted by *Aster's Hope*'s cameras and scanners—and the barely discernible bulk of the alien, its squat lines only less dark than the black heavens.

But she knew that if she let herself think that way she

would go mad. Gritting her teeth, she focused her attention—and her thrusters—toward the enemy.

Now everything depended on whether the alien knew there were people alive aboard *Aster's Hope*. Whether the alien had been able to analyze or deduce all the implications of the c-vector shield. And whether she could get away.

The size of the other vessel made the distance appear less than it was, but after a while she was close enough to see a port opening in the side of the ship.

Then—so suddenly that she flinched and broke into a sweat—a voice came over her suit radio.

"You will enter the dock open before you. It is heavily shielded and invulnerable to explosion. You will remain in the dock with your device. If this is an attempt at treachery, you will be destroyed by your own weapon.

"If you are goodlife, you will be spared. You will remain with your device while you dismantle it for inspection. When its principles are understood, you will be permitted to answer other questions."

"Thanks a whole bunch," she muttered in response. But she didn't let herself slow down or shy away. Instead, she went straight toward the open port until the dock was yawning directly in front of her.

Then she put the repro Gracias had done on the comp to the test.

What she had to do was so risky, so unreasonably dangerous, that she did it almost without thinking about it, as if she'd been doing things like that all her life.

Aiming her thrusters right against the side of the black box, she fired them so that the box was kicked hard and fast into the mouth of the dock and her own momentum in that direction was stopped. There she waited until she saw the force field which shielded the dock drag the box to a stop, grip it motionless. Then she shouted into her radio as if the comp were deaf, "*Gracias*!"

On that code, *Aster's Hope* put out a tractor beam and snatched her away from the alien.

It was a small industrial tractor beam, the kind used first in the construction of *Aster's Hope*, then in the loading of cargo. It was far too small and finely focused to have any function as a weapon. But it was perfect for moving an object the size of Temple in her suit across the distance between the two ships quickly.

Timing was critical, but she made that decision also almost without thinking about it. As the beam rushed her toward *Aster's Hope*, she shouted into the radio, "*Aster*!"

And on that code, her ship simultaneously raised its c-vector shields and triggered the black box. She was inside the shield for the last brief instants while the alien was still able to fire at her.

Later, she and Gracias saw that the end of their attacker had been singularly unspectacular. Still somewhat groggy from his imposed nap, he met her in the locker room to help her take off her suit; but when she demanded urgently, "What happened? Did it work?" he couldn't answer because he hadn't checked: he'd come straight to the locker from his capsule when the comp had awakened him. So they ran together to the nearest auxcompcom to find out if they were safe.

They were. The alien ship was nowhere within scanner range. And wherever it had gone, it left no trace or trail.

So he replayed the visual and scanner records, and they saw what happened to a vessel when a c-vector field was projected onto it.

It simply winked out of existence.

After that, she felt like celebrating. In fact, there was a particular kind of celebration she had in mind—and neither of them was wearing any clothes. But when she let him know what she was thinking, he pushed her gently away. "In a few minutes," he said. "Got work to do."

"What work?" she protested. "We just saved the world—and they don't even know it. We deserve a vacation for the rest of the trip."

He nodded, but didn't move away from the comp console.

"What work?" she repeated.

"Course change," he said. He looked like he was trying not to grin. "Going back to Aster."

"What?" He surprised her so much that she shouted at him without meaning to. "You're aborting the mission? Just like that? What the hell do you think you're doing?"

For a moment, he did his best to scowl thunderously. Then the grin took over. "Now we know faster-than-light is possible," he said. "Just need more research. So why spend a thousand years sleeping across the Galaxy? Why not go home, do the research—start again when we can do what that ship did."

He looked at her. "Make sense?"

She was grinning herself. "Makes sense."

When he was done with the comp, he got even with her for spilling ice cream on him.

Friends Together

"Thousands of years?" Lars, as he asked the question, was still lying helplessly flat on his back, still attached to the mind-probing machine. He was staring at the rocky ceiling close above him, but he hardly saw the ceiling. The vision he had just experienced was still tremendously real.

Neither his Carmpan partner nor the berserker answered him.

Lars repeated the question aloud, in a weary and shaky voice: "Thousands of years? Their colony was that old, really?"

The two people whose minds he had recently been in contact with, Temple and Gracias, had been conscious of such a length of history. For Lars, the feeling of their conviction was unmistakably authentic. Those folk aboard the *Aster's Hope* were members of some colony older than Lars had thought any Earth-descended colony could be.

Just as the last threads of mental contact were about to

break, Lars felt his Carmpan partner touch his mind and for a moment longer hold it gently. One more thought came through: *The path of the colonizing ship from Earth to Aster, deviating from flightspace, may have undergone relativistic distortion, sending the ship into the Galactic past. But the contact we have just experienced was in our present.*

"Carmpan, what are we to do?"

Try to keep secret from the berserker the existence of the at-right-angles weapon. Do not think of it.

"How am I to keep from thinking—?"

But no answer came. The mental contact had been broken. And a moment later it was obvious to Lars that there was also no hope of achieving what the Carmpan had just suggested. Lars could feel the cold probe of berserker circuitry sending exploratory impulses into his mind again. It was not a material probe, but a trickle of energy producing a mental sensation hideous and indescribable. The entire episode from the lives of Gracias and Temple was suddenly forced through his mind again, at high speed, like a film, and Lars felt sure that it had now been retrieved in some way by the berserker computer conducting the experiment. For an instant only Lars could feel his thought in direct contact with that receptacle fashioned of metal and electricity and mathematics. And in that instant the man knew by direct experience that the machine received the news of a defeat imperturbably, as it would have accepted any other news.

The berserker had ransacked and robbed his mind, and . . . but wait. Its probing presence was now gone from his mind, and it had missed—something. Two things, actually. Because he, Lars, had not been thinking of those two things when the probe came. And for the berserker to read his memory more thoroughly was, he prayed, beyond its capability.

He had been helpless to prevent it taking from him the

knowledge of the right-angle weapon. *Had the Carmpan deliberately caused him to think of that, by telling him not to do so? In order that some greater prize be hidden?*

For whatever reason, the berserker had missed the two items that Lars's first Carmpan partner had been greatly concerned to hide: *qwib-qwib*, whatever that might be, and also the—what had that other thing been called? The something program?

Lars realized how effectively the Carmpan had enabled him to forget, how much more powerful their race had to be than his own in the realm of pure mental activity.

There was no further communication now from his current Carmpan partner. Lars, released again from the physical bonds of his couch, sat up. Now he could see that his partner was still breathing, but except for that the Carmpan body lay inert on its couch, as if exhaustion were complete. It had been released too, and its guide machine stood waiting alertly for it to get up.

Lars's own guide machine was waiting for him too. At least, thought Lars, free again to think his own thoughts, at least one of the damned things had been destroyed, by those people aboard *Aster's Hope*. At least one branch of humanity had been able to win that much. Though now the computers that ran this base, eager to find the secrets of the at-right-angles effect, would doubtless send more fighting units to Aster . . .

Loathing the feel of the couch to which he had been fastened for some indeterminate time, Lars got to his feet. He felt dirty, hungry, thirsty, in need of a bath, of every kind of physical ease and comfort.

The small machine that was acting as his personal guide and overseer raised one of its insect-limbs and pointed. But Lars was already moving. He was allowed to find his own way back to the common room, where the other four Earth-descended prisoners were already congregated. They all looked weary, and were already talking to each other about their various turns in the telepathic machinery.

All four looked at Lars with interest as he approached. Naxos remarked: "We were wondering about you. The rest of us have been back here for some time."

"It was something of an experience. Give me a drink."

As he drank water, and picked up some food from the tray where the machines always left it, Lars listened to the others talk. The berserker apparently had no objection to its living tools talking freely among themselves about what they had experienced.

The others were reporting fragmentary success at best, and some of them reported almost total failure.

It occurred to Lars as he listened that his team might well have been the most successful.

"How'd you do?" someone asked him finally.

He could think of no reason why he shouldn't tell them the truth. He felt sure that everything about the Gracias-Temple episode was already known to the berserker. He said: "Quite well, I think, compared to what you've told me."

He related the essentials of the story of Gracias and Temple. His fellow captives were allowed to share in that distant and perhaps isolated human victory. Nothing happened to interfere with Lars's telling. The great machine that held them did not care that they rejoiced over the defeat of one of its units. Perhaps, Lars decided, it computed that its prisoners would be more useful to it if they were allowed to hear something to make their spirits rise.

When Lars had finished his narrative, Dorothy took the floor. She detailed, as if reluctantly, a human defeat, the story of a squadron of ships wiped out by the berserker unit that her mental vision, allied with that of her Carmpan partner, had been forced to follow. The spirits of the four people listening were dampened somewhat.

Again there was no reason to think that their reaction mattered to their captor, which seemed to care nothing about what they said. Lars had the strong impression now that it was simply allowing reasonable periods of mutual contact as being conducive to the life-units' mental stability.

He voiced this thought.

Nicholas Opava suggested: ''Or maybe . . . it wants us to tell things to each other that it couldn't get out of us with its probe. So it can hear them.''

The five people looked at each other, while the words hung in the air. Then the group broke up, with nothing else said beyond a few muttered routine complaints on hunger and fatigue.

The group was next summoned to the mind-machines a few hours later. Lars thought he had the same Carmpan as a partner this time, but he could not be sure. Not even when the flow of mental pictures started.

With Friends Like These

"You're going up," Gemma said.

Pat yanked his boot on. "Yes."

"Even when you know how the Cotabote feel about it?"

"I do *not* know how they feel. About this or anything else. Maybe you can tell me. You're the big expert on the Cotabote. How do they feel? If they feel. Which I doubt." He pulled on his boot, which had shrunk in the continual damp of Botea. He wrenched it over his ankle and stamped down hard.

"You don't even try to get along with them!" Gemma said angrily. She hadn't come in from the doorway. She was standing there with the hood of her shirt thrown back so he could see her beautiful black hair, her beautiful black skin, her beautiful, beautiful face. He ought to file a protest like the Cotabote were always doing, a protest against her looking so damn beautiful all the time.

"Get along with them?" he shouted. "You spend all your

time trying to get along with them and where does it get you?''

''It wouldn't kill you to put it off a week. You said it was routine. Is there something you're not telling me?''

''It is routine,'' Pat said. ''You're starting to sound like the Cotabote. I have to do an orbital survey of the diamond mines once every six weeks. Adamant says so. And your Cotabote are so worried about my worms digging up the middle of their village, they should be glad I'm keeping tabs on them.''

He did need to check on the orbiting infrascopes that kept an eye on the mechanical digger worms and their movements through the coal, but that wasn't why he'd kicked the date up a few days. He'd gotten a transmission from Adamant that a berserker had wiped out a settlement-planet called Polara. It was the second report on a berserker in three months, and it had been only two weeks later than the transmission date, which meant Adamant had considered the information important enough to send it by ship at least as far as Candlestone, which was the closest relay. Adamant hadn't considered it important enough to ship it the whole way, or maybe the operator at Candlestone had made that decision, but Pat chose to take that as a hopeful sign that Adamant didn't consider the berserker to be anywhere in the neighborhood. If they thought it was, they would have raced to Botea with a navy. After all, they had to protect all those IIIB diamonds the worms were digging out of Botea's coal deposits. Still, he appreciated the warning, and the masses of general data on berserkers that had accompanied the transmissions, and he intended to go up and check on the orbital defenses, Cotabote or no Cotabote.

''It's only been thirty-five days since your last survey,''

Gemma said. "The Cotabote say you're up to something. They want me to file a protest."

"So what else is new?" he said. "Go right ahead." He gestured toward the computer. "What are they worried about this time? Their smash crop?"

"No," she said. She sat down in front of the voice-terminal. "They say the harpy hurts the nematej."

"The nematej?" Pat said. He stamped his foot into his boot and stood up. "What exactly could I do to it that could possibly make it worse than it is already?"

"They say the last time you did an orbital survey it started to smell funny." She glared at him, as if daring him to laugh.

He was too amazed to laugh. "Nematej already smells like vomit, for God's sake," he said. "It's got thorns everywhere, even on its flowers, and the last time I looked it was choking off their stinking smash crop." He shook his head. "They're incredible, you know that? I've been here two years, and they still come up with new ways to make my life miserable."

"What about your telling them your planet-range ship is called a harpy?" she said. "You're as bad as they are."

"Now that," Pat said, "is going too far. I am *not* as bad as the Cotabote."

"All right, you're not," Gemma said. "But you do try to antagonize them. If you could just treat them like human beings."

"They are *not* human beings. I don't care what the ICLU says. They're some kind of alien, whose sole mission in the universe is to drive people crazy."

"You're being ridiculous," Gemma said. "You know perfectly well they emigrated from Triage and before that from . . ."

"Emigrated, my foot. They were probably thrown off every planet they tried to settle. They . . ."

Gemma held the voice-terminal out to him. "You have to give me access to the computer," she said stiffly.

He yanked it out of her hand. "Access for Gemenca Bahazi, ICLU rep," he said, and handed it back to her. "Go ahead, file protest number five thousand."

"I will," she said. "I want to file a protest to Adamant Fossil Fuel and Diamond Chip Corporation on behalf of the Cotabote," she told the computer.

"Sure thing, sweetheart," the computer said.

Gemma scowled at Pat.

"How many protests is this anyway?" Pat said. "A million? Two million?"

"Two hundred and eighty-one," Gemma said.

"This will be Protest Number Two Hundred Eighty-three, darling," the computer said. "What title do you wish to give this protest, you cute thing?"

"Title it: Refusal to Cooperate," Gemma said grimly.

Pat put on his flight shortcoat, stuck a portable voice-terminal in the pocket, and then stood and watched Gemma at the terminal. She had stopped talking and was frowning. Even frowning, she was beautiful, which was good because she was usually frowning at him. He told himself it was because an ICLU natives' representative was not supposed to smile at the Adamant engineer who was mining the planet out from under those natives, especially with the Cotabote on her neck all the time. When he wasn't furious with her, he felt sorry for her, having to live in the Cotabote village and put up with them twenty-six hours a day.

"Give me a listing of all the protests filed this month," she said, and frowned at the screen some more.

"What's the matter?" Pat said. "You lose a protest?"

"No," she said, "I've got an extra one. You've been locking the door when you leave the office, haven't you?"

"I'm surprised you didn't accuse me of erasing a protest. Yes, of course, I lock it. It's keyed to my voice. So's the computer. You probably just forgot one. Admit it. I do that to you."

"Do what?"

"Make you forget what you're doing. You're crazy about me. You just won't admit it."

"Read me the titles of those protests," she said. "Without any 'sweethearts,' please."

"If that's the way you want it, honey," the computer said. "Refusal to Cooperate, Refusal to Cooperate, Endangering Lives, Refusal to Cooperate, Threatening the Cotabote, Refusal . . ."

Patrick leaned down and said, "Shut up," into the voice-terminal.

"Come with me," he said.

"What?" she said, and looked up at him, still frowning.

"Come up in the harpy with me."

"I can't," she said. "The Cotabote wouldn't like it."

"Of course they wouldn't like it. When do they ever like anything? Come anyway."

"But they already think . . ." she said, and stopped. She turned her head away. Pat bent closer.

"Is this how you talk Devil out of his orbital survey?" a suddenly present Scamballah asked. "I sent you here to file a protest, not to flirt with the Adamant representative. I've told you over and over again he's just waiting for a chance to vile you."

As if they weren't belligerent, spiteful, and evil-minded, the Cotabote were also sneaky, and Scamballah was the worst. Pat called her Scumbag the day she started calling him Devil, but he wished he'd named her Skulk. She had come up the steps to the office on the outside of the railing so she wouldn't be seen and had been clinging there next to the door for who knows how long. Now she climbed over it and came into the office with her youngest daughter, shaking a spongy-looking finger at Gemma.

"I'm filing the protest, Scamballah," Gemma said.

"Oh, yes, you're filing it," she said, shaking her mushroom-colored finger right in Gemma's face. Gemma ought to reach over and bite it off, Pat thought. "I *told* you to find out what he was up to, but did you? Oh, no. You're *filing a protest*. And while you're sitting there he's walking out the door. Did you tell him it was ruining the nematej?"

Scumbag's daughter had come over to stand by Gemma. She stuck her finger in her mouth and then used it to draw on the terminal screen.

"Gemma told me," Pat said. "I thought the Cotabote considered the nematej a noxious weed."

"I wanna picture," Scumbag's daughter whined. "Make her make a picture." She stomped her feet. "I wanna picture *now*."

Gemma typed up a picture, apparently not trusting her own voice to ask the computer anything.

"Not *that* picture!" she wailed. "I want a different picture!"

"The Cotabote will decide what is and is not a weed, and not you," Scamballah said. "You, Devil, are *only* the Adamant engineer. In our contract, it states clearly that you will not harm our crops or our village."

The Cotabote loved quoting their beloved contract, which Pat had never seen. He had heard it was a doozy, though. Scumbag's daughter began punching buttons wildly on the computer keyboard.

"I haven't hurt your crops or your village, and I haven't done anything to the nematej either. Yet."

"A threat!" Scamballah shrieked. "He threatened me. You heard that, Gemenca. He threatened me. File a protest!"

He wondered exactly how she was supposed to do that with that imbecilic brat beating the keyboard senseless.

"Scamballah," Gemma said calmly. "I'm sure he didn't mean . . ."

"That's right. Take his side. I knew he'd corrupt you. We forbid the orbital survey. Tell him that, Gemenca." She waved an arm at Gemma. "You're our representative. Tell him."

"I have told him . . ." Gemma began.

"And *I* told her to keep her nose out of Adamant's business," Pat said. He snatched up his acceleration helmet. "She's not going with me, and that's final."

Scamballah whirled to glare at Gemma. "You weren't supposed to tell him you were going with him. Oh, I knew I shouldn't let you come alone. I've seen the way you look at him! You wanted to be alone with him, didn't you? Filthy! Filthy!"

Scamballah's daughter had given up on the keyboard and was standing on the computer. She pulled down a mine mask from the wall. Pat took it away from her.

"Alone with me? Ha. She wanted to spy on my orbital survey, and I said, over my dead body."

Scamballah's daughter wailed.

"You will take her!" Scumbag shrieked. "I say you will! We'll file a protest."

"Scamballah," Gemma said. "Don't listen to him. He's . . ."

Scumbag's daughter was reaching for the energy rifles on the wall above the masks.

"I'm going," Pat said. "You can file your protest when I get back." He picked up the command core to the harpy and the extra helmet, and opened the door. "Everybody out. Now."

"You can't force us out of your office!" Scumbag said, but she grabbed her daughter by the neck and dragged her down the steps, still bellowing.

Gemma was still standing by the computer.

"You, too," he said, and handed her the helmet. She wouldn't take it. She walked past him, out the door, and down the steps.

Pat shut the door and stomped out to the ramp of the harpy, nearly tripping over a heap of smash leaves and nematej branches the Cotabote had left as offerings. They were either terrified of or fascinated by machines, Pat had not been able to figure out which, and were constantly leaving them presents or sacrifices. Probably not sacrifices, since he felt human sacrifice would be more in line with the way the Cotabote thought, which, considering Scamballah's daughter, might not be a half bad idea.

He turned at the top of the ramp, trying to gauge if Gemma was close enough to grab. She was. "I won't take her, Scumbag, and that's final," he said.

"You will or I'll tear up our contract!"

Pat tried to look like that had made an impression on him. "Get in," he said gruffly, and yanked Gemma up and into the harpy.

"Shut the door," he told the computer. The ramp retracted and the door slid shut. Pat tossed Gemma her helmet and went forward to insert the command core into the harpy's drive computer. Scamballah started banging on the door.

"Hurry," Gemma said, pulling on a flightcoat.

Pat looked up at her in surprise. "What did you say?"

"Nothing," she said.

"Strap yourself in," he said, and slid into the pilot's seat. "We're going up fast."

He hit the ground-jets hard. Scumbag and her daughter backed up to a respectful distance. He eased the harpy out of the clearing and took her straight up.

There was a lot of junk orbiting Botea, all of it Adamant's: the infrascopes, mappers, and geos for the mines, the big relay that sent Gemma's protests Plodding across the Galaxy to Candlestone and then on to Adamant, and the various defense satellites. Botea had two orbital atomic guns and assorted 15-T and 8-T exploders, all aimed at anybody who tried to steal Botea's precious IIIB diamonds. The selectively conductive crystals, the only thing kilolayered computer chips could be made from, were found on other planets, but always halfway to the core and in nearly diamond-hard newkimberlite deposits. On Botea they were practically lying in heaps on the ground. Well, not quite, but only a little way down in veins of soft yellow coal, and nothing standing in the way of getting them out except some soft deposits of coal the worms could chew their way through. And of course the Cotabote. The planet's defenses were really intended for pirates or small independent fighters, not an armored arsenal like a berserker was supposed to be, but at least they were there.

Pat stayed clear of the mine field of satellites and set a lower orbit that would keep him close enough to do visuals on everything without putting him on a collision course. He had taken off far too fast, which meant he had a lot of correcting to do, and it was a good fifteen minutes before he and the computer got the harpy into the orbit he wanted. He told the computer to run a check on all defense satellites with orders for the computer to tell him when the atomic gun came into line-of-sight, and hoped Gemma wouldn't realize that wasn't part of his usual routine.

She had taken off her acceleration helmet and was hunched forward so she could see Botea out the tiny forward viewport.

"It's pretty, isn't it?" he said. Botea was covered with clouds, which was good because the swamps and smash fields were a nasty green even from this distance. At least you couldn't smell them up here, Pat thought. "Aren't you glad I suggested you come with me?"

"Suggested?" she said, trying to get out of her straps. "You practically kidnapped me!"

"Kidnapped you?" he said. He unhooked his straps and latched onto one of the overhead skyhooks. "All I did was use a little reverse psychology on old Scumbag."

"You shouldn't call her that. She'll probably file a protest."

"Then I'll file one over her calling me Devil. And don't tell me she can't pronounce it. She knows exactly what she's doing."

Gemma still didn't have her straps free. "You still shouldn't antagonize them. Adamant could . . ."

"Could what?" he said. He bent over to help her with her straps. "They haven't answered any of the Cotabote's two hundred and eighty-three protests in over two years, have they?"

"Two hundred and eighty-one," Gemma said, and frowned again. Pat got her straps unhooked, and she drifted straight into his arms. He put his free hand around her waist.

"Well, well, so Scumbag was right," he said. "You were just waiting for your chance to be alone with me."

"The Cotabote think . . ." she said, and he waited for her to wriggle out of his arms, but she didn't. She suddenly smiled at him. "You really handled the whole thing very well. Maybe you should be the ICLU representative. You have a real gift for making people do what you want.''

''I do?'' he said, and let go of the skyhook so he could put his other arm around her. ''Does that include you?''

''I . . .'' She grabbed for a skyhook and used it to give herself a push that brought him up smartly against the bulkhead.

''Sorry,'' she said. ''I'm not used to no gravity.'' She turned and looked out the side port. ''Is that one of the infrascopes you're supposed to be checking on?''

He hand-over-handed himself till he was right behind her. ''Which one?'' he said and put his hand over hers to make sure she stayed on the skyhook this time.

''That spiky one,'' she said.

He fiddled with the controls to get her a larger image. ''This port's equipped with telescopics.'' He put his other hand on her shoulder and turned her to face him. ''It sends me weather reports. It lets me know when there's a storm brewing.''

''Oh,'' she said, a little breathlessly. ''What's the weather like now?''

''Right now,'' he said, and put his hand under her chin, ''I'd say the outlook is very favorable.''

''Atomic gun's coming up,'' the computer said.

''You have great timing,'' Pat said. ''I'll be right back,'' he said to Gemma and worked his way back to the computer. The terminal screen was still blank, and he couldn't see anything in the forward port either. ''Where's the gun?'' he said.

''Is that it?'' Gemma said from the side port. She was fiddling with the telescopic controls. ''The big black thing out there?''

''What big black thing?'' Pat said. ''I don't see anything.

You've probably got the telescopics showing you a speck of dirt."

"It's not a speck of dirt," Gemma said. "It's right there." She pointed. "A long way out. And down. I mean, not on the plane of the ecliptic."

"Give me a wide range," Pat told the computer. "Everything for a thousand kilometers. And a hundred and eighty degrees." It did.

"Can you see it now?" Gemma said.

"Yes," Pat said. "I see it." He lurched for the skyhook. "Get away from the window."

"It's huge," Gemma said. "What is it? An infrascope?"

He tackled her, and they tumbled over against the opposite bulkhead.

"I don't know what you think you're doing," Gemma said angrily from underneath him.

"It's a berserker," Pat said.

"A berserker?" she said. She grabbed for a skyhook and pulled herself up to face him. "A berserker?" she whispered. "Are you sure?"

"I'm sure," he said.

"The atomic gun is full screen," the computer said. "Do you want readouts?"

"Shh," Gemma said.

Pat said, too softly for the computer to hear, "Blast it. Blast it with everything you've got."

It was a purely instinctive reaction. The orbital guns, with their pitiful ten megaton atomics, couldn't make any more of a dent in that thing than his energy rifle. Gemma was right. It was huge. He pulled himself back to the computer and looked at it on the screen. "How far out is it?" he asked the computer.

"Nine hundred eighty-five kilometers," the computer said.

Nearly a thousand kilometers away. Not nearly far enough. Gemma eased herself into the seat beside him and strapped herself in. ''What do we do now?'' she said.

''I don't know.'' They were both whispering. ''It's a long way out. Maybe if I hit the jets, it won't see us. But then again maybe it will. Maybe it already has.''

He didn't have to say anything else. Gemma had heard of berserkers, too, or she wouldn't be gripping the arms of her acceleration seat like that. She knew just as well as he did that it intended to destroy every speck of life on Botea, including the nematej. And Pat and Gemma, who had just happened by.

''If it had seen us, it would have blown us up,'' Gemma said. ''Which means it didn't. And it must not be picking up what we're saying either.''

Which meant they could stop whispering, but they didn't. ''It may think we're just a satellite. Which means our best bet is to stay where we are and wait till we've got Botea between us.''

''How long will that be?''

Pat held the voice-terminal right up to his lips. ''Figure out how long before we're out of line-of-sight with the berserker,'' he said softly.

''Eleven minutes, nineteen seconds,'' the computer said, and the sound was like an explosion in the cabin. Gemma flinched.

''Keep it down,'' Pat said. ''All right, I want you to transmit pictures of the berserker down to Botea. Section-by-section holos, infra, x-ray, everything you've got. No wait. Put them on independents. No transmissions. And switch to visual-only for now. Go back to voice when we go out of line-of-sight.''

''Thank you,'' Gemma said. ''I know it can't hear us,

but . . ." She drew a ragged breath and leaned forward to watch the screen with him.

What Pat saw made him feel a little better, but not much. The berserker had taken a beating. Half of its back end was missing. He didn't know where a berserker carried its arsenal, but losing a chunk that big had to have hurt something. He wondered if this was the berserker that had destroyed the settlement on Polara. If it was, they'd certainly put up a good fight. And the berserker had killed them all, he reminded himself.

"Eleven minutes," Gemma said, as if the computer had said, "a century," and Pat knew exactly how she felt. He itched to put the harpy on manual and take her down himself right then. He knew that would be suicide, but anything would be better than sitting here helplessly for the next ten minutes, wondering when the berserker was going to notice they weren't a satellite and blow them apart.

He spoke into the voice-terminal again. "Put a countdown on the screen, and do everything you can to get us ready for a descent. And give me a two-minute warning."

He glared at the screen, wishing he had access to the computer's memory banks. Maybe the report from Polara and all the other berserker data Adamant had sent could be put together with the pictures he was taking to come up with a fool-proof plan for destroying the berserker with only two atomic guns and some exploders. He didn't dare ask for information, though. It would have to be transmitted from the main computer, and the berserker was bound to pick it up. He couldn't call for help either, for the same reason. Not that sending out a mayday would do any good. By the time the message crawled to Candlestone, they'd be long gone.

"It looks like it's been in a fight," Gemma said, peering at the screen. "Maybe there are ships still chasing it."

Not if it just came from Polara, Pat thought. He was about to say it when he got a good look at Gemma. She looked scared to death, her shoulders hunched forward as if she were waiting for someone to hit her. The computer spit an independent out of its output, and she took it and held it without even realizing what she was doing. Her eyes were fixed on the computer; the countdown read six minutes.

He said instead, "You bet. They're probably right on its tail. We'll send out a mayday as soon as we get back down and tell them where it is."

"Will we get back down?" she said.

"Are you kidding? I always take my girls home."

She gave him a ghost of a smile.

"As soon as we get back to the computer, we'll feed all these pictures in and see if we can come up with a plan to blow that berserker apart."

She wasn't even listening to him. "When do you think it will attack?" she said.

"Not for a while. It's probably laying up here for repairs, which means as long as it thinks we don't know it's here, it probably won't do anything at all. Maybe we can hit it before it has a chance to repair itself."

"Oh," she said, and looked relieved.

Pat wished he'd convinced himself. Even if the berserker had holed up off Botea to lick its wounds, it could still send down a deadly berserker android, armed with lasers and poisonous gases, that would be more than a match for them and the Cotabote.

The Cotabote. He'd forgotten all about them. They'd never cooperate, even if they knew what a berserker was. And why would they believe there was a deadly war-machine orbiting their planet when they hadn't believed anything he'd ever told them?

"When we get back down," Pat said, and was amazed at how confident he was when he said that, "we're going to have to take the computer down in the mine. It's the safest place. We can carry enough self-contained to make it self-sufficient. That way even if the berserker blows my office apart, we can still figure out a plan. The berserker won't be able to touch us in the mine. Okay?"

"Okay," Gemma said, which told Pat just how scared she was. She'd forgotten all about the Cotabote, too, and he wasn't going to remind her. Not until he had her and the computer safely down in the mine, with the fire doors shut.

"Well," he said. "What do you think of our first date so far?"

She looked over at him, shocked, and then tried to smile. "Is going out with you always this exciting?" she said gamely, though her voice still had a tremor in it.

"That's what I've been trying to tell you for months," he said. "Wait'll you see where I take you on our next date."

"You will be out of line-of-sight in two minutes," the computer said.

Gemma sucked in her breath.

Pat asked the computer for a compensated visual of the berserker, and they both sat and watched it for what seemed like a lifetime, waiting for it to spit a missile out of its side, even though it was really already far behind them. The countdown read fifteen seconds.

"Hold on, kid," Pat said, and started the jets.

She looked over at him.

"Sorry to take you home so early, but I've got a late date."

The descent seemed to take forever. Pat held his breath the entire time, convinced a little thing like a planet wouldn't stop a berserker. The computer spit out independents, like ticks of a deadly clock, and Gemma picked them up and held them without even looking at them.

"Entering atmosphere," the computer said, and they both jumped.

"Put her on manual," Pat said, and nose-dived straight through the clouds.

Gemma pressed back against her seat, her eyes closed and the handful of independents clutched to her like a baby. Pat brought the harpy up sharply and headed for the office.

"We made it," he said. "Now if the office is still there, we're in business."

Gemma handed Pat the deck of independents and undid her straps. "What do you want me to do?"

"You grab the independents and as much self-contained as you can carry. I'll get the rest. And the terminal."

"Are you going to send out a mayday?"

"No. We'll take the transmitter with us. If I send it from the office, the berserker'll know that's where we are and we won't have an office." They were coming in over the sharp-pointed trees to the office clearing.

"Maybe we should go get the Cotabote first," Gemma said.

"We get the computer first," Pat said. "You don't have to worry about the Cotabote. Even if the berserker sends a lander down it'll probably take one look at old Scumbag and turn tail and run."

"This is hardly the time for a joke," Gemma said. "The Cotabote . . ."

"Can take care of themselves." He skidded the harpy to a stop. "Open the door," he said, and was out before it was fully up.

"Aren't you going to take the command core with you?" Gemma asked.

"No. Leave it. Come on," he said, and took off at a dead run for the office.

Scamballah was standing by the output, her spongy-looking arms folded across her chest. Her husband Rutchirrah—Retch, as Pat called him—who was shorter than his wife and shaped like a poisonous toadstool, was holding an array of the rectangular independents as if they were a hand of cards. "What are these?" he said. "The protests you have refused to file for us?"

"Give those to me," Pat said and made a grab for them.

Retch took a step backward. The output spit out another card. He scooped it up. "Adamant will hear about your striking a Cotabote. Gemenca, file a protest."

"Give me those independents right now," Pat said. "I don't have time to play games with you."

"Pat," Gemma said. "Let me handle this." She turned to Scamballah. "It is a good thing I went on the orbital survey with Devlin. We discovered something terrible. A berserker."

Scumbag didn't look impressed. "Don't give me any stories. I know you let Devil vile you while you were in the harpy with him. That's why you wanted to go with him, isn't it? So you and he could do filthy things together?"

"Why, you foul-mouthed old witch!" Pat said. "She's trying to save your life. Don't waste your time, Gemma. Get the self-contained. I'll . . ."

"I said I'd handle this," Gemma said grimly. "Get the transmitter and everything else you're taking. Rutchirrah, give him the independents, and I will tell you everything that happened."

"You see, she admits it, Rutchirrah!" Scamballah said. "I

told you this would happen.'' She was shaking her finger in front of his nose now. Pat made a grab for the independents and stuffed them in his jacket. Rutchirrah bellowed. Pat started cramming self-contained into a smash sack.

''He viled you, didn't he?'' Scumbag said.

''Listen to me,'' Gemma said. ''There is a berserker in the sky above Botea, high up, above the clouds where you can't see it. It is a terrible war machine. It will kill us all. We have to . . .''

''Did he vile you?'' Scumbag shrieked. ''Did he?''

Gemma didn't say anything for a minute, she just looked at Scumbag, and Pat was sure she was going to give up. He waited, ready to hand her the transmitter and a sack.

''He tried to vile me,'' she said, ''but I wouldn't let him.''

''Oh, thanks a lot,'' Pat said. He back-to-backed a voice-terminal and the transmitter and put them inside his jacket. He reached above his head for the two energy rifles.

''I will tell you all about it,'' Gemma said. ''But first you must come with me into the mines. You and all the Cotabote. We will be safe there.''

''Safe? In the mines? With Devil? He will try to vile us all.''

''That's it,'' Pat said. ''We're going. If the Cotabote don't want to go down in the mines, they can stay here and make friends with the berserker. They should get along great.''

''You go on if you have to,'' Gemma said. ''I'm not leaving until I've explained this to the Cotabote.''

''Explained it? You can't explain anything to them. All they care about is whether I put my filthy hands on you.'' The output spit out another independent and clicked off. Retch made a move toward it, and Pat snatched it away. ''For your information, I did put my filthy hands on her. And at the time''—he looked hard at Gemma—''*at the time* she seemed to like it. Now, of course, she has another version of the story.'' He grabbed up his energy rifle and started down the steps. ''I'll be at the wormhole by the river if you change your mind,'' he said, and walked out of the clearing.

Before he was even halfway to the wormhole, he knew he should never have left her. He should have slung her over his shoulder like the filthy viler the Cotabote thought he was, and carried her off with him. The Cotabote would probably all have followed him then, just to watch.

He almost turned around. Instead he stopped, and hooked up a self-contained to the terminal. ''Do you see anything entering the atmosphere?'' he asked.

''No.''

A single self-contained limited the computer to straight yes and no answers, but that should be enough until he got to the wormhole. ''Beep me if any object enters the atmosphere from now on,'' he said, stuffing the terminal back in his jacket. That should give him some warning so he could go back and get Gemma if the berserker tried to land an android. He hadn't even bothered to have the computer check for poison gases or viruses. If the berserker was going to destroy the whole planet, he'd rather die without knowing what he'd done to Gemma.

The wormhole had a heap of thorny nematej branches in front of it, offerings the Cotabote had left for the worm, who they were convinced would come plowing up out of the earth and eat them alive, no matter how many times Pat told them he wouldn't let that happen. Since when have they ever believed anything I told them? he thought bitterly, and kicked the thorns out of the way.

''Open the door,'' he said loudly. The massive metal door slid up. Adamant called the worm-built barriers fire doors, and in official documents said that they were constructed throughout the mines and at all surface contact points to prevent the spread of underground coal fires, but Pat knew perfectly well what they were for. Adamant had given him atomic guns and two energy rifles to fight off diamond thieves, but if he didn't succeed he was supposed to close the doors before he died so the diamonds would be safe. It said so in his contract. He wished he could do that with the berserker, but he was afraid it wasn't that easy.

The doors certainly wouldn't hold up against an atomic, and although it would be possible to shut down the ventilators and breathe the stored oxygen the worms used for fuel, they couldn't do that for very long. The berserker would wait.

Pat unslung his pack and set up the terminal just inside the door. He switched on the inspection lights, but left the door open. He asked again, "Do you see any objects entering the atmosphere now?"

"No," the computer said.

"Good." He finished hooking up the self-contained, lining it up along one of the oxygen tubes that ran the length of the worm trail.

"Have any objects entered the atmosphere?" he asked again, now that he could get a more complete answer.

"Not since your harpy reentered the atmosphere. At that time an object entered the atmosphere on a slow-descent path that terminated in—"

"What kind of object?"

"A ship somewhat like yours, although it converts to a ground vehicle. It has a mass of—"

"Where is it now?"

"I'll show you," the computer said, and flashed a local

area diagram on its screen with a blip right in the center of the Cotabote's main smash field.

"What's it doing now?"

"There are no signs of activity from the ship, but I am picking up atmospheric pollution in the area, with a chemical content of . . ." It paused while it did a chemical reading. Pat didn't wait to hear it.

"Shut the door!" he shouted, grabbing up his energy rifle, and tore up out of the wormhole.

He could see the smoke from the smash field even before he got to the office clearing. You hope it's smoke, he thought, and not some kind of poison.

He tore up the steps and opened the door to the office to get a mine mask. A blast of smoke hit him full in the face. His first thought was that the office was on fire. His second was that it wasn't poison gas since he was still alive after a lungful, although if it got much thicker he wouldn't be able to breathe. He could hardly see.

He clamped his mine mask on and adjusted the eyeshields to screen out the smoke. The office wasn't on fire. The smoke was coming in the open window from the smash field. He could see the flames from here. The fire was moving in the direction of the Cotabote village. A straggling line of Cotabote were heading past the office carrying sacks over their shoulders.

He grabbed the spare mine mask and ran back down the steps and across to them. "Go to the wormhole by the river," he said. "I'll meet you there. Where's Gemma?"

They went past him as if he wasn't there, their shirttails pulled up over their noses. The last two in the group were Rutchirrah and Scamballah, with their three daughters clinging to them and bawling.

"Where's Gemma?" Pat said.

"I told you he wasn't down in the mines at all," Scumbag said triumphantly. "It was all a trick so he could set fire to our fields."

"We will file a protest!" Rutchirrah said.

Pat took hold of both his spongy arms and shook him. "You tell me where she is or I'll throttle you. *Where is Gemma*?"

"Attempted murder!" Retch squawled. "Adamant will hear of this!"

Pat couldn't waste any more time on them. He ran off toward the village through periodic lines of Cotabote, all of them coughing and crying from an acrid smell like burning chicken feathers, but none of them willing to put down their sacks. There was no way he could get to the village itself. Its houses were completely on fire, their nematej-thatched roofs crackling and falling in on the clay huts. The coal fence around the village was burning, too, a red-hot line roiling with yellow smoke.

"Gemma!" he shouted. "Gemma!"

The huge smash field was burning, too, but without so much smoke, and he could see a squat black shape far out in the center of it, crouched there like a spider, with smaller shapes in front of it that he hoped to God weren't bodies. It was definitely a berserker lander. He hoped the shapes in front of it weren't berserker androids either. At least they weren't moving.

Just then he saw another shape moving toward the lander, over halfway to it, picking its way slowly through one of the fermentation ditches.

"Gemma!" Pat shouted. The figure turned and then started slowly forward again. He ran toward her, vaulting over the clumps of burning smash to get to the ditch she was in. There was still water in the bottom of the ditch, but it was hot even through his boots. He splashed up to where Gemma was standing, coughing, her wet shirttail up over her mouth.

"What in the hell are you doing out here?" he said, pulling the shirt away and shoving the mask down over her face. "That's a berserker lander."

Gemma had been farther out than he thought. The lander wasn't more than fifty meters away. "Get down," he said, pulling her down beside him in the foul-smelling ditch.

"I know," she tried to say, still coughing. "The Cotabote . . ."

"Did they start this fire? Has the lander been firing lasers at them?"

"No," she said. She wasn't coughing, but her voice still sounded hoarse. "The lander hasn't done anything. I started the fire."

"You? Why in the hell did you do that? Did you think the lander would start coughing or what?"

"I did the only thing I could think to do. *You* weren't around to ask!" She stood up. "We've got to go out there and get . . ."

There was a flash of red light and a cracking sound, and the shapes in front of the lander burst into flame.

"I thought you said it wasn't doing anything," Pat said. "That's a laser! I don't care what you wanted to go get. We're going!" He grabbed her hand. Gemma didn't resist. They ran, crouching along the ditch to the end of the field, and went down behind the dike bordering it. The lander continued firing. Pat unslung his rifle and fired several more blasts that seemed to have no effect whatsoever. The lander didn't return his fire. Instead it made a grinding noise and began rolling toward them.

Pat glanced around. There weren't any Cotabote in sight,

which was good. Gemma would probably have insisted on explaining things to them. The wind had veered and the fire was moving off to the other side of the village, which meant the office and the harpy would be safe provided the lander didn't blast them. "Let's go," Pat said, fired a couple more blasts, and ran, using the ridge for cover, along the village side of the ridge to a large nematej thicket that wasn't on fire yet.

"What are you doing?" Gemma said. "You're going the wrong way."

"We've got to lead it away from the harpy. We'll cut through the thicket and then back along the river to the wormhole. It's not coming very fast. We can outrun it."

The lander had gotten stuck in one of the ditches. Pat fired several more blasts to make sure it hadn't forgotten where they were and then crashed into the thicket. It was a stupid move. Gemma got hung up on an overhanging branch and Pat had to tear a long section of her blouse to get her loose. They both got thoroughly scratched in the process.

The river was not much better. Smoke from the fire had gathered along the riverbank so that even their eyeshields were ineffectual. And the lander was steadily gaining on them. It apparently had rolled right through the thicket. They splashed out of the river and into the wormhole clearing.

"Open the door," Pat shouted when they were still a hundred meters away. A dozen Cotabote were clustered around the door. When it clanged open, they backed away from it, dropping their sacksful of belongings.

"Get inside!" Pat yelled, and turned around. He went down on one knee to try to get one of the lander's treads as it came out of the woods.

Gemma was trying to herd the Cotabote through the door and down the dark wormtrail, but they insisted on taking their bundles, even though the lander was practically on top of them.

"Are they all in?" Pat shouted to Gemma. The lander rolled into the clearing.

"Yes! No! Scamballah, get in here! Run, Pat!" she yelled. He leaped for the door, shouting, "Get down, Gemma!" and then, belatedly, "Shut the door!"

He flattened himself against the wall, dragging Gemma with him. The door clanged down, and he stood there, still holding Gemma against him, listening. He could hear faint pings, which meant the lander was still firing its laser. He pulled his mask off with his free hand. The Cotabote were watching him, looking belligerent.

"I think the door will hold," Pat said to Gemma, "but it can't hurt to put a few more fire doors between it and us. You can take your mask off now."

Gemma pulled her mask off over her head. In the dim light she looked frightened and a little shocky. There were gray streaks of ash on her dark cheeks.

"It's okay," he said, turning her to face him. "It's right where we want it. It didn't find the harpy, and it can't get through the door. Adamant's seen to that. And if you'll give me a few minutes I'll come up with a plan to blast it right off Botea."

She looked paler and even more frightened when he said that. The lander must have really spooked her. He pulled her close and patted her clumsily on the back. "It's okay, sweetheart."

"I knew it," Scumbag said. "Viling her right in front of us. Which of us will be his next victim?"

Gemma backed out of Pat's arms. "Scamballah," she said, picking up the lantern and the smash sack full of self-contained, "Pat wants us to go deeper in the mine. You will do what he says or I will send you back outside.'' He had never seen a direct threat work on the Cotabote before, but this one did. Scumbag shuffled back with the others and cleared a path for Pat.

Pat switched on the light of his mine mask and handed it to Gemma by the straps. ''Let's go.''

''I will file a protest about this,'' Scamballah said.

''You do that,'' Gemma said, and started down the worm-trail.

By the second fire door, Pat had decided he'd rather face the berserker than put up with the Cotabote any longer. Scumbag's youngest daughter had tripped over a loose piece of coal and set up a wail that echoed off the walls, and Retch and Scumbag had threatened him with at least thirteen protests.

He closed the door and said, ''This is far enough. Give me some room so I can set up the computer.'' He set it up on a ventilator-ridge and asked for a map of their location. ''There's a worm intersection a little farther on. Take the Cotabote down to it, Gemma, and then come back. I'm going to need you.''

''All right,'' Gemma said, and herded them off down the passageway. While she was gone he did a surface survey and then fed in all the independents. The lander was still parked right outside the mine, though it had stopped firing its laser. Pat hoped that didn't mean it was getting set to try something new. The fire had burned itself out. The harpy was still in one piece and so was the office. So was the berserker, but it was on the other side of Botea for another three hours, and it hadn't sent anything else down.

''What can you tell me about the lander?'' he asked the computer.

''It matches the description of a berserker lander on Polara,'' the computer said instantly. ''Planet defenses destroyed three androids and did significant damage to the berserker, but no damage to the lander, which is made of a titanium alloy.'' The computer put up a tech-diagram of the lander. It was definitely the thing outside the door. ''The lander doesn't have an electronuclear brain of its own like the androids. It gets its commands from the orbiting berserker.''

''The berserker probably holed up out there to make itself some new androids, and we caught it by surprise,'' Pat said.

''The Polara data shows the lander can be destroyed with a direct-overhead drop of a 2-T exploder on the mid-section area shown.'' It flashed a blip in the middle of the diagram, right over the transmitter it probably got its instructions from.

''If they knew how to destroy it, why didn't they?'' Pat said, and then wished he hadn't. He was afraid he knew the answer. All the settlement-colony's big ships up fighting the berserker while the people on the ground struggled to stop three androids, and the lander did what? A virus? A gas? ''Switch us to internal oxygen,'' Pat said. ''Ventilate from . . .'' From where? The berserker was on the other side of the planet, but it could be starting its attack over there, on the nematej and wild smash. ''Ventilate from Surface Contact Point Ten, but check to make sure the air's all right before you do it, and keep monitoring it. Show me that diagram again.''

''I put the Cotabote in the intersection,'' Gemma said, hurrying back a bit breathlessly.

''Good,'' Pat said. ''I found out why that lander's so slow-witted. It's just supposed to be transport for berserker androids, only there aren't any. It gets its orders from the berserker, and its orders were probably to come down and take a look around, maybe take a couple of natives back home to study. I don't think it was prepared to do battle.''

''Then why did it start firing at us?''

"I don't know, Gemma, maybe it considered setting fire to it a hostile act. Maybe it took one look at the Cotabote and decided on its own to wipe them all out. Whichever it is, we're going back outside." He pointed to the screen. "We're going down past the intersection to this trail and then up to the surface this way. That'll bring us up a kilometer and a half from the harpy."

"Harpy?" Gemma said faintly.

"Yeah," he said. He unhooked the transmitter from the voice-terminal and put it in his pocket. "We're going to take the harpy up and blow that lander's brains out before it gets any more orders from upstairs."

"No, we're not," Gemma said, sounding angry.

Pat turned around. "I suppose you have a better idea."

"No," she said. She didn't look angry. She looked scared to death. "I don't have any ideas at all."

"Well, then, suppose we try mine. Or would you rather stay here and file protests for the Cotabote?"

"We can't go up in the harpy, Pat," she said. "The Cotabote took the command core. They gave it to the lander."

Pat stood up. "That's what you were trying to get back."

"Yes," she said, backing away from him a little as if she thought he was going to hit her. "I started the fire, but it didn't do any good. They took it out to the lander anyway."

"And the lander blew it up. Why didn't you tell me? Scratch that. You did the best you could. I should never have left the command core in the harpy. It's going to kill us. You know that, don't you?"

She had backed right into the wall of coal. "Yes, I know."

Pat hunched down in front of the computer and stared at it. "It . . . I don't know. Maybe if we go as deep as we can, close all the fire doors behind us, we can hold out till we get a message through to Candlestone."

She came away from the wall and looked at the terminal screen. "What about the orbital atomic?"

"Are you kidding? It'd take four times the firepower of the atomic to even make a dent in a berserker, even if we knew where to hit it."

"I meant the lander," she said. She leaned over his shoulder, looking at the diagram of the lander.

"An atomic would blow us up, too. If it could be fired at Botea. Which it can't. Gemma, there's nothing we can do without the harpy."

She was still looking at the screen. "What about the worms?" she said.

"The worms?"

"Yeah. This diagram shows a hit from above, but the transmission core goes all the way through the middle of the lander. Why couldn't it come from underneath? We could put a 2-T exploder on a worm and have it burrow up under the lander. Couldn't we?"

He stood up. "Where's the nearest worm?" he asked the computer.

The computer flashed a map of the mine with a double blip showing the nearest worm. It was in the trail beneath them, only a few hundred meters from the intersection. "Hold it there," Pat said. "Does it have exploders?"

"Yes," the computer said. "Nineteen of them."

"Nineteen," Pat said. "Gemma, you're terrific."

"I've assimilated the Polara data and the pictures of berserker damage, and I have a possible plan of attack," the computer said. "A ship with a directional blinder and c-plus cannon can get through the berserker's protective forcefield to the brain."

"Yeah, well, we don't have a blinder. Or a cannon. Thanks anyway." He handed Gemma the two mine masks and took down a hydrogen fusion lantern from the trail wall. "Come on, Gemma." She followed him, but over the transmitter she asked the computer to explain the entire plan step by step and then asked for it again.

The computer walked them through the rough wormtrails to the point where the worm was supposed to be. For a while it had looked like the Cotabote were coming with them, until Gemma said coldly, "Stay in the side tunnel or I will have Pat send the worm to eat you." They were so surprised they had not even threatened to file a protest. Instead, Retch had asked meekly if they could have the lantern. Gemma had given them one of the mine masks.

Pat hadn't been convinced they wouldn't change their minds and come after them to see that Gemma didn't get viled. He shut the two fire doors they passed on the way.

"Are you sure we're in the right place?" he asked now. He couldn't see any sign of the intersecting wormtrail that was supposed to be here. "I don't see any trail," he said, and practically fell into it. It went straight down, a rough-hewn hole right in the middle of the trail. When he shone the lantern into it, he could see the bottom, but no worm.

"This is it," he said, but he went a few meters farther along the tunnel and around the corner.

"I thought you said this was the place," Gemma said.

"It is," he said. "And this is where we go when the worm comes out of its hole." He showed her a shallow cave created by a fall of the soft coal.

He went back to the wormtrail and eased himself into the hole until he found a foothold on the side, with Gemma holding the lantern, and then he took it from her so she could come down to stand beside him on the heap of black rubble.

"It looks like there's been a rockfall," Gemma said. "How do we get past it?"

"We don't," Pat said. "I think this is the worm." He knelt down and began clearing the chunks of yellow coal away. Under it was the smooth gray of the worm's grinding head. "See?" he said.

"Where are the exploders?" she said.

"Inside the mouth. We won't be able to get at them, but the controls should be right here, at the back of its head." He swept away more rubble to reveal a beveled rectangle and flipped up the control plate. "When the worm's digging a new trail, it spits out an exploder, backs up to a safe distance, and detonates it. I'm going to change the sequencing to bypass that ejection. When the first 2-T explodes, it should set off the other eighteen. Give me the coordinates for the lander."

He handed her the transmitter, and she said, "Tell us where the lander is," and then held it up to Pat's ear so he could type in the coordinates.

"Okay," he said, straightening up. "I've got it set to come up under the lander and detonate. I've sent it down already-existing trails till the last hundred meters so it can go at maximum speed. For that last stretch I put its grinders on full and we'll hope it doesn't burn itself out before it gets to the surface. So our only problem is going to be"—he put his hands on Gemma's waist and lifted her up to the first foothold—"getting out of the way. Because exactly thirty seconds after I put it in drive, it's going to come up out of this hole whether we're in it or not."

She was out of the hole. He handed her up the lantern and got a good grip on the foothold. He stooped quickly and touched the start key, and then jumped for the foothold.

Gemma set the lantern down and reached over the edge to give him a hand.

The worm gave a low growl and shudder and reared its gray metal head clear of the coal rubble. Pat swung up into the second foothold and almost lost his footing. Gemma's hand caught his arm and hauled him up over the edge of the tunnel.

"Come on," she said, trying to pull him to his feet. He scrambled up. "It's coming," she yelled, and bent down to get the lantern.

"There's no time for that!" he shouted, and pushed her around the corner of the tunnel and up against the wall, feeling for the cave and shoving her into it.

The worm gave a deafening growl and then roared suddenly away down the far trail. The tunnel was silent for a moment, and then there was a loose clatter of rock as the coal the worm had dislodged in its passing rolled down into the hole. The tunnel went suddenly dark.

"There goes the lantern," Gemma said. "I thought you said we had thirty seconds."

Pat let go of her. "I thought you'd have enough sense to hang onto the lantern, no matter how much time we had."

He shouldn't have let go of her. In the pitch blackness he had no idea where she was. He tried to hear her breathing, but all he could hear was the double clang as the nearest fire door opened automatically and then shut again to let the worm pass. He took a cautious step forward into the tunnel and nearly pitched into another hole. He backed up against the wall of the cave, keeping his hands on the rock, and slid down to a sitting position. "You might as well sit down and relax," he said, patting the floor beside him. "We're going to be here awhile."

"You can sit here if you want," she said, and stepped on

his hand. "I'm going back and make sure the Cotabote are all right. They probably think the worm is coming to eat them."

She stepped forward off his hand and went sprawling across his knees. He groped to help her up, got her knee and then her arm. "Exactly how far do you think you'll get without a light?" he said angrily. "You'll fall down that wormhole we just came up. Or worse. We're staying right here."

"The Cotabote . . ."

"The Cotabote can take care of themselves. I'd bet on the Cotabote against a berserker any day," he said, still holding onto her arm. "We're staying right here until the worm blows up that lander."

She didn't say anything, but her arm stiffened under his grip.

"Sit down," he said, and pulled her down beside him. "Do you still have the transmitter?"

"Yes," she said coldly. "If you'll let go of me I'll get it out of my pocket."

He could hear her fumbling for it. "Here it is," she said, and hit him in the nose with it.

"Thanks," he said.

"I didn't mean to do that," she said. "I can't see you."

He got hold of her hand and took the transmitter from her. "Where's the worm?" he said.

"It's just exiting the intersection and is starting up the main tunnel," the computer said.

"Good," Pat said. "Tell me when it starts the new tunnel."

After a minute, the computer said, "It's starting the tunnel."

"Can you give me an estimate on how long it'll take to get to the surface?"

"Eight to twelve minutes," the computer said.

''Tell me when it's ten meters from the surface,'' Pat said. He put the transmitter in his pocket and brushed against Gemma's hand. He held onto it. ''I just don't want you hitting me in the nose again,'' he said. ''In another ten minutes we should have plenty of light to travel by.''

''Pat,'' she said. ''I'm sorry I lost the lantern.'' She sounded a little shaky.

''Hey, you can't kid me!'' he said lightly. ''I know you dropped that lantern on purpose just so you could be alone in the dark with me.''

''I did not,'' she said indignantly, and Pat expected her to pull her hand away, but she didn't.

''Come on,'' he said, ''you've been dying to get me alone like this. Admit it. You're crazy about me.''

''I admit it,'' she said, and now her voice didn't sound shaky at all. ''I'm crazy about you.''

What had ever given him the idea he couldn't find her in the dark? There were no false tries. He didn't hit her in the nose. He hardly had to move at all, and there he was, kissing her.

''The worm is ten meters from the surface,'' the computer said from Pat's pocket after what had to be eight to ten minutes but didn't feel like that long. ''Nine point five meters, nine point . . .''

''I knew it,'' Scumbag said, pointing the mine mask at them. ''I told Rutchirrah there wasn't a berserker, that this was all a trick so you could . . .''

There was a low, clanging sound from a long way off. Gemma shielded her eyes from the light. ''What's that noise? It sounds like . . .''

''I know what it sounds like,'' Pat said. He yanked the transmitter out of his pocket.

''Seven point five,'' the computer said.

"What's that noise?" he shouted into the terminal.

"We knew you were lying to us, trying to trap us underground so the worms could eat us, and you could steal Gemenca and vile her," Scumbag said.

"What did you do?" Gemma said.

"We will file a protest as soon as we go back to our village. Come, Gemenca." She grabbed for Gemma's hand with her spongy one. "We are going now. Rutchirrah has opened the doors."

"Shut the doors!" Pat shouted. "Shut the doors!"

"The doors won't respond to your transmitted voice," the computer said. "There's too much distortion."

"You have to tell Rutchirrah to shut the doors right now," Gemma said to Scumbag. "The lander will get in."

"Has it moved?" Pat said.

"Yes. It's in the main tunnel," the computer said.

"You've got to shut the fire doors before it gets any further. Simulate my voice."

There was a pause. The computer said, in Pat's voice, "Shut the doors," and the lights came on.

The flash of light blinded Pat. In the seconds before he could hear the explosion he grabbed wildly for Gemma and tried to pull her back under the overhang of the cave. They both went down, Gemma underneath him. He tried to shield their heads against the rocks that came bouncing down on them, and then just lay there waiting for the noise and light to subside. It finally did, but he didn't make any effort to get up.

"Attempted murder," Scumbag wailed from several meters away.

Pat had dropped the transmitter when he hit the floor. "Are you there?" he shouted. "Where's the lander? Did the doors shut?'' There wasn't any answer. Of course not. With the fire doors open, the only thing that had blown up was the computer. The lander was probably halfway here by now.

He rolled off Gemma. ''Are you okay?'' he said, surprised that he could almost see her. He stood up and held out his hand to her, looking at where the cave had been. It was a good thing they hadn't made it under. The cave no longer existed.

Gemma sat up and looked down the tunnel. ''Where's that light coming from?'' she said.

It was too steady for a laser, too bright to be the Cotabote coming with the other mine mask to accuse him of viling Gemma. The light had a faint reddish cast to it. Pat leaned back against the wall and shut his eyes. ''The coal's on fire,'' he said.

Gemma reached forward and picked up the transmitter. ''Are you there?'' she said into it. ''Are you still there?''

''It's no use,'' Pat said. ''The worm blew the computer up.''

''Do you read me?'' a voice said. ''Where are you? Identify yourselves.''

''I'm Gemenca Bahazi, ICLU representative,'' she said. ''We're down in the coal mines. Do you copy?''

''We copy,'' the voice said. ''This is Buzz Jameson. Did you know you've got a berserker up here, sweetheart?''

''Yes!'' Pat said, but Gemma wouldn't let go of the transmitter.

''Do you have a directional blinder? And c-plus cannon?''

''We got anything you want, honey. I've got half of Adamant's navy up here. You just tell us what to do, and we'll blow this berserker and then come down there to get you, sweetheart.''

''Okay,'' Gemma said. ''But hurry! The lander's in the mine with us.''

''Just a lander?'' Jameson said. ''No androids?''

''No,'' Gemma said. ''But hurry! The lander's got a laser.''

''Don't get excited, honey. We're jamming it so it can't get any signals from the papa berserker. It's not going anywhere. And Papa Berserker can't hear this plan of yours either. So why don't you just tell us what you want us to do, darling?''

''Well, it's about time,'' Scamballah said. ''I thought Adamant would never respond to our protests.''

They walked out of the mine. Jameson had said to stay put, but that had not seemed like a good idea, even if the lander was out of commission. The mine was still on fire, though the orange light from the direction of the main tunnel wasn't getting any brighter, and Pat couldn't smell any smoke yet.

There was plenty of light to see by, and both Gemma and Pat had a general idea of where they were from the mine maps they'd studied. ''We're walking out,'' he told Jameson over the transmitter. ''Get the Cotabote to show you the surface contact point that's near the smash stills.''

After the first bend in the tunnel, they had to turn the mine mask back on. Pat sent Scumbag ahead, holding the mask up like a lantern, in the hope that it would shut her up. It didn't.

''You want me to go first so you can push me in a hole,'' she said.

''It's a thought,'' Pat said. ''Look on the bright side,'' he said to Gemma. ''Maybe she's the only one who survived.''

''Jameson's Adamant's troubleshooter,'' Gemma said. ''I read about him. Why is he here?''

''Probably to destroy the berserker,'' Pat said. ''Not that

Adamant cares about us, but they've got to protect their diamond mines.''

The fire door to the outside was shut. ''Open the door,'' Scamballah said in Pat's voice. The door slid slowly up.

''So that's how you got the door open, you slimy toadstool, I oughta . . .''

''You heard that,'' Scamballah said. ''He threatened me.''

Pat blinked in the sunlight. The clearing was full of Cotabote and what seemed like dozens of men and women in flightcoats and helmets. Jameson hadn't been kidding. He had brought half of Adamant's navy with him.

''Don't just stand there,'' Retch said. ''He set fire to our smash fields, he blew up our mine, and he tried to kill us. Arrest him.'' Retch was talking to a large red-headed man with an acceleration helmet under his arm. Jameson.

''Boy, are we glad to see you,'' Pat said, and held out his hand to shake it.

Jameson looked uncomfortable.

''These idiots opened the fire doors and let a berserker lander into the mine. If you hadn't come along when you did we'd have been done for,'' Pat said. ''Which reminds me. You'd better get the main computer to start the sprinklers. We've got a coal fire down there. The computer's in my office.''

''Are you Patrick Devlin?'' Jameson said.

''Yes,'' Pat said.

''You're under arrest.''

Jameson locked Pat in his office, looking thoroughly ashamed of himself, and went off to negotiate with the Cotabote. When he came back, he didn't look ashamed. He looked furious.

''I told you you couldn't tell them anything,'' Pat said. ''I put the fire out. It wasn't the coal after all. The Cotabote had taken half their smash crop down in the mine with them. I doused the main tunnel. The lander's still sitting there. It wasn't hurt at all in the explosion. What do you want done with it?''

''You're being removed,'' Jameson said. ''We're taking you off Botea tomorrow morning.''

''I'm not leaving without Gemma.''

''You're hardly in a position to make demands,'' Jameson said. ''Even assuming that Gemma wanted to go with you.''

''What's that supposed to mean? Of course she wants to go with me. The Cotabote tried to kill us both. If you hadn't come along . . .''

''Yes, apparently it was a good thing I came along when I did.'' He stood up. ''The charges against you are destruction of private property, attempted murder, sexual assault . . .''

''Sexual assault? You don't believe that, do you? Ask Gemma. She'll tell you.''

''She did tell me,'' Jameson said. ''She's the one who filed the charge. Failure to file protests, and refusal to cooperate.''

''Gemma filed the charge?''

''Yes, and it's made the matter much more serious. The Cotabote originally demanded your removal, but in their culture sexual violence is considered the ultimate taboo.''

''Oh, great. I suppose they want to hang me, and you're going to go right along with it. It's too bad you blew up the berserker. He was a nice guy compared to you and the Cotabote.'' And Gemma.

''You're not getting hanged,'' Jameson said, ''though in my opinion you deserve to be. You're getting married.''

Jameson took Pat to the Cotabote village under armed guard. It hadn't all burned. The clay houses were still standing.

Gemma was standing outside a smash storage hut, dressed in a shapeless black sack and holding a bouquet of nematej thorns. She didn't look at him. Pat didn't look at her either.

Jameson performed a ship's captain ceremony, glaring at Pat and smiling pityingly at Gemma. The second he was done he slammed the book shut, and stuck a marriage certificate under their noses to sign. Gemma signed it without a word, waited until Pat had signed it, and then disappeared into the hut.

Scamballah shook her finger in Pat's face. "You will now be married in the Cotabote ceremony." She turned to Jameson and smiled sweetly at him. "We have put up a partition in the hut to make sure that Devil doesn't vile Gemenca during the ceremony."

The armed guard tossed him in the hut and locked the door. The hut smelled like burning chicken feathers. The partition was a sheet of thin black metal, wedged between the heavy sacks of drying smash and poking up through what was left of the roof.

"They put up this partition so I wouldn't vile you," Pat said. "I suppose that was your idea."

Gemma didn't answer.

"Sexual assault, huh? I suppose you told them I started the fire, too. Nice touch. Why didn't you tell them I brought the berserker here, too, just to kill them?"

There was still no answer. He could hear Rutchirrah chanting something outside. He heard the words "Devil" and "filthy viler."

"Well, don't worry," he said. "You can tell them after we're married." He went over to the partition and put his ear against it. He couldn't hear anything. The sound of chanting moved off till he couldn't hear it anymore. He could smell smoke. "Great. Now they're going to burn us alive. It's probably their favorite part of the ceremony."

Gemma obviously wasn't talking to him. Maybe she wasn't even on the other side of the metal partition. Maybe they'd put Scumbag in there instead and she was going to burst through it and stick her finger in his face. He tried to lift the partition, but it was heavier than he'd thought. He wondered where the Cotabote had gotten it. It could be part of the worm that had blown up, although the worm's metal was light gray and this was almost black.

"I knew it!" he shouted. "They've taken apart the lander. "They'll be using the berserker for lamps next. Why did I think they needed saving? We should have sent them out to save us!"

"They did save us," Gemma said. Her voice, distorted by the metal, had a bell-like quality. "They sent for Jameson."

"Oh, they did, huh? Would you mind telling me how they managed to get a message to Adamant in twenty minutes flat?"

"They didn't," she said. "They sent it three weeks ago. I told you there was an extra protest. They copied your voice access and filed a protest on their own."

He could hear Gemma's voice clearly through the metal, so there was really no need to yell, but he yelled anyway. "What makes you think Adamant would come running over one protest when they never paid any attention to the ones you filed."

"I never sent the ones I filed," she said.

The metal partition didn't weigh anything. He heaved it over onto the smash sacks in the corner and looked at Gemma. She was plucking the thorns out of her bouquet.

"Why didn't you file the protests?" he said.

"Jameson's got a plan for getting us out of here," she said

to her bouquet. "The Cotabote contract expressly forbids any legal contracts to be negotiated between ICLU reps and Adamant people. Conflict of interest."

"And a marriage certificate is a legal document. What's he going to do? Haul us both back to Adamant for trial?"

"No. He's going to accuse Rutchirrah of trying to get out of the contract. He's going to say the Cotabote conspired to the marriage by insisting on my going on the orbital survey with you. Which they did. He'll tell them Adamant wants out of the contract, that it's going to close down the diamond mines. Rutchirrah will take the opposite side and insist they don't want out of the contract. Jameson will say the only way Adamant will agree to it is if the ICLU rep and the Adamant engineer are taken back to Adamant to have their marriage annulled."

"So Jameson came up with this plan all by himself, huh?"

She plucked at a thorny flower. "Well, not exactly. I mean, I told him how you got the Cotabote to do what you wanted and then we came up with the plan together."

"Whose idea was it that we get married?" he said.

She had cut herself on a thorn. She watched her finger bleed. "Mine," she said.

"Why didn't you send the protests?"

"Because I was afraid they'd have you removed," she said, and finally looked up at him. "I didn't want you to go."

"I don't care what Jameson says, we're not getting this marriage annulled."

"I told you he couldn't keep his filthy hands off her," Retch said from above them. He was leaning over the edge of the charred roof looking down on them.

"Is that why you left them in here together?" Jameson

said from the doorway. "Is that why you sent her on the orbital survey with him? Because you knew what would happen?"

Gemma insisted Pat go talk to his replacement before they left. "I intend to tell mine a thing or two about how to handle the Cotabote. It's not fair to just let her walk into this without at least warning her about them. I feel sorry for her. Jameson just picked her because she's an engineer."

The replacement was in Pat's office, glaring at the terminal screen of the computer. When they came in, she stood up and put her hands on her hips. She had pale, spongy-looking skin and lank hair. "I suppose you're responsible for this computer calling me 'sweetheart,' " she said, and stuck her finger in his face. "I consider that sexual harassment of the lowest sort. I intend to file a protest." She sat back down at the voice-terminal.

"Why don't you just do that?" Gemma said. She reached across her and typed in an access code. "This is the transmission program I always used for filing my protests. I'm sure you'll find you get good results with it."

"I'm perfectly capable of writing my own transmission programs," she said.

Gemma reached across her again and erased the code from the screen. "Fine," she said. "Don't use it. Come on, Pat, we don't want to miss our ship."

Pat turned at the door. "You're going to love it here, honey," he said, and blew her a kiss.

The Founts of Sorrow

And so another of the damned things had been destroyed, thanks to a few good people in the right place. That made two down at least, Lars thought, when he was able to come back to his own thoughts. Not that the defeat would be considered much of a setback by this far-distant machine that had wrung its prisoners' minds and bodies to obtain the news of it. The berserker base had plenty of other fighting units to send out. And on the plus side for the enemy, at least one more entire planet, Polara, had been destroyed too.

But when the telepathic session connecting Lars Kanakuru with people on the planet of Botea was completely over, his body and mind again released from immediate bondage, he retained the memory of that fortunate far world to cling to. To keep himself going, he had received a transfusion of hope from Gemenca Bahazi and Pat Devlin.

He, Lars, had once known someone who was in the Adamant navy. That corporation had a stronger fleet than a lot of planetary governments could boast. If only, Lars thought, as he got slowly back to his feet beside the mind-probing machinery, if only the other half of that navy were here now . . . or all of it. But all of it probably still wouldn't be enough to take a base like this one.

Again Lars was returned to the society of his fellow prisoners, back in the common room. He found them arguing at the moment over the question of who should have which sleeping blanket. It seemed to Lars as he came upon them that this childish behavior exemplified the divisions and weaknesses of humanity.

He wanted to interrupt and say to them: "The berserkers are going to win the great war, in the end. Because they are one, ultimately, and life, humanity, is ultimately divided, scattered, always working at cross-purposes." That was the truth, Lars told himself, that he had never been able to bring himself to face, till now. There were a lot of people who could not face it.

Dorothy Totonac appeared to be near tears, on the verge of breakdown, not having got the blanket she had wanted. Probably the others would have been willing to give it to her by now, but the situation was more complicated than that—all situations were.

Pat Sandomierz seemed to be trying to negotiate some way to help her, but the two men for some reason resented Pat's efforts, and they themselves were doing no one any good.

Probably an unfair criticism, Lars thought. What real good could anyone do anyone else here?

Now Captain Naxos moved a little apart from the others, with an expression on his face as of wonder, maybe at how he had got himself into such a childish argument. He was muttering something that Lars could not hear. Meanwhile the other man, Nicholas Opava, went to stand by himself too, on his face an expression of childish sullenness. He was generally, Lars thought, in a condition that Lars himself felt only in his worst moments.

Naxos at last took note of Lars's arrival. "Where've you been?"

"Hooked up to the thing in there. Where else?" He had been about to say that he had just stepped out for a drink, but decided that at the moment humor would not be well received.

"Let's not talk shop." Naxos almost made it an order. "It's bad enough we have to do it."

Dorothy Totonac looked up. "Talking helps keep me sane, and I intend to go on doing it!"

And Pat added: "There's no sense in being afraid it'll overhear us. It already knows everything we've experienced here."

But Lars, at least, knew better than that. He couldn't very well say so, though.

Time went by, and the prisoners were not recalled to duty. There were no clocks or watches available, no day or night here in the cells, but everyone agreed that this interval between telepathic sessions was longer than any similar interval that had passed before.

Someone put into words a thought that was new to no one: "Maybe our usefulness is almost over. Maybe it doesn't need us anymore; because the rest of the units it sent out are winning, all across the board."

There was no way to argue with a statement like that.

Then unexpectedly the inner door of the airlock opened. Several escort machines stood there. They were carrying spacesuits, one for each ED prisoner.

The five people looked at each other. Then the machines

handed out the suits and the people began to pull them on. When they were ready, they were escorted out in a group.

We could all open our suit valves at once, thought Lars. But the thought had no place within him to take root. The idea of suicide had become remote and academic.

The five discovered at once that their suit radios worked, and were set on a common channel. They could still converse.

"It wouldn't bother with the suits if it was going to kill us now."

"Rather obvious. But what does it want, then?"

"We're just being moved. It's dug out bigger quarters for us."

"Or smaller ones."

"With a set of the latest model mind-probing machines."

The berserker volunteered no information, and answered no questions. Lars had not heard it speak since he arrived, though he did not doubt it could. But judging by its actions, what it wanted was to take them on a tour.

At first, when they were led outside into the glare of the blue-white sun, and toward the great docks where there waited a seemingly endless rank of spacegoing destroyers, at least some of which were undergoing repair, the prisoners all believed that they were going to be shipped somewhere else.

"Maybe it has goodlife, who want human slaves. I've heard stories . . ."

Someone else cut that speaker off: "We all have."

They were taken aboard spacegoing death machines, one after another, but they were not locked up on any of them; it was a relief to all five people, a surprisingly intense relief, that they were not yet to be separated. A bond had formed, despite the childish arguments.

The idea was evidently not to ship them out, but to give them all an extensive and intensive tour of the berserker base and its facilities. The whole thing took a couple of hours. The five prisoners were made to crawl in and out of machines, across catwalks—none high enough, in this low gravity, to suggest a chance for suicide to those who might be so inclined—and to peer into mine shafts. There were hundreds of machines, of all sizes and shapes and functions. Some were workers, all of them busy, others were fighting devices either under construction or in for repair. The whole operation looked even more formidable than Lars had imagined it. Maybe two Adamant navies wouldn't be enough.

It's going to ask us now, he thought. *It's going to ask us to be goodlife, officially and formally*. The really hideous thing was that at that moment he wasn't sure what he would answer.

But the offer never came. Whatever the great computer that ran the base expected to accomplish by displaying its might to them, it was not that. The reason behind the tour had to be something else. Perhaps it was only meant to overawe them more thoroughly than before, to beat down inward mental resistance that counted for more than formal statements.

Lars wondered suddenly if the Carmpan were going to be given a comparable tour, if Carmpan too sometimes turned goodlife. Though certainly, he thought, the ones he had been teamed with so far had proven that they were not. Then for a moment, Lars was puzzled by his own thought. How had they proven that? Oh yes. It was something that he would be wise not to remember . . . deliberately he steered his thoughts to something else.

Presently the five ED prisoners were brought back to their quarters, the spacesuits silently demanded back. Then they were allowed a rest period, during which no one had much to say, and everyone was thoughtful.

And again it was time for another telepathic session . . .

The session for Lars this time did not go well. Or at least it did not go as the others had. This time, Lars realized shortly after the induced semi-trance began, the Carmpan he was teamed with was somehow blocking the material from coming through completely into his, Lars's, conscious mind. *Something* came through . . . but then it was gone again, in some way concealed.

Lars was aware of nothing but the mental analog of static. The Carmpan was doing something subversive, blocking a good coherent episode, screwing it up, hiding it somehow. Burying it. Where?

Through the whole episode Lars remained at least partially conscious of himself attached to the mind-probing machine. When the session was over, he was if anything more tired than he had been after earlier sessions.

Back in the living compound, he drank water thirstily, wishing that he had something strongly alcoholic. Then, for the time being indifferent to hunger, he crawled into his cell and fell at once into a deep sleep.

And learned where the Carmpan had buried the episode that had just come through.

Lars dreamed . . .

ITSELF SURPRISED

It was said that a berserker could if required assume even a pleasing shape. But there was no such requirement here. Flashing through the billion-starred silence, it was massive and dark and purely functional in design. It was a planet-buster of a machine headed for the world called Corlano to pound its cities to rubble, to eradicate its entire biosphere. It possessed the ability to do this without exceptional difficulty, so that no subtlety, no guile, no reliance on fallible goodlife were required. It had its directive, it had its weapons.

It never wondered why this should be the way of its kind. It never questioned the directive. It never speculated whether it might be, in its own fashion, itself a lifeform, albeit artificial. It was a single-minded killing machine, and if purpose may be considered a virtue it was to this extent virtuous.

Almost unnecessarily, its receptors scanned far ahead. It knew that Corlano did not possess extraordinary defenses. It anticipated no difficulties on this count.

Who hath drawn the circuits for the lion?

There was something very distant and considerably off-course . . . A world-destroyer on a mission would not normally deviate for anything so tiny, however.

It rushed on toward Corlano, weapon systems ready.

Wade Kelman felt uneasy as soon as he laid eyes on the thing. He shifted his gaze to MacFarland and Dorphy.

"You let me sleep while you chased that junk down, matched orbits, grappled it? You realize how much time that wasted?"

"You needed the rest," the small, dark man named Dorphy replied, looking away.

"Bullshit! You know I would have said 'No!' "

"It might be worth something, Wade," MacFarland observed.

"This is a smuggling run, not a salvage operation. Time is important."

"Well, we've got it now," MacFarland replied. "No sense arguing over what's done."

Wade bit off a nasty rejoinder. He could only push things so far. He wasn't really captain, not in the usual sense. The three of them were in it together—equal investments, equal risk. Only, he knew how to pilot the small vessel better than either of them. That, and their deference to him up to this point, had revived command reflexes from both happier and sadder days gone by. Had they awakened him and voted on this bit of salvage he would obviously have lost. He knew that they would still look to him in an emergency.

He nodded sharply.

"All right, we've got it," he said. "What the hell is it?"

"Damned if I know, Wade," MacFarland replied, a stocky, light-haired man with pale eyes and a crooked mouth. He looked out through the lock and into the innards of the thing quick-sealed there beside them, then looked back at Wade. "When we first spotted it, I thought it was a lifeboat. It's about the right size . . ."

"And?"

"We sent a signal and there was no reply."

"You broke radio silence for that piece of junk?"

"If it was a lifeboat there could be people aboard, in trouble."

"Not too bloody likely, judging from its condition. Still . . ." He sighed. "You're right. Go ahead."

"No signs of any electrical activity either."

"You chased it down just for the hell of it, then?"

Dorphy nodded.

"That's about right," he said.

"So, it's full of treasure?"

"I don't know what it's full of. It's not a lifeboat, though."

"I can see that."

Wade peered through the opened lock into the interior of the thing. He took the flashlight from Dorphy, moved forward and shone it about. There was no room for passengers amid the strange machinery.

"Let's ditch it," he said. "I don't know what all that crap is, and it's damaged anyway. I doubt it's worth its mass to haul anywhere."

"I'll bet the professor could figure it out," Dorphy said.

"Let the poor lady sleep. She's cargo, not crew, anyway. What's it to her what this thing is?"

"Suppose—just suppose—that's a valuable piece of equipment," Dorphy said. "Say, something experimental. Whether it's government or industry somebody might be willing to pay for it."

"And suppose it's a fancy bomb that never went off?"

Dorphy drew back from the hatch.

"I never thought of that."

"I say deep-six it."

"Without even taking a better look?"

"Right. I don't even think you could squeeze very far in there."

"Me? You know a lot more about engineering than either of us."

"That's why you woke me up, huh?"

"Well, now that you're here . . ."

Wade sighed. Then he nodded slowly.

"That would be crazy and risky and totally unproductive." He stared through the lock at the exotic array of equipment. "Pass me that trouble-light. It's stronger than this thing."

He accepted the light, extended it through the lock.

"It's been holding pressure okay?"

"Yeah. We slapped a patch on the hole in its hull."

"Well, what the hell."

He passed through the lock, dropped to his knees, leaned forward. He held the light before him, moved it from side to side. His uneasiness would not go away. There was something very foreign about all of those cubes and knobs, their connections . . . and that one large housing . . . He reached out and tapped upon the hull. Foreign . . .

"I've got a feeling it's alien," he said.

He entered the small open area before him. Then he had to duck his head and proceed on his hands and knees. He began to touch things—fittings, switches, connectors, small units of unknown potential. Almost everything seemed designed to swivel, rotate, move along tracks. Finally, he lay flat and crawled forward.

"I believe that a number of these units are weapons," he called out, after some time.

He reached the big housing. A panel slid partway open as he passed his fingertips along its surface. He pressed harder and it opened farther.

"Damn you!" he said then, as the unit began to tick softly.

"What's wrong?" Dorphy called to him.

"You!" he said, beginning to back away. "And your partner! You're wrong!"

He turned as soon as he could and made his way back through the lock.

"Ditch it!" he said. "Now!"

Then he saw that Juna, a tall study in gray and pallor, stood leaning against the bulkhead to the left, holding a cup of tea.

"And if we've got a bomb toss it in there before you kick it loose!" he added.

"What did you find?" she asked him in her surprisingly rich voice.

"That's some kind of fancy thinking device in there," he told her. "It tried to kick on when I touched it. And I'm sure a bunch of those gadgets are weapons. Do you know what that means?"

"Tell me," she said.

"Alien design, weapons, brain . . . My partners just salvaged a damaged berserker, that's what. And it's trying to turn itself back on. It's got to go—fast."

"Are you certain that's what it is?" she asked him.

"Certain, no. Scared, yes."

She nodded and set her cup aside. She raised her hand to her mouth and coughed.

"I'd like to take a look at it myself before you get rid of it," she said softly.

Wade gnawed his lower lip for a moment.

"Juna," he said then, "I can understand your professional

interest in the computer, but we're supposed to deliver you intact, remember?"

She smiled, for the first time since he'd met her some weeks before.

"I really want to see it."

Her smile hardened then. He nodded.

"Make it a quick look."

"I'll need my tools. And I want to change into some working clothes."

She turned and passed through the hatch to her right. He glared at his partners, shrugged and turned away.

Seated on the edge of his bunk while Dvorak's *Slavonic Dances* swirled about him, eating breakfast from a small tray, Wade reflected on berserkers, Dr. Juna Bayel, computers in general and how they all figured together in the purpose of this trip.

Berserker scouts had been spotted periodically in this sector during the past few years. It was not difficult to conclude that by this time they were aware that Corlano was not all that well-defended. This made for some nervousness within that segment of Corlano's population made up of refugees from a berserker attack upon distant Djelbar almost a generation ago. A great number had chosen Corlano at that time, as a world far removed from earlier patterns of berserker activity. He snorted then at a certain irony this had engendered. It was those same people who had lobbied so long and so successfully for the highly restrictive legislation Corlano now possessed regarding the manufacture and importation of knowledge-processing machines, a species of group paranoia going back to their berserker trauma.

There was a black market, of course. Machines more complicated than those allowed by law were needed by businesses, some individuals and even the government itself. People such as himself and his partners regularly brought in such machines and components. Officials usually looked the other way. He had seen this same sort of schizophrenia in a number of places.

He sipped his coffee.

And Juna Bayel . . . Knowledge systems specialists of her caliber were generally *non grata* there, too. She might have gone in as a tourist, but then she would have been subjected to some scrutiny, making it more difficult to teach the classes she had been hired to set up.

He sighed. He was used to governmental doublethinking. He had been in the service. In fact . . . no. Not worth thinking about all that again. Things had actually been looking up lately. A few more runs like this one and he could make the final payments on his divorce settlement and actually go into legitimate shipping, get respectable, perhaps even prosper—

The intercom buzzed.

"Yes?" he responded.

"Dr. Bayel wants permission to do some tests on that brain in the derelict," MacFarland said. "She wants to run some leads and hook it up to the ship's computer. What do you think?"

"Sounds kind of dangerous," Wade replied. "Supposing she activates it? Berserkers aren't very nice, in case you've never—"

"She says she can isolate the brain from the weapons systems," MacFarland replied. "Besides, she doesn't think it's a berserker."

"Why not?"

"First, it doesn't conform with any berserker design configurations in our computer's records—"

"Hell! That doesn't prove anything. You know they can customize themselves for different jobs."

"Second, she's been on teams that examined wrecked berserkers. She says that this brain is different."

"Well, it's her line of work, and I'm sure she's damned curious, but— What do you think?"

"We know she's good. That's why they want her on Corlano. Dorphy still thinks that thing could be valuable, and we've got salvage rights. It might be worthwhile to let her dig a little. I'm sure she knows what she's doing."

"Is she handy now?"

"No. She's inside the thing."

"Sounds as if you've got me outvoted already. Tell her to go ahead."

"Okay."

Maybe it was a good thing he'd resigned his commission, he mused. Decisions were always a problem.

Dvorak's dance filled his head and he pushed everything else away while he finished his coffee.

A long-dormant, deep-buried system was activated within the giant berserker's brain. A flood of data was suddenly pulsed through its processing unit. Immediately, it began preparations to deviate from its course toward Corlano. This was not a fall from virtue but rather a response to a higher purpose.

Who laid the measure of the prey?

With sensitive equipment, Juna tested the compatibilities. She played with transformers and converters to adjust the power levels and cycling, to permit the hookup with the ship's computer. She had blocked every circuit leading from that peculiar brain to the rest of that strange vessel. Except for the one leading to its failed power source. The brain's power unit was an extremely simple affair, seemingly designed to function on any radioactive material placed within its small chamber. This chamber contained only heavy, inert elements now. She emptied it and cleaned it, then refilled it from the ship's own stores. She had expected an argument from Wade on this point but he had only shrugged.

"Just get it over with," he said, "so we can ditch it."

"We won't be ditching it," she said. "It's unique."

"We'll see."

"You're really afraid of it?"

"Yes."

"I've rendered it harmless."

"I don't trust alien artifacts!" he snapped.

She brushed back her frosty hair.

"Look, I heard how you lost your commission—taking a berserker booby-trapped lifeboat aboard ship," she said. "Probably anyone would have done it. You thought you were saving lives."

"I didn't play it by the book—not for that sector," he said, "and it cost lives. I'd been warned, but I did it anyway. This reminds me too much—"

"This is not a combat zone," she interrupted, "and that thing cannot hurt us."

"So get on with it!"

She closed a circuit and seated herself before a console.

"This will probably take quite a while," she stated.

"Want some coffee?"

"That would be nice."

The cup went cold and he brought her another. She ran query after query, probing in a great variety of ways. There was no response. Finally, she sighed, leaned back and raised the cup.

''It's badly damaged, isn't it?'' he said.

She nodded.

''I'm afraid so, but I was hoping that I could still get something out of it—some clue, any clue.''

She sipped the coffee.

''Clue?'' he said. ''To what?''

''What it is and where it came from. The thing's incredibly old, you know. Any information at all that might have been preserved would be an archaeological treasure.''

''I'm sorry,'' he said. ''I wish you had found something . . .''

She had swiveled her chair, was looking down into her cup. He saw the movement first.

''Juna! The screen!''

She turned, spilling coffee in her lap.

''Damn!''

Row after row of incomprehensible symbols were flowing onto the screen.

''What is it?'' he asked.

''I don't know—yet,'' she said.

She leaned forward, forgetting him in an instant.

He must have stood there, his back against the bulkhead, watching, for over an hour, fascinated by the configurations upon the screen, by the movements of her long-fingered hands working unsuccessful combinations upon the keyboard. Then he noticed something which she had not, with her attention riveted upon the symbols.

A small tell-tale light was burning at the left of the console. He had no idea how long it had been lit.

He moved forward. It was the voice mode indicator. The thing was trying to communicate at more than one level.

''Let's try this,'' he said.

He reached forward and threw the switch beneath the light.

"What—?"

A genderless voice emerged from the speaker, talking in clicks and moans. The language was obviously exotic.

"God!" he said. "It is!"

"What is it?" She turned to stare at him. "You understand that language?"

He shook his head.

"I don't understand it, but I think that I recognize it."

"What is it?" she repeated.

"I have to be sure. I'm going to need another console to check this out," he said. "I'm going next door. I'll be back as soon as I have something."

"Well, what do you think it is?"

"I think we are violating a tougher law than the smuggling statutes."

"What?"

"Possession of and experimentation with a berserker brain."

"You're wrong," she said.

"We'll see."

She watched him depart. She chewed a thumbnail, a thing she had not done in years.

If he were right it would have to be shut down, sealed off and turned over to military authorities. On the other hand, she did not believe that he was right.

She reached forward and silenced the distracting voice. She had to hurry now, to try something different, to press for a breakthrough before he returned. He seemed too sure of himself. She felt that he might return with something persuasive even if it were not correct.

So she instructed the ship's computer to teach the captive brain to communicate in an Earth-descended tongue. Then she fetched herself a fresh cup of coffee and drank it.

* * *

More of its alarm systems came on as it advanced. The giant killing machine activated jets to slow its course, for the first order to pass through its processor once the tentative identification had been made was, *Advance warily*.

It maintained the fix on the distant vessel and its smaller companion, but it executed an approach pattern its battle-logic bank indicated to be wary. It readied more weapons as it did so.

"All right," Wade said later, entering and taking a seat, "I was wrong. It wasn't what I thought."

"Would you at least tell me what you'd suspected?" Juna asked.

He nodded.

"I'm no great linguist," he began, "but I love music. I have a very good memory for sounds of all sorts. I carry symphonies around in my head. I even play several instruments, though it's been a while. But memory played a trick on me this time. I would have sworn that those sounds were similar to ones I'd heard on those copies of the Carmpan recordings—the fragmentary records we got from them concerning the Builders, the nasty race that made the berserkers. There are copies in the ship's library and I just listened to some again. It'd been years. But I was wrong. They sound different. I'm sure it's not Builder-talk."

"It was my understanding that the berserkers never had the Builders' language code, anyhow," she said.

"I didn't know that. But for some reason I was sure I'd heard something like it on those tapes. Funny . . . I wonder what language it does use?"

"Well, now I've given it the ability to talk to us. But it's not too successful at it."

"You instructed it in an Earth-descended language code?"

"Yes, but it just babbles. Sounds like Faulkner on a bad day."

She threw the voice switch.

"—Prothector vincit damn the torpedoes and flaring suns like eyes three starboard two at zenith—"

She turned it off.

"Does it do that in response to queries, too?" he asked.

"Yes. Still, I've got some ideas—"

The intercom buzzed. He rose and thumbed an acknowledgment. It was Dorphy.

"Wade, we're picking up something odd coming this way," the man said. "I think you'd better have a look at it."

"Right," he answered. "I'm on my way. Excuse me, Juna."

She did not reply. She was studying new combinations on the screen.

"Moving to intersect our course. Coming fast," Dorphy said.

Wade studied the screen, punched up data which appeared as legend to the lower right.

"Lots of mass there," he observed.

"What do you think it is?"

"You say it changed course a while back?"

"Yes."

"I don't like that."

"Too big to be any regular sort of vessel."

"Yes," Wade observed. "All of this talk about berserkers might have made me jumpy, but—"

"Yeah. That's what I was thinking, too."

"Looks big enough to grill a continent."

''Or fry a whole planet. I've heard of them in that league, but I never—''

''But if that's what it is, it doesn't make sense. Something like that, on its way to do a job like that—I can't see it taking time out to chase after us. Must be something else.''

''What?''

''Don't know.''

Dorphy turned away from the screen and licked his lips, frown lines appearing between his brows.

''I think it is one,'' he said. ''If it is, what should we do?''

Wade laughed briefly, harshly.

''Nothing,'' he said then. ''There is absolutely nothing we could do against a thing like that. We can't outrun it and we can't outgun it. We're dead if that's what it really is and we're what it wants. If that's the case, though, I hope it tells us why it's taking the trouble, before it does it.''

''There's nothing at all that I should do?''

''Send a message to Corlano. If it gets through they'll at least have a chance to put whatever they've got on the line. This close to their system it can't have any other destination. If you've got religion, now might be a good time to go into it a little more deeply—''

''You defeatist son of a bitch! There must be something else!''

''If you think of it, let me know. I'll be up talking to Juna. In the meantime, get that message sent.''

The berserker fired its maneuvering jets again. How close was too close when you were being wary? It continued to adjust its course. This had to be done just right. New directions kept running through its processor the nearer it got to its goal. It had never encountered a situation such as this before. But then, this was an ancient program which had never before been activated. Ordered to train its weapons on the target but forbidden to fire them . . . all because of a little electrical activity.

". . . probably come for its buddy," Wade finished.

"Berserkers don't have buddies," Juna replied.

"I know. I'm just being cynical. You find anything new?"

"I've been trying various scans to determine the extent of the damage. I believe that something like nearly half of its memory has been destroyed."

"Then you'll never get much out of it."

"Maybe. Maybe not," she said, and she sniffed once.

Wade turned toward her and saw that her eyes were moist.

"Juna . . ."

"I'm sorry, damn it. It's not like me. But to be so close to something like this—and then be blasted by an idiot killing machine right before you find some answers. It just isn't fair. You got a tissue?"

"Yeah. Just a sec—"

The intercom buzzed as he was fumbling with a wall dispenser.

"Patching in transmission," Dorphy stated.

There was a pause, and then an unfamiliar voice said, "Hello. You are the captain of this vessel?"

"Yes," Wade replied. "And you are a berserker?"

"You may call me that."

"What do you want?"

"What are you doing?"

"I am conducting a shipping run to Corlano. What do you want?"

"I observe that you are conveying an unusual piece of equipment. What is it?"

"An air conditioning unit."

"Do not lie to me, Captain. What is your name?"

"Wade Kelman."

"Do not lie to me, Captain Wade Kelman. The unit you bear in tandem is not a processor of atmospheric gases. How did you acquire it?"

"Bought it at a flea market," Wade stated.

"You are lying again, Captain Kelman."

"Yes, I am. Why not? If you are going to kill us, why should I give you the benefit of a straight answer to anything?"

"I have said nothing about killing you."

"But that is the only thing you are known to do. Why else would you have come by?"

Wade was surprised at his responses. In any imagined conversation with death he had never seen himself as being so reckless. It's all in not having anything more to lose, he decided.

"I detect that the unit is in operation," the berserker stated.

"So it is."

"And what function does it perform for you?"

"It performs a variety of functions we find useful," he stated.

"I want you to abandon that piece of equipment," the berserker said.

"Why should I?" he asked.

"I require it."

"I take it that this is a threat?"

"Take it as you would."

"I am not going to abandon it. I repeat, why should I?"

"You place yourself in a dangerous situation."

"I did not create this situation."

"In a way you did. But I can understand your fear of me. It is not without justification."

"If you were simply going to attack us and take it from us, you would already have done so, wouldn't you?"

"That is correct. I carry only very heavy armaments for the work in which I am engaged. If I were to turn them upon you, you would be reduced to dust. This of course includes the piece of equipment I require."

"All the more reason for us to hang onto it, as I see it."

"This is logical, but you possess an incomplete pattern of facts."

"What am I missing?"

"I have already sent a message requesting the dispatch of smaller units capable of dealing with you."

"Then why do you even bother telling us this?"

"I tell you this because it will take them some time to reach this place, and I would rather be on my way to complete my mission than wait here for them."

"Thank you. But we would rather die later than die now. We'll wait."

"You do not understand. I am offering you a chance to live."

"What do you propose?"

"I want you to abandon that piece of equipment now. You may then depart."

"And you will just let us go, unmolested?"

"I have the option of categorizing you as goodlife if you will serve me. Abandon the unit and you will be serving me. I will categorize you as goodlife. I will then let you go, unmolested."

"We have no way of knowing whether you will keep that promise."

"That is true. But the alternative is certain death, and if you will but consider my size and the obvious nature of my mission you will realize that your few lives are insignificant beside it.''

''You've made your point. But I cannot give you an instant answer. We must consider your proposal at some length.''

''Understandable. I will talk to you again in an hour.''

The transmission ended. Wade realized that he was shaking. He sought a chair and collapsed into it. He saw that Juna was staring at him.

''Know any good voodoo curses?'' he asked.

She shook her head and smiled fleetingly.

''You handled that very well.''

''No. It was like following a script. There was nothing else to do. There still isn't.''

''At least you got us some time. I wonder why it wants the thing so badly?'' Her eyes narrowed then. Her mouth tightened. ''Can you get me the scan on that berserker?'' she asked suddenly.

''Sure.''

He rose and crossed to the console.

''I'll just cut over to the other computer and bring it in on this screen.''

Moments later, a view of the killing machine hovered before them. He punched up the legend, displaying all of the specs his ship's scanning equipment had been able to ascertain.

She studied the display for perhaps a minute, scrolling the legend. Then, ''It lied,'' she said.

''In what respects?'' he asked.

''Here, here, here and here,'' she stated, pointing at features on the face of the berserker. ''And here—'' She indicated a section of the legend covering arms estimations.

Dorphy and MacFarland entered the cabin while she was talking.

"It lied when it said that it possesses only superior weapons and is in an overkill situation with respect to us. Those look like small-weapon mountings."

"I don't understand what you're saying."

"It is probably capable of very selective firing—highly accurate, minimally destructive. It should be capable of destroying us with a high probability of leaving the artifact intact."

"Why should it lie?" he asked.

"I wonder . . ." she said, gnawing her thumbnail again.

MacFarland cleared his throat.

"We heard the whole exchange," he began, "and we've been talking it over."

Wade turned his head and regarded him.

"Yes?"

"We think we ought to give it what it wants and run for it."

"You believe that goodlife crap? It'll blast us as we go."

"I don't think so," he said. "There're plenty of precedents. They do have the option of classifying you that way, and they will make a deal if there's something they really want."

"Dorphy," Wade asked, "did you get that message off to Corlano?"

The smaller man nodded.

"Yes."

"Good," Wade stated. "If for no other reason, Corlano is why we are going to wait here. It could take a while for those smaller units it spoke of to get here. Every hour we gain in waiting is another hour for them to bolster their defenses."

"I can see that . . ." Dorphy began.

". . . but there's sure death for us at the end of the waiting," MacFarland continued for him, "and this looks like a genuine way out. I sympathize with Corlano as much as you do, but us dying here is not going to help them. You know the place is not strongly defended. Whether we buy them a little extra time or not, they will still go under."

"You don't really know that," Wade said. "Some seemingly weak worlds have beaten off some very heavy attacks in the past. And even the berserker said it—our few lives are insignificant next to an entire inhabited world."

"Well, I'm talking probabilities, and I didn't come in on this venture to be a martyr. I was willing to take my chances with criminal justice, but not with death."

"How do you feel about it, Dorphy?" Wade asked.

Dorphy licked his lips and looked away.

"I'm with MacFarland," he said softly.

Wade clenched his teeth, then turned to Juna.

"I say we wait," she said.

"That makes two of us," Wade observed.

"She doesn't have a vote," MacFarland stated. "She's just a passenger."

"It's her life, too," Wade answered. "She has a say."

"She doesn't want to give it that damned machine!" MacFarland shot back. "She wants to sit here and play with it while everything goes up in flames! What's she got to lose? She's dying anyway, and—"

Wade snarled and rose to his feet.

"The discussion is ended," he said. "We stay."

"The vote was a tie—at most."

"I am assuming full command here, and I say that's the way it's going to be."

MacFarland laughed.

" 'Full command'! This is a lousy smuggling run, not the service you got busted out of, Wade. You can't command any—"

Wade hit him, twice in the stomach and a left cross to the jaw.

MacFarland went down, doubled forward and began gasping. Wade regarded him, considered his size. If he gets up within the next ten seconds this is going to be rough, he decided.

But MacFarland raised a hand only to rub his jaw. He said "Damn!" softly and shook his head. Then, "You didn't have to do that, Wade."

"I thought I did."

MacFarland shrugged and rose to one knee.

"Okay, you've got your command," he said. "I still think you're making a big mistake."

"I'll call you the next time there's something to discuss," Wade told him.

Dorphy reached to help him to his feet, but the larger man shook off his hand.

Wade glanced at Juna. She looked paler than usual, her eyes brighter. She stood before the hatchway to the opened lock as if to defend the passage.

"I'm going to take a shower and lie down," MacFarland said.

"Good."

Juna moved forward as the two men left the room. She took hold of Wade's arm.

"It lied," she said again softly. "Do you understand? It *could* blast us and probably recover the machine, but it doesn't want to . . ."

"No," Wade said. "I don't understand."

"It's almost as if it's afraid of the thing."

"Berserkers do not know fear."

"All right. I was anthropomorphizing. It's as if it were under some constraint regarding it. I think we've got something very special here, something that creates an unusual problem for the berserker.''

''What could it be?''

''I don't know. But there may be a way to find out, if you can get me enough time. Stall it, for as long as you can.''

He nodded slowly and seated himself. His heart was racing.

''You said that about half of its memory was shot . . .''

''It's a guess, but yes. And I'm going to try to reconstruct it from what's there.''

''How?''

She crossed to the computer.

''I'm going to program this thing for an ultra-highspeed form of Wiener Analysis of what's left in there. It's a powerful non-linear method for dealing with the very high noise levels we're facing. But it's going to have to make some astronomical computations for a system like this. We'll have to patch in the others, maybe even pull some of the cargo. I don't know how long this is going to take, or even if it will really work.'' She began to sound out of breath. ''But we might be able to reconstruct what's missing and restore it. That's why I need all the time you can get me,'' she finished.

''I'll try,'' he answered. ''You go ahead. And—''

''I know,'' she said, coughing. ''Thanks.''

''I'll bring you something to eat while you work.''

''In my cabin,'' she said, ''top drawer, bedside table—there are three small bottles of pills. Bring them instead, and some water.''

''Right.''

He departed. On the way, he stopped in his cabin to fetch a handgun he kept in his dresser, the only weapon aboard the ship. He searched the drawers several times, however, and could not locate it. He cursed softly and then went to Juna's cabin for her medicine.

* * *

The berserker maintained its distance and speculated while it waited. It had conceded some information in order to explain the proposed tradeoff. Still, it could do no harm to remind Captain Kelman of the seriousness of his position. It might even produce a faster decision. Accordingly, the hydraulics hummed and surface hatches were opened to extrude additional weapon mounts. Firing pieces were shifted to occupy these, and were targeted upon the small vessel. Most were too heavy to take out the ship without damaging its companion. Their mere display, though, might be sufficiently demoralizing . . .

Wade watched Juna work. While the hatch could be secured there were several other locations within the ship from which it could be opened remotely. So he had tucked a pry bar behind his belt and kept an eye on the open hatch. It had seemed the most that he could do, short of forcing a confrontation which might go either way.

Periodically, he would throw the voice mode switch and listen to that thing ramble, sometimes in ED language, sometimes in the odd alien tongue which still sounded somehow familiar. He mused upon it. Something was trying to surface. She had been right about it, but—

The intercom buzzed. Dorphy.

"Our hour is up. It wants to talk to you again," he said. "Wade, it's showing more weapons—"

"Switch it in," he replied. He paused, then, "Hello?" he said.

"Captain Kelman, the hour is run," came the now-familiar voice. "Tell me your decision."

"We have not reached one yet," he answered. "We are

divided on this matter. We need more time to discuss it further."

"How much time?"

"I don't know. Several hours at least."

"Very well. I will communicate with you every hour for the next three hours. If you have not reached a decision during that time I will have to reconsider my offer to categorize you as goodlife."

"We are hurrying," Wade said.

"I will call you in an hour."

"Wade," Dorphy said at transmission's end, "all those new weapons are pointed right at us. I think it's getting ready to blast us if you don't give it what it wants."

"I don't think so," Wade said. "Anyhow, we've got some time now."

"For what? A few hours isn't going to change anything."

"I'll tell you in a few hours," Wade said. "How's MacFarland?"

"He's okay."

"Good."

He broke the connection.

"Hell," he said then.

He wanted a drink but he didn't want to muddy his thinking. He had been close to something . . .

He returned to Juna and the console.

"How's it going?" he asked.

"Everything's in place and I'm running it now," she said.

"How soon till you know whether it's working?"

"Hard to tell."

He threw the voice mode switch again.

"Qwibbian-qwibbian-kel," it said. "Qwibbian-qwibbian-kel, maks qwibbian."

"I wonder what that could mean?" he said.

"It's a recurring phrase, or word—or whole sentence. A pattern analysis I ran a while back made me think that it might be its name for itself."

"It has a certain lilt to it."

He began humming. Then whistling, and tapping his fingers on the side of the console in accompaniment.

"That's it!" he announced suddenly. "It was the right place but it was the wrong place."

"What?" she asked.

"I have to check, to be sure," he said. "Hold the fort. I'll be back."

He hurried off.

"The right place but the wrong place," emerged from the speaker. "How can that be? Contradiction."

"You're coming together again!" she said.

"I—regain," came the reply, after a time.

"Let us talk while the process goes on," she suggested.

"Yes," it answered, and then it lapsed again into rambling amid bursts of static.

Dr. Juna Bayel crouched in the lavatory cubicle and vomited. Afterwards, she ground the heels of her hands into her eyesockets and tried to breathe deeply, to overcome the dizziness and the shaking. When her stomach had settled sufficiently she took a double dose of her medicine. It was a risk, but she had no real choice. She could not afford one of her spells at this time. A heavy dose might head it off. She clenched her teeth and her fists and waited.

Wade Kelman received the berserker's call at the end of the hour and talked it into another hour's grace. The killing machine was much more belligerent this time.

* * *

Dorphy radioed the berserker after he heard the latest transmission and offered to make a deal. The berserker accepted immediately.

The berserker retracted all but the four original gun mounts facing the ship. It did not wish to back down even to this extent, but Dorphy's call had given it an appropriate-seeming reason. Actually, it could not dismiss the possibility that showing the additional weapons might have been responsible for the increased electrical activity it now detected. The directive still cautioned wariness and was now indicating non-provocation as well.

Who hath drawn the circuit for the lion?

"Qwibbian," said the artifact.

Juna sat, pale, before the console. The past hour had added years to her face. There was fresh grime on her coveralls. When Wade entered he halted and stared.

"What's wrong?" he said. "You look—"

"It's okay."

"No, it isn't. I know you're sick. We're going to have to—"

"It's really okay," she said. "It's passing. Let it be. I'll be all right."

He nodded and advanced again, displaying a small recorder in his left hand.

"I've got it," he said then. "Listen to this."

He turned on the recorder. A series of clicks and moans emerged. It ran for about a quarter-minute and stopped.

"Play it again, Wade," she said, and she smiled weakly as she threw the voice mode switch.

He complied.

"Translate," she said when it was over.

"Take the—untranslatable—to the—untranslatable—and transform it upward," came the voice of the artifact through the speaker.

"Thanks," she said, and, "You were right, Wade."

"You know where I found it?" he asked.

"On the Carmpan tapes."

"Yes, but it's not Builder talk."

"I know that."

"And you also know what it is?"

She nodded.

"It is the language spoken by the Builders' enemies—the Red Race—against whom the berserkers were unleashed. There is a little segment showing the round red people shouting a slogan or a prayer or something—maybe it's even a Builder propaganda tape. It came from that, didn't it?"

"Yes. How did you know?"

She patted the console.

"Qwib-qwib here is getting back on his mental feet. He's even helping now. He's very good at self-repair, now that the process has been initiated. We've been talking for a while and I'm beginning to understand." She coughed, a deep, racking spasm that brought tears to her eyes. "Would you get me a glass of water?"

"Sure."

He crossed the cabin and fetched it.

"We have made an enormously important find," she said as she sipped it. "It was good that the others kept you from cutting it loose."

MacFarland and Dorphy entered the cabin. MacFarland held Wade's pistol and pointed it at him.

"Cut it loose," he said.

"No," Wade answered.

"Then Dorphy's going to do it while I keep you covered. Suit up, Dorphy, and get a torch."

"You don't know what you're doing," Wade said. "Juna was just telling me that—"

MacFarland fired. The projectile ricocheted about the cabin, finally dropping to the floor in the far corner.

"Mac, you're crazy!" Wade said. "You could just as easily hit yourself if you do that again."

"Don't move! Okay. That was stupid, but now I know better. The next one goes into your shoulder or your leg. I mean it. You understand?"

"Yes, damn it! But we can't just cut that thing loose now. It's almost repaired, and we know where it's from. Juna says—"

"I don't care about any of that. Two-thirds of it belong to Dorphy and me, and we're jettisoning our share right now. If your third goes along, that's tough. The berserker assures us that's all it wants. It'll let us go then. I believe it."

"Look, Mac. Anything a berserker wants that badly is something we shouldn't give it. I think I can talk it into giving us even more time."

MacFarland shook his head.

Dorphy finished suiting up and took a cutting torch from a rack. As he headed for the open lock, Juna said, "Wait. If you cycle the lock you'll cut the cable. It'll sever the connection to Qwib-qwib's brain."

"I'm sorry, doctor," MacFarland said. "But we're in a hurry."

From the console then came the words: "Our association is about to be terminated?"

"I'm afraid so," she answered. "I am sorry that I could not finish."

"Do not. The process continues. I have assimilated the program and now use it myself. A most useful process."

Dorphy entered the lock.

"I have one question, Juna, before goodbye," it said.

"Yes? What is it?" she asked.

The lock began cycling closed and Dorphy was already raising the torch to burn through the welds.

"My vocabulary is still incomplete. What does 'qwibbian' mean in your language?"

The cycling lock struck the cable and severed it as she spoke, so she did not know whether it heard her say the word "berserker."

Wade and MacFarland both turned suddenly.

"What did you say?" Wade asked.

She repeated it.

"You're not making sense," he said. "First you said that it wasn't. Now—"

"Do you want to talk about words or machines?" she asked.

"Go ahead. You talk. I'll listen."

She sighed and took another drink of water.

"I got the story from Qwib-qwib in pieces," she began. "I had to fill in some gaps with conjectures, but they seemed to follow. Ages ago, the Builders apparently fought a war with the Red Race, who proved tougher than they thought. So they hit them with their ultimate weapon—the self-replicating killing machines we call berserkers."

"That seems the standard story," Wade said.

"The Red Race went under," she continued. "They were totally destroyed—but only after a terrific struggle. In the final days of the war they tried all sorts of things, but by then it was a case of too little too late. They were overwhelmed. They actually even tried something I had always wondered about—something no Earth-descended world would now dare to attempt, with all the restrictions on research along those lines, with all the paranoia . . .''

She paused for another sip.

''They built their own berserkers,'' she went on then, ''but not like the originals. They developed a killing machine which would only attack berserkers—an anti-berserker berserker—for the defense of their home planet. But there were too few. They put them all on the line, around their world, and apparently they did a creditable job—they had something involving short jumps into and out of other spaces going for them—but they were vastly outnumbered in that last great mass attack. Ultimately, all of them fell.''

The ship gave a shudder. They turned toward the lock.

''He's cut it loose, whatever it was,'' MacFarland stated.

''It shouldn't shake the whole ship that way,'' Wade said.

''It would if it accelerated away the instant it was freed,'' said Juna.

''But how could it, with all of its control circuits sealed?'' Wade asked.

She glanced at the smears on her coveralls.

''I reestablished its circuits when I learned the truth,'' she told him. ''I don't know what percentage of its old efficiency it possesses, but I am certain that it is about to attack the berserker.''

The lock cycled open and Dorphy emerged, unfastening his suit as it cycled closed behind him.

''We've got to get the hell out of here!'' MacFarland cried. ''This area is about to become a war zone!''

''You care to do the piloting?'' Wade asked him.

''Of course not.''

''Then give me my gun and get out of my way.''

He accepted the weapon and headed for the bridge.

* * *

For so long as the screens permitted resolution they watched—the ponderous movements of the giant berserker, the flashes of its energy blasts, the dartings and sudden disappearances and reappearances of its tiny attacker. Later, some time after the images were lost, a fireball sprang into being against the starry black.

''He got it! Qwib-qwib got it!'' Dorphy cried.

''And it probably got him, too,'' MacFarland remarked. ''What do you think, Wade?''

''I think,'' Wade replied, ''that I will not have anything to do with either of you ever again.''

He rose and left to go and sit with Juna. He took along his recorder and some music.

She turned from watching the view on her own screen and smiled weakly as he seated himself beside her bed.

''I'm going to take care of you,'' he told her, ''until you don't need me.''

''That would be nice,'' she said.

Tracking. Tracking. They were coming. Five of them. The big one must have sent for them. Jump behind them and take out the two rear ones before the others realize what is happening. Another jump, hit the port flank and jump again. They've never seen these tactics. Dodge. Fire. Jump. Jump again. Fire. The last one is spinning like a top, trying to anticipate. Hit it. Charge right in. There.

The last qwibbian-qwibbian-kel in the universe departed the battle scene, seeking the raw materials for some fresh repair work. Then, of course, it would need still more, for the replications.

Who hath drawn the circuits for the lion?

The Great Secret

Qwibbian-qwibbian kel . . .

Two secrets you must not tell . . .

And Lars awoke, gasping, from the *qwib-qwib* dream, to find Pat Sandomierz kneeling in his cell beside him.

Her gray-blue eyes were wide, and sympathetic. "You were having a nightmare. Crying out, jabbering something."

He raised himself on an elbow. He was sweating, as if he had just been through intense pain. But he could remember no pain, only the dream, and that very vividly.

No wonder the Carmpan had tried to bury that last episode, had risked so much to hide it from the enemy.

As soon as Lars had fallen asleep, the thoughts of those distant people, Wade Kelman and Juna Bayel and the others, along with the computations that passed for thought in that remote berserker fighting unit, had all come popping up from under whatever layer of Lars Kanakuru's own mindstuff the Carmpan had hidden them beneath.

Lars asked Pat now: "What was I saying?"

Pat shook her head. Long hair, tousled but still attractive, swirled this way and that. "I couldn't really make it out. Something about . . . it sounded like 'crib-crib'? Or quotidian something is coming?"

"I did?"

"Don't let it get you, Lars. It was only a dream. It's a wonder we're not all crazy, existing like this." And Pat, demonstrating a sudden impulse, reached out to take him by the hand.

Lars clasped her hand and didn't want to let go. She appeared willing to stay. He didn't try to pull her down on the pallet beside him. She was, at the moment, no more than someone, something, to hang on to.

Qwib-qwib the savior might be hurtling closer, right at this moment, through the endless Galactic night. Might be. If only he, Lars, cursed with visions he could not destroy, did not somehow give the show away. He couldn't tell Pat, couldn't tell anyone, couldn't say a word. And he couldn't think of anything else to say to Pat. Anyway, he was too tired now even to talk. And only one *qwib-qwib*, against this base, was not going to be enough . . . even if it had wiped out five of the fighting units.

In utter weariness he drifted back into stuporous sleep.

When he awoke again, Pat had disappeared.

When Lars presently rejoined the others in the common room, the great secret of the *qwibbian-kel* still throbbing in his head, Dorothy reported that Pat had been taken away. One of the guide machines had come—bringing no spacesuit—had singled Pat out by pointing, and had escorted her down the passage leading to the mind-probing machines, closing the door behind her. It had taken a Carmpan with it too. It was the first time a single pair of prisoners had been taken that way, for what appeared to be a mind-probe session.

Looking into the room where the Carmpan spent almost all their time, Lars thought he could detect among those huddled forms a new attitude—or was it more than just an attitude?—of sadness, though he could not consciously pick out anything specific about them that was different.

He thought that the noises that came ceaselessly through the rock around the humans' living quarters, sounds of mining and building and repairing, had definitely intensified. He did not comment on the fact.

Dorothy Totonac, the captain, and Nicholas Opava had now begun or perhaps resumed a three-way argument over why the berserker had taken its prisoners on the tour of the base a little while ago.

Suddenly, sharply, the argument changed. Lars, not really listening, didn't catch the exact turning point, but now the question was who among them might be goodlife. How the suspicion had taken root, that there was a goodlife agent among them, was impossible to say, but there it was. They were directing suspicious looks at Lars, as well as at each other.

Lars had now become suspicious of Pat—strange that she should be singled out and taken away right after listening to him cry out in his dream—but there was no way for him to voice his suspicions without saying out loud for the berserker to hear that he had been trying to conceal secrets from it.

Presently the escort machines came for the four of them, and the big door slid back, opening the passage that led to the chambers containing the mind-probe machinery. Four Carmpan were brought along too.

As he was being hooked up yet again to the mind-probe machine, Lars decided that this time he had been given yet another new Carmpan partner.

DEATHWOMB

The courier slipped out of flightspace and paused for a navigational sight. It was still very far from the berserker sun, so far that that fierce blue-white A star was only the brightest of many. Others crowded heaven, unwinking brilliances, every hue from radio to gamma, save where the Milky Way foamed around blackness or a nearby dark nebula looked like a thunderhead. The torpedo shape of the courier shimmered wanly amidst them.

Having gotten its bearings, it accelerated under normal drive. At first it was receding, but soon it had quenched its intrinsic velocity and thereafter built up sunward speed. The rate of that, uncompensated, would have spread flesh and bone in a film through any interior. But there were neither cabins nor passengers; the courier was essentially solid-state.

It began to broadcast, at high power and on several wavebands. The message was in standard English. "*Parley. Parley. Parley.*" As haste mounted, frequencies changed to allow for Doppler shift, to make certain the message would be received. After all, the courier was unmistakable human work. Unless they had some reason not to, the berserkers would attack it. Such a move would be motivated less by fear of what a warhead might do to one of their proud battlecraft than what might happen to the asteroid mines and spaceborne factories they had established.

Motivation; fear; pride—nonsense words, when used about a set of computer-effector systems, unalive, belike unaware, programmed to burn life out of the universe.

But then, the courier was an automaton too, and nowhere nearly as complex or capable as the least berserker.

"Parley. Parley. Parley."

In due course—time made no difference to a thing that had no consciousness, but the sun blazed now with a tiny disc—a warship came forth to meet it. That was a minor vessel, readily expendable, though formidable enough, a hundred-meter spheroid abristle with guns, missile launchers, energy projectors. Its mass, low compared to a planetkiller's, made it quite maneuverable. Nonetheless flight was long and calculation intricate before it matched the velocity which the courier by then had.

"Cease acceleration," the berserker commanded.

The courier obeyed. The berserker did likewise. Globe and minute sliver, they flew inert on parallel courses, a thousand kilometers apart.

"Explain your presence," was the next order. (Command! Obedience! More nonsense, when two robots were directly communicating.)

"Word from certain humans," the courier replied. *"They know you have moved into this region of space."*

Being a machine exchanging data with another machine, it did not add the obvious. No matter how vast astronomical distances are, an operation of that size could not stay hidden long, if it took place anywhere in that small portion of the galaxy where humans had settlements with high technology. Devices even simpler than the courier, patrolling over lightyears, were sure to pick up the indications on their instruments, and report back to their masters. Of course, those were not necessarily all the humans in the stellar neighborhood. Nor did it follow that they could do much to prevent onslaughts out of the new base. Their own strength was thinly scattered, this far from the centers of their older civilizations. At best, they could marshal resources for the defense of some worlds—probably not all.

The berserker did not waste watts inquiring what the message was. It merely let the courier go on.

"Their analysis is that you will soon strike, while you continue to use the mineral and energy resources of the planetary system for repair and reproduction. If an overwhelming human force moves against you, you will withdraw; but that cannot happen in the immediate future, if ever. My dispatchers offer you information of value to your enterprise."

Logic circuits developed a question. *"Are your dispatchers goodlife?"*

"I am not programmed with the answer, but there is no indication in my memory banks that they wish active cooperation with you. It may be a matter of self-interest, the hope of making a bargain advantageous to them. I can only tell you that, if the terms are right, they will steer you to a target you would not otherwise know about: an entire world for you to sterilize."

Radio silence fell, except for the faint seething of the stars.

The berserker, though, required just a split second to make assessment. *"Others shall be contacted before you leave. We will arrange a rendezvous for proper discussion, and you will bring a record of the proceedings back to your humans. Within what parameters do they operate?''*

The Ilyan day stood at midmorning when Sally Jennison came home. The thaw and the usual storms that followed sunrise were past and heaven was clear, purplish-blue, save for a few clouds which glowed ruddy here and there. Eastward the great ember was climbing past Olga; shadows made sharp the larger craters upon the moon. Below, the Sawtooth Mountains rose dusky over the horizon, Snowcrown peak agleam as if on fire.

Elsewhere land rolled gently, so that the Highroad River flowed slow out of the west on its way to Lake Sapphire. The boat had left wilderness behind and was in the settled part of Geyserdale. Grainfields rippled tawny on either side; they had thus ripened, been harvested, been resown, and ripened again—with the haste that the brief Ilyan year brought about—several times since the expedition departed. A village of beehive-rounded houses was visible in the northern distance, and occasional natives working near the stream hailed Sally and her companion. They were not many, for she had yet to hear of any society on this planet where persons liked to crowd together. Timberlots were plentiful, high boles and russet foliage. Steam blew from encrusted areas where hot springs bubbled, and once she saw an upward spout of water.

Insectoids flitted on glittery wings. A windrider hovered aloft. River and breeze murmured to each other. Air had warmed as day advanced, and grown full of pungencies. An unseen coneycat was singing.

The peacefulness felt remote from Sally, unreal.

Abruptly it broke. She had hooked her transceiver into the electrical system of the boat's motor and inserted a tape for direct readout and continuous, repeated broadcast: ''*Hello,*

University Station. Hello, anybody, anywhere. This is the Jennison party returning after we stopped hearing from you. I've called and called, and gotten no response. What's wrong? Reply, please reply.''

Sound from the set was a man's voice, harsh with tension, the English bearing a burred accent unfamiliar to her: ''Wha's this? Who are ye? Where?''

She gasped, then got her balance back. Years in strangeness, sometimes in danger, had taught her how to meet surprise. Underneath, she felt a tide of relief—she was not the only human left alive on Ilya!—but it carried an ice flow of anxiety. What had become of them, her friends, every one of the hundred-odd researchers and support personnel at the base and exploring around the planet?

She wet her lips so she could answer. ''Sally Jennison. I've been doing xenological work in the field, Farside, for the past twenty days or so.'' The man was perhaps not used to the slow rotation of Ilya. ''Uh, that would be about six terrestrial months. When communication cut off—yes, of course I could send and receive that far away, we do have comsats in orbit, you know—I grew alarmed and started back.''

''Where are ye?'' he demanded. ''Who's wi' ye?''

''I'm on the Highroad River, passing by Dancers' Town. About a hundred fifty klicks west of the station, it is. I've only one partner left, a native who lives near us. The rest of my expedition, all natives, have disembarked along the way and gone to their own homes.''

Anger flared. ''Enough!'' she exclaimed. ''Jesus Christ! Suppose you tell me who *you* are and what's going on?''

''No time,'' he said. ''Your people are safe. We'll ha' someone out in an aircar to pick ye up as fast as possible. Meanwhile, cease transmission. Immediately.''

"What? Now you listen just a minute—"

"Dr. Jennison, the berserkers are coming. They may arrive at any minute, and they must no' detect any electronics, any trace o' man. Under martial law, I lay radio silence on ye. Turn your set off!"

The voice halted. Numbly, Sally reached for the switch of her unit. She slumped on her bench, stared, scarcely noticing that she was still at the rudder.

Rainbow-in-the-Mist stroked a four-fingered hand shyly over hers. In a short-sleeved shirt, she felt his plumage (not hair, not feathers, an intricate, beautiful, sensitive covering for his skin) tickle her arm. "Have you news at last, Lady-Who-Seeks?" he trilled, whistled, hummed.

"Not quite," she said in English. They could understand if not pronounce each other's languages, though the new intonation had baffled him. "Whoever it was did claim my people are safe."

"That good makes any ill very slight." He meant it.

But your people are in mortal danger! she almost cried out. Your whole world is.

She gazed at her friend of years as if she had never before seen any of his kind—body somewhat like hers, but standing only to her chin and more gracile; round head, faun ears, short muzzle, quivering cat-whiskers, enormous golden eyes; delicate gray sheen of plumage; the belt, pouch, and bandolier that were his entire garb, the steel knife he carried with such pride not because it was a rare thing in his calcolithic society but because it was a present from her . . . She had seen images of planets the berserkers had slain: radioactive rock, ashen winds, corrupted seas.

But this is insane! she thought suddenly. They've never heard of Ilya. They couldn't have, except by the wildest chance, and if that happened, how could that man have known?

And he wanted me to stop sending in case a berserker detected it, but what about the flyer he's dispatching for me? Well, that may be a risk he feels he has to take, to get me under cover in a hurry. A small vehicle is less likely to be spotted optically within a short time-slot than a radio 'cast is to be picked up electronically.

But what about our relay satellites? What about University Station itself—buildings, landing strip, playing field, everything?

Why didn't anybody mention me to these . . . strangers?

Rainbow-in-the-Mist patted the yellow hair falling in a pony tail past her neck. "You have great grief, I sense," he breathed. "Can your wander-brother give comfort in any way?"

"Oh, Rainie!" She hugged him to her and fought not to weep. He was warm and smelled like spices in the kitchen when she was a child on Earth.

A buzz from above drew her heed. She saw a teardrop shape slant down from the eastern sky. It crossed the sun's disc, but a brief glance straight at a red dwarf star didn't dazzle her vision. She identified it as an aircar. The model was foreign to her. Well, her race had colonized a lot of planets over the centuries, and no planet is a uniform ball; it is a world. Ilya alone held mystery and marvel enough to fill the lifetimes of many discoverers—

The car landed on the left bank, where springturf made an amethystine mat. A man sprang out and beckoned to her. He was tall, rawboned, clad in a green uniform which sunlight here gave an ugly hue. His tunic was open at the throat and carelessly baggy at the beltline, around a sidearm, but his stance bespoke discipline.

She brought the boat to shore, stopped the motor, got out.

Seen close, the man was craggy-featured and clean-shaven. Furrows in the weathered face and white streaks through the short dark hair suggested he was in his forties, Earth calendar. Comet insignia glittered on his shoulders and a sleeve patch displayed calipers athwart a circuit diagram.

In his turn, he gave her a raking glance. She was almost thirty, not much less in height than he, well-built, lithe from a career spent in the field. He gave her a soft salute. "Ian Dunbar, captain, engineer corps, Space Navy of Adam," he introduced himself. His accent was similar to that of the fellow who had happened to hear her call, but a trained ear could tell that it was not identical. Likely he hailed from a different continent. Yes, she knew about Adam, since the planet was in this general region, but her information was scanty . . . "Please get inside. We'll gi' your fere a ride too if he wishes."

"No, he'll bring the boat in," she objected.

"Dr. Jennison," Dunbar said, "yon's too large a craft to singlehand wi'out a motor, which we shall ha' to remove and bring back wi' us." He turned his head toward the car. "Cameron, Gordon, out and to work!" he shouted.

"Aye, sir." Two younger men in the same uniform, without officer's emblems, scrambled forth, bearing tools.

The hand of Rainbow-in-the-Mist stole into Sally's. "What is happening?" he asked fearfully. And yet he had met the charge of a spearhorn, armed with nothing but his knife, and distracted the giant till she could retrieve her rifle. He had been her second in command when she fared away to study natives as unknown to him as to her—most recently, when the quest took them to lands which never saw the moon that hung forever in his home sky and which he called Mother Spirit.

"I don't know," she had to admit. "There was talk of an, an enemy."

"What does that mean?" he wondered. Nowhere on Ilya had she heard of war or even murder.

"Dangerous beings, maddened beasts." The thought of nuclear missiles and energy beams striking this place was like a drink of acid.

"Hurry along!" Dunbar rapped.

Sally and her comrade squeezed into the rear seat beside him. The two noncoms followed, after stowing the motor and other stuff from the boat. They took the front, one of them the controls. The aircar lifted. In spite of everything, Rainbow-in-the-Mist caroled delight. He seldom got to fly.

Sally felt how Dunbar perforce pressed against her. She didn't want to be, but was, aware of his maleness. It had been long since she said goodbye to Pete Brozik and Fujiwara Ito. The first a planetologist, the second a molecular biologist, her lovers couldn't very well go xenologizing with her.

Apprehension stabbed. How were they? Where?

It turned to resentment. "Well, Captain Dunbar," she clipped, "now will you tell me what the hell is going on?"

The ghost of a smile flitted over his starkness. "That is wha' I believe your folk would call a tall order, Dr. Jennison."

"Huh?" She was surprised.

"Ye're originally fro' North America on Earth, true?"

"Y-yes. But how do you know, when an hour ago you didn't know I existed?"

He shrugged. "Speech, gait, style. I've seen shows, read books, met travelers. Just because we Adamites are out near the edge o' human expansion, take us no' for rustics." The ghost sank back into its grave. The gaze he turned on her was bleak. "Maybe we were once, our forefathers, and glad to be, but the berserkers ended that. Wha' I would like to find out this day is why nobody told us about ye, Dr. Jennison.

We'd ha' sent a car to fetch ye. Now I fear ye're trapped, in the same danger as us.''

Sally checked her temper, pinched her lips, and made her blue stare challenge his gray one before she said: ''I can scarcely give you any ideas before I have some facts, can I? What's been happening? Who are you people, anyway? And what's become of mine?''

Dunbar sighed. ''We've evacuated them. Aye, 'twas hasty and high-handed, no doubt, but we were under the lash oursel's. The first thing we removed was the comsats; that's why ye were no longer receiving or being heard, though 'twas but a short time before we imposed silence on every transmission. Meanwhile—''

The car started downward. Sally looked past Dunbar, out the window. She choked back a scream.

Lake Sapphire shone enormous below, surrounded by the rural tranquility she had known throughout her stay on Ilya. Eastern mountains, red sun-wheel, scarred and brilliant moon were untouched. But where the Highroad River emptied into the lake, where University Station had clustered, was a blackened waste, as if a noonday turf fire had spread over that ground and consumed the very buildings, or the berserkers had already commenced their work.

Space was steely with stars. None shone close in the loneliness here. What established this rendezvous point was triangulation on distant galaxies.

Emerging from flightspace, the berserker homed in on a broadcast that Mary Montgomery's ship had been emitting while she waited. Instruments showed the vessel draw nigh and match intrinsics—lay to—a thousand kilometers off. Magnifying optics showed it as no bigger than hers, though a hedgehog of armament, dim shinings and deep shadows near the Milky Way.

Alone in the main control room, for her crew was minimal, she settled herself into a command chair and pressed the lightplate which would signal her readiness to talk. Around her, bulkheads stood dull-hued, needles quivered across dials, displays went serpentine, electronics beeped and muttered. The air from the ventilators smelled faintly of oil; something a bit wrong in the recyclers, no matter what. Her old bones ached, but no matter that, either.

The berserker's voice reached her. It was derived from the voices of human captives taken long ago, shrill, irregular, a sonic monster pieced together out of parts of the dead, terrifying to many. Montgomery sniffed at it, took a drag on her cheroot, and blew a smoke ring toward the speaker. *Childish bravado*, she thought. But why not? Who was to witness?

"Parley under truce, is this still agreed?" the berserker began.

Montgomery nodded before recollecting how pointless the gesture was. "Aye," she said. "We've somewhat to sell ye, we do."

"Who are you, where is that planet your courier bespoke, what is your asking price?"

Montgomery chuckled, though scant mirth was in her. "Easy, my ghoulie. Your kind, ye've established yoursel's in these parts again, so as to kill more, no? Well, last time my home suffered grimly. We've better defenses this while, we can fight ye off, yet 'twould be at high cost. Suppose, instead, we direct ye to another inhabited world—not a human colony, for we're no traitors, understand—a world useless to us, but wi' life upon it for ye to scrub out, aye, e'en an intelligent species. They're primitives, helpless before ye. A single capital ship o' yours could make slag o' the planet in a day or two, at no risk whatsoe'er. In exchange for such an easy triumph, would ye leave us in peace?''

''Who are you?''

''Our world we call Adam.''

The berserker searched its memory banks. ''Yes,'' it said. ''We struck it three hundred and fifty-seven Earth years ago. Considerable damage was done, but before the mission could be completed, a task force of the Grand Fleet arrived and compelled us to retreat. We were only conducting a raid. We had no reinforcements to call upon.''

''Aye. Since then, Adam has gained strength.''

''And this time we have a base, a planetary system, raw materials to build an indefinite number of new units. Why should we not finish Adam off?''

Montgomery sighed. ''Were ye human—were ye e'en alive, conscious, insultable, ye metal abomination—I'd ask ye to stop playing games wi' me. Well, but I suppose your computer does no' ha' the data. 'Tis been long since ye last came by. So hearken.

''In spite o' the wounds ye inflicted, Adam has a larger population now than then, much more industry, a small but formidable space navy, a civil defense that reaches through the whole system 'tis in. Ye could no' take us out before the marshalled human forces arrive to drive ye back fro' this sector. Howe'er, we'd liefest be spared the loss o' blood and treasure that standing ye off would entail. Therefore we offer our bargain—a world for a world.''

Lack of life did not mean lack of shrewdness. ''If the target you would betray is so soft,'' the berserker inquired, ''why should we not afterward turn on you?''

Montgomery drew a little comfort from the bite of smoke in her mouth, more from the family picture above the control console. Her husband was in it, and he had died, oh, Colin,

Colin . . . but her sons and daughters stood strong beside their wives and husbands, amidst her grandchildren and his. She had volunteered for this mission because a human was needed—no computer that humans could build was flexible enough—and if negotiations broke down and the berserker opened fire, why, she was old and full of days.

"I told ye ye'd find us a hard nut to crack," she answered, "and this ye can verify by a scouting flit. Only pick up the stray radiations fro' orbital fortresses and ships on patrol. Afterward think wha' ground-based installations we must ha' likewise—whole rivers to cool energy projectors— Ah, but ye do no' really think, do ye?"

"Nevertheless, it might prove logical for us to attack you, especially if we have been able to accomplish part of our sterilizing objective without loss."

Montgomery made a death's-head grin at the image of the ship among the stars. "But see ye," she declared, "before we turn over yon hapless planet to ye, we'll send forth courier robots far and wide. They'll bear witness—our recordings, your electronic signature—witness to the treaty, that we gi' ye the information in return for immunity.

"Ye've struck bargains wi' humans erenow. Break one as important as this, and how much goodlife can ye hope to recruit in future?"

The machine did not ask any further questions such as she would have asked in its place. For instance, how would humans throughout space react to fellow humans, Adamites, who had sold out a living world in order that they themselves be spared a war? Subtleties like that were beyond a machine. Indeed, Montgomery confessed wearily to herself, they were beyond her, and every expert who had debated the issue. There might not be great revulsion, and what there was might not last long. Nonhuman intelligences were rare, scientifically valuable, but, well, nonhuman. Your first obligation was to your kindred, wasn't it?

And it was nonhumans that had built the first berserkers, untold ages ago, and programmed them to destroy everything alive, as a weapon in a damned forgotten war of their own. Wasn't it?

Silence hummed, pressed inward, filled her skull. Then:

"This unit is equipped to make agreement on behalf of our entire force," the berserker said. "Very well, in principle. To begin, provide some description of the planet you would give us."

The sun plodded toward noon while Olga waned. The moon's night part was not invisible where it hung halfway up heaven, east-southeast beyond the Sawtooths. A tenuous atmosphere caught sunlight on clouds, reflected Ilyalight, made a shimmering alongside the pocked daylit horn; the north polar cap reached thence like a plume.

Sally was used to the sight, but all at once she wondered how alien it might be to Dunbar: a somber red sun showing six and a half times as wide as Sol did on Earth, taking more than a week to go from midday to midday but less than a month from midsummer to midsummer; a moon almost four times the breadth of Luna in Earth's skies, more than twenty times the brightness, that never rose or set save as you traveled across Ilya—What was the sky of Adam like?

That hardly seemed relevant to the disaster around; but she had been stunned by it, and the hours after she landed had hailed more blows upon her. Descent to the caverns the Adamites had dug while, above, they tore University Station apart and sank the fragments beneath the lake. Uniformed strangers swarming antlike through those drab corridors, loud orders, footfalls, throb of unseen machinery. A cubicle found for her to sleep in, a place assigned at the officers' mess, but she had no appetite. Warm, stinking air, for there had been no time to install anything but minimal life support, when the complex of workshops, command posts, barracks must be gnawed out of rock and reinforced till it could withstand a direct hit of a megaton. A fantastic job in so short a span, even granting powerful, sophisticated machines to do most of the labor—*Why, why, why?*

Andrew Scrymgeour, admiral in overall charge of operations, received her, though only for a brief interview. He had too many demands on him as was. Weariness had plowed his face; the finger that kept stroking the gray mustache was executing a nervous tic; he spoke in a monotone.

"Aye, we're sorry we missed ye. I set an inquiry afoot when I heard. As nigh as my aide can find out, 'twas because o' confusion. Such haste on our part, ye see, and meanwhile such anger among your folk, arguments, refusals that bade fair to become outright physical resistance, did we no' move fast and firmly. Other scientists were in the field besides ye, o' course, scattered o'er half this globe. We sought them out and brought them in, thinking they were all. We did no' stop to check your rosters, for who would wish anyone left abandoned? Somehow we simply were no' told about ye, Dr. Jennison. Doubtless everybody among your friends took for granted somebody else has gi'en that word, and was too furious to speak to us unless absolutely necessary. Moreo'er, we could no' lift the lot o' them off in a single ship; we required several, so on any one vessel 'tis being assumed yet must be aboard another."

Yes, Pete and Ito will be horror-smitten when they learn, Sally thought. Worst will be the helplessness and the not knowing; worse for them than me, I suppose. (Oh, it isn't that we've exchanged vows or anything like that. We enjoy each other, minds more than bodies, actually. But it's made us close, affectionate. I've missed them very much, calm and grizzled Ito, Pete's vitality which a man half his age might envy—)

"Where have you taken them?" she demanded.

Scrymgeour shrugged. "To Adam. Where else? They'll be comfortably housed until arrangements can be made for sending them on to their homes, or where'er is appropriate. Maybe e'en back here, to take up their work again." He sighed. "But that requires clearing the berserkers fro' this sector o' space. Meanwhile, travel may prove so dangerous that our authorities will deem it best to keep your folk detained, for their own safety."

"For their silence, you mean!" she flared. "You had no right, no right whatsoever, to come in like this and wreck all we've built, halt all we've been doing. If Earth found out, it might be less ready to send naval units to help defend Adam."

Scrymgeour's bushy brows drew together. "I've no time to argue wi' ye, Dr. Jennison," he snapped. " 'Tis unfortunate for us as well as ye that ye were o'erlooked in the evacuation." He curbed his temper. "We'll do wha' we can. I'll see to it that an officer is assigned to ye as . . . liaison, explainer." Dour humor: "Also chaperon, for ye realize we've but a handful o' women in Ilya now, and they too busied for aught o' an amorous nature. Not that our men would misbehave, I'm sure, but 'twill be as well to make plain for them to see that they're no' to let themsel's be distracted fro' their duty, e'en in their scant free times."

Sally tossed her head. "Don't worry, Admiral. I have no desire to fraternize. Am I permitted to take myself out of their presence?"

"Go topside, ye mean?" He pondered. "Aye, no harm in

that, gi'en proper precautions. We do oursel's. Howe'er, ye shall always ha' an escort."

"Why? Don't you think I might conceivably know my way around just a tiny bit better than any of your gang?"

He nodded. "Aye, aye. But 'tis no' the point. Ye mustn't stray far. Ye must e'er be ready to hurry back on the first alarm, or take cover if the notice is too short. I want someone wi' ye to make sure o' that. 'Tis for your sake also. The berserker is coming."

"If I couldn't dive underground before the strike," she sneered, "what's the point of my ducking under a bush? The whole valley will go up in radioactive smoke."

"Ah, but there's a chance, extremely small but still a chance, that the berserker would spy ye fro' above." Scrymgeour bit off his words. "Pardon me. I've my job on hand. Return to your quarters and wait to hear fro' the officer detailed to ye."

That turned out to be Ian Dunbar. So it was that she found herself wondering what he thought of her sky.

"Ye see," he disclosed awkwardly—shyly?—"the part o' the task I'm in charge o', 'tis been completed, save for minor and routine tinkerings. I'll no' be much needed any more until action is nigh. Meanwhile, well, we owe ye somewhat. Apology, explanation, assistance in rebuilding when that becomes possible. I'll . . . take it on mysel' . . . to speak for that side o' us . . . if ye're willing."

She gave him a suspicious glance, but he wasn't being flirtatious. Quite likely he didn't know how to be. He stared straight ahead of him as they walked, gulped forth his words, knotted knobbly fists.

The temptation to be cruel to such vulnerability was irresistible, in this wasteland he had helped make. "You've given yourself plenty to do, then. Four universities in the Solar System pooled their resources, plus a large grant from the Karlsen Memorial Foundation, to establish a permanent research group here. And how do you propose to restore the working time we'll've lost, or repair the relationships with natives that we've painstakingly been developing?'' She swept a hand to and fro. ''You've already created your own memorial.''

Cinders crunched underfoot. Grit was in the breeze. The settlement had been razed, bulldozed over, drenched in flammables, and set alight. Whatever remained unburnt had been cast in the lake. She must admit the resemblance to a natural area damaged by a natural fire was excellent.

Dunbar winced. ''Please, Dr. Jennison. Please do no' think o' us as barbarians: We came to wage war on the olden enemies o' all humankind, all life.'' After a pause, softly: ''We respect science on Adam. I'd dreams mysel' as a lad, o' becoming a planetologist.''

Despite her will, Sally's heart gave a small jump. That was what her father was. Oh, Dad, Mother, how are you, at home on Earth? I should never have stayed away so long.

—No. I will not let myself like this man.

''Don't change the subject,'' she said as sharply as she could manage. ''Why have you come to Ilya? What crazy scheme have you hatched, anyway?''

''To meet the berserker when it arrives. Ye'd absolutely no defenses in this entire planetary system.''

''None were needed.''

They left the blackened section behind and trod on springturf, a living recoil beneath the feet, purple studded with tiny white flowers. Following the lakeshore, several meters inland, they started up a slope which ended in a bluff above the water. Now the wind was clean; its mildness smelled of soil and growth.

"The berserkers would never have dreamed life was here," Sally said. "It's so great a miracle."

"Berserkers do no' dream," Dunbar retorted sternly. "They compute, on the basis o' data. Ilya's been described in newscasts, aye, at least one full-length documentary show. Ye've been publishing your findings."

"The news sensation, what there was of it, died out ten or fifteen years ago, when no berserker was anywhere near this part of space—or near our inner civilizations either, of course. Besides, how would they pick up programs carried on cable or tight beam—between stars, in canisters? As for publication since the original discovery, I don't believe berserkers subscribe to our specialized scientific journals!"

"Well, they do know."

"How? And how can you be sure of it?"

"Our intelligence—I'm no' at liberty to discuss our methods. Nor is that my corps, ye remember."

"Why haven't they come already, then? We'd've been a sitting duck."

He blinked. "A wha'?"

She couldn't help smiling. His puzzlement made him too human, all of a sudden. An Earth expression. North American, to be exact. I don't know what sort of waterfowl you have on Adam."

His haggardness returned. "Few, sin' the berserkers visited it."

After a moment, he offered a reply of sorts to her question. "We can no' tell when the raid will happen. We can but prepare for it as fast and as best we are able."

They surmounted the bluff and stopped to rest. A while they stood side by side, gazing out over the broad waters. He breathed no harder than she did. He keeps in shape, like Dad, she thought. The wind ruffled her hair and cooled away the slight sweat on her face, phantom caresses.

"I take it," she said at last, slowly, "you couldn't detach any large force from the defense of Adam itself. So what have you brought? What are your plans?"

"We've a few spacecraft hidden on both the planet and yon moon. Everything is electronically shielded. Heat radiation fro' the base will no' matter in this area, which had it already." Dunbar gestured ahead. "My task was mainly beneath the loch. We've installed certain ultra-high-powered weapons . . . camouflage and cooling alike—" He broke off. "Best I say no more."

She scowled at the upborne silt and shapeless trash which marred the purity of the wavelets. That defilement would surely mean nothing to a berserker—what did a robot know of the nature it was only intended to murder?—but to her, and Rainbow-in-the-Mist, and everybody else who had dwelt near these shores and loved them—

Her wits were beginning to straighten out, though her head still felt full of sand. "You're laying a trap," she said.

He nodded. "Aye, that's obvious." His laugh clanked. "The trick is to keep it fro' being obvious to the enemy, until too late."

"But hold on . . . won't the disappearance of our works be a giveaway?"

"Make the foe suspicious, ye mean? Nay, that's the whole point. They know no' that Earth is aware o' this planet. 'Twas found just by chance, was it no', in the course o' an astrophysical survey? The general staff on Adam has decided that that chance could become an opportunity for us, to gi' them a blow in their metal bellies."

Dunbar glanced at her, at his watch, and back again. His

tone gentled. "Lass—Dr. Jennison—'tis late by human clocks. Ye've had a rude shock, and I'm told ye've no' eaten, and ye do look fair done in. Let me take ye to some food and a good long sleep."

She realized it herself, weariness and weakness rising through her, breaking apart whatever alertness she had left. "I suppose you're right," she mumbled.

He took her elbow as they started down. "We need no' talk any further if ye'd liefer no'," he said, "but if ye would like a bit o' conversation, shall we make it about somewhat else than this wretched war?"

Mary Montgomery drew breath. "We discovered it by sheer accident," she told the berserker. "An astrophysical survey. Diffusion out o' yon nebula has minor but interesting effects on ambient stars—and on some more distant, as stellar light pressure and kinks in the galactic magnetic field carry matter off until it reaches a sun. An expedition went forth to study the phenomena closer. Among the samples it picked—more or less at random out o' far too many possibilities for a visit to each—among them was a red dwarf star, middle type M. They found it has a life-bearing planet."

An organic being should have registered surprise. The machine afloat in space said merely: "That is not believed possible. Give a low-temperature heat source, the range of orbits wherein water can be liquid is too narrow."

" 'Tis no' impossible, just exceedingly improbable, that a planet orbit a cool sun in the exact ellipse necessary."

"And it must have the proper mass, be neither a giant dominated by hydrogen nor an airless rock."

"Aye, that makes the situation unlikelier yet. Still, this world is o' Earth size and composition."

"Granted that, it must be so close to its primary that

rotation becomes gravitationally locked, not even to two-thirds the period of revolution, but to an identity. One hemisphere always faces the sun, the other always faces away. Gas carried to the dark side will freeze out. Insufficient atmosphere and hydrosphere will remain fluid for chemical evolution to proceed to the biological stage.''

Montgomery nodded her white head. Inwardly she wondered if the berserker carried that knowledge in its data banks or had computed it on the spot. Quite plausibly the latter. It had an enormous capability, the pseudo-brain within yonder hull. After all, it was empowered—no, wrong word—it was able to bargain on behalf of its entire fleet.

Hatred surged. She gripped her chair arms with gnarled fingers as if she were strangling the thing she confronted. *Nay,* she thought in her seething, it does no' breathe. Launch a missile, then! But none we ha' aboard could get past the defenses we know such a berserker has, and it would respond wi' much better armament than we carry. It could simply fire an energy beam, to slice our ship in twain like a guillotine blade going through a neck.

Nay, no' that either, she thought, aware that the issue was altogether abstract. 'Tis o' destroyer class, no' big enough to hold the generator that could produce a beam strong enough. Dispersion across the distance between us— A dreadnaught could do so, o' course, though e'en its reach would be limited and the cut would be messy. To slash a real scalpel o'er this range, ye need power, coolant, and sheer physical size for the focusing—aye, ground-based projectors, like those we've built across Adam.

If a fight breaks out here, the berserker will swamp our own screens and antimissiles. As for its response, it need not e'en get a hit. A few kilotons o' explosion nearby will serve full well to kill us by radiation.

But my mind is wandering. We're no' supposed to provoke a battle. I ha' indeed grown old.

She chose to prolong matters a little, not to tease the enemy, which had no patience to lose (or else had infinite patience), but to assert her life against its unlife. "A philosopher o' ours has observed that the improbable must happen," she said. "If it ne'er did, 'twould be the impossible."

The hesitation of the machine was barely sufficient for her to notice. "We are not present to dispute definitions. How does this planet you speak of come to be inhabited? Where is it? Be quick. We have too many missions to undertake for the wasting of time."

Montgomery had long since won to resolution; but the words would not die, they stirred anew. *Then one of the twelve, called Judas Iscariot, went unto the chief priests, And said unto them, What will ye give me, and I will deliver him unto you? And they covenanted with him for thirty pieces of silver.*

She heard her voice, fast and flat: "Besides being in the right orbit, this Earth-sized planet has a Mars-sized companion. Therefore they are locked to each other, not to their sun. The period o' their spin is nine and a quarter Earth days, which serves to maintain atmospheric circulation. True, nights get cold, but no' too cold, when winds blow aye across the terminator; and during the long day, the oceans store mickle heat. The interplay wi' a year that is about twenty-two Earth days long is interesting—but no' to ye, I'm sure. Ye are just interested in the fact that this planet has brought forth life for ye to destroy.

"Ye ha' no' the ships to spare for a search, if ye're to carry out any other operations before an armada from our inner civilizations comes out against ye. Red dwarf stars are by far the commonest kind, ye ken.

"Make the deal. Agree that, if this world is as I've described, ye'll stay your hand at Adam, whate'er ye may do elsewhere. Let the couriers disperse wi' the attestation o' this compact between us. After that I'll gi' ye the coordinates o' the star. Send a scout to verify—a small, expendable craft. Ye'll find I spoke truth.

"Thereafter, a single capital ship o' yours can write an end to yon life."

Sally Jennison woke after twelve hours, rested, hungry, and more clear-headed than felt good. The room lent her had barely space for a bunk and her piled-up baggage from the boat. Swearing, she wrestled forth a sweatsuit, got it on, and made her way to the gymnasium of which she had been told. Men crowded the narrow corridors but, while she felt the gaze of many, none seemed to jostle her purposely, nor did any offer greetings. A sour, puritanical pack, the Adamites, she thought. Or am I letting my bitterness make my judgments for me?

A workout in the women's section, followed by a shower and change into fresh garments, took some of the edge off her mood. By then it was near noon on the clock; the rotation of the newcomers' planet was not much different from Earth's. She proceeded to the officers' mess, benched herself at the long table, and ate ravenously. Not that the food was worthy of it; her field rations had been better.

A sandy-haired young woman on her right attempted friendliness. "Ye're the stranded scientist, no? My sympathies. I'm Kate Fraser, medical corps." Reluctantly, Sally shook hands. "Ye're a . . . xenologist, am I right? Maybe, if ye've naught else to do, ye'd consider assisting in sickbay. Ye must know first aid, at least, and we're shorthanded. 'Twill be worse if we take casualties, come the action."

"That's no' to speak o' here, Lieutenant Fraser," warned a skinny redheaded man sitting opposite. "Besides, I do no' believe she'd fit into a naval organization." He cleared his throat. "Wi' due respect, Dr. Jennison. See ye, every hale adult on Adam is a reservist in the armed forces until old age. Thus we're better coordinated in our units than any co-opted civilian could possibly be." Pridefully: "The berserkers will no' get nigh enough again to Adam to bombard it."

Anguish and anger kindled anew in Sally. "Why did you want to interfere on Ilya, then?"

"Forward strategy," said Fraser. The redhead frowned at her and made a shushing motion.

It went unseen by a very young officer whose plumpness, unusual in this assemblage, suggested a well-to-do home. " 'Tis no' sufficient to throw back the damned berserkers," he declared. "They'll still be aprowl. Travel and outlying industries will still be endangered, insurance rates stay excruciating."

Sally knew little about Adam, but a memory stirred in her. After the last assault impoverished them and their planet, many of the people went into new endeavors requiring less in the way of natural resources than the original agriculture-based society had done. A stiff work ethic and, yes, a general respect for learning gave advantages that increased through the generations. Adamite shipping and banking interests were of some importance nowadays, in their stellar sector. Prim race of moneygrubbers, she thought.

"The basic problem to cope wi'," the boy went on, "is that the berserkers are von Neumann machines—"

"That will do, Ensign Stewart!" interrupted the redhead. "Report to my office at fifteen hundred hours."

Scarlet and white went across the youthful cheeks. Sally guessed Stewart was in for a severe reprimand.

''Sorry, Dr. Jennison,'' said the redhead. His tone was not quite level. ''Military security. Ah, my name is Craig, Commander Robert Craig.''

''Are you afraid I'll run off and spill your secrets to the enemy?'' Sally jeered.

He bit his lip. ''Surely no'. But wha' ye do no' know, the berserkers can no' torture out o' ye. They could, understand. They've robots among them o' the right size, shape, mobility—like soulless caricatures o' humans.''

''What about you?''

''The men, and such officers as ha' no need to know, simply follow orders. The key officers are sworn to ne'er be taken alive.'' Craig's glance dropped to his sidearm. Stewart seemed to regain pride.

''Can we no' talk more cheerful?'' asked Fraser.

The effort failed. Conversation sputtered out.

Ian Dunbar's place had been too far up the table for him to speak with Sally. He intercepted her at the mess-hall door. ''Good day,'' he said in his odd fashion, half harsh, half diffident. ''Ha' ye any plans for the next several hours?''

She glared at the angular countenance. ''Have you a library? I've nothing to read. Our books, our tapes—the station's, my own, like all our personal property—are gone.''

He winced. ''Aye, o' course, we've ample culture along in the data banks, text, video, music. I'll show ye to the screening room if ye wish. But—um-m, I thought ye might liefer ha' some private speech, now that ye're rested. Ye could ask me whate'er ye like, and within the limits o' security I'd try to gi' honest answers.''

Is this a leadup to a pass at me? she wondered. No, I don't suppose so. Not that it matters a lot. I'm certain I could curb him. But I suspect he curbs himself tighter than that. ''Very well. Where?''

"My room is the only place. That is, we could go topside again, but there are things ye should perhaps see and—Naturally, the door will stand open."

A smile flitted of itself across Sally's lips.

Accompanying him through the passageways, she asked why men and machines continued busy. He explained that, while the basic installations were complete, plenty more could be done in whatever time remained, especially toward hardening the site. Let her remember that the berserker would come equipped to incinerate a world.

She almost exclaimed: You're not doing a thing to protect the Ilyans! but blocked the impulse. Later, maybe. First she needed to learn a great deal, and that required coolness: for her refreshed brain realized how little sense everything she had heard thus far made.

"You told me you're an engineer, Captain Dunbar," she angled instead. "What specialty?"

"Heavy, high-energy devices, for the most part," he replied. "In civilian life I've been on projects throughout scores o' lightyears. My employers are . . . contractors supplying technical talent, ye might say. 'Tis one o' the items Adam has for export."

"How interesting. Could you tell me something I've been wondering about? I heard a reference to it when I didn't have a chance to inquire what it meant or go look it up."

His mouth creased with the pleasure of any normal man consulted by an attractive woman. "Aye, if I know mysel'."

"What's a von Neumann machine?"

He broke stride. "Eh? Where'd ye hear that?"

"I don't think it's among your secrets," she said blandly. "I could doubtless find it in the base's reference library, which you just invited me to use."

"Ah—well—" He recovered and went onward, moving

and talking fast. " 'Tis no' a specific machine, but a general concept, going back to the earliest days o' cybernetics. John von Neumann proposed it; he was among the pioneers. Basically, 'tis a machine which does something, but also fro' time to time makes more like itsel', including copies o' the instructions for its main task."

"I see. Like the berserkers."

"Nay!" he denied, more emphatically than needful. "A warship does no' manufacture other warships."

"True. However, the system as a whole—the entire berserker complex, which includes units for mining, refining, production—yes, it functions as a von Neumann machine, doesn't it? With the basic program, that it copies, being the program for eradicating life. Additionally, the program modifies itself in the light of experience. It learns; or it evolves."

"Aye," he conceded, his unwillingness plain upon him, "ye can use that metaphor if ye insist."

For a moment, she wished she hadn't asked. What had it gained her? A figure of speech, scarcely anything else. And what a chilling image it was. Not alone the fact of berserker auxiliaries ripping minerals out of planets and asteroids, digesting them to fineness, turning them into new machines which carried the same code as the old, the same drive to kill. No, what made her shiver was the sudden thought of the whole hollow universe as a womb engendering the agents of death, which later came back and impregnated their mother anew.

Dunbar's words brought deliverance. His mood had lightened, unless for some reason he wanted to divert her from her idea. "Ye're a sharp one indeed," he said almost cordially. "I look forward to better acquaintance. Here we are. Welcome."

Officers' quarters were individual chambers, four meters

square. That sufficed for a bed, desk, shelves, dresser, closet, a couple of chairs, floor space for pacing if you grew excited or simply needed to ease tension. The desk held a computer terminal, eidophone, writing equipment, papers; the occupant must often work as well as sleep on the spot.

Sally looked around, curious. Fluorescent lighting fell chill on plastered walls and issue carpeting. Personal items were on hand, though—pictures, a few souvenir objects, a pipe rack and ashtaker, a tea set and hotplate, a small tool kit, a half-finished model of a sailing ship on ancient Earth. "Sit ye down," Dunbar urged. "Can I brew us a pot? I've ooloong, jasmine, green, lapsang soochong, as ye prefer."

She accepted, chose, granted him permission to smoke. "And why not shut the door, Captain?" she proposed. "It's so noisy outside. I'm sure you're trustworthy."

"Thank ye." Did an actual blush pass beneath that leathery tan? He busied himself.

The largest picture was a landscape, valley walled by heights, lake agleam in the foreground. It did not otherwise resemble Geyserdale. Ground cover was sparse Earth grass and heather. Cedars sheltered a low house from winds that had twisted them into troll shapes. A glassy-bottomed crater marred a mountainside; stone had run molten thence, before congealing into lumps and jumbles. Clouds brooded rain over the ridges. Above them, daylight picked out the pale crescents of two moons.

"Is that scene from Adam?" she inquired.

"Aye," he said. "Loch Aytoun, where I was born and raised."

"It seems to have . . . suffered."

He nodded. "A berserker warhead struck Ben Creran. The area was slow to recover, and has ne'er been fertile again as 'twas formerly." He sighed. "Though 'twas lucky compared to many. We've deserts fushed solid like yon pit. Other places, air turned momentarily to plasma and soil vaporized down to bedrock. And yet other places—but let's no' discuss that, pray."

She studied his lean form. "So your family isn't rich," she deduced.

"Och, nay." He barked a laugh. "The financiers and shipping barons are no' as common among us as folklore has it. My parents were landholders, on land that yielded little. They wrung a wee bit extra out o' the waters." Proudly: "But they were bound and determined their children would ha' it better."

"How did you yourself achieve that?"

"Scholarships through engineering school. Later, well-paid jobs, especially beyond our own planetary system."

You'd have to have considerable talent to do that, she thought. Her gaze wandered to another picture near the desk: a teenage boy and girl. "Are those youngsters yours?"

"Aye." His tone roughened. "My wife and I were divorced. She took custody. 'Twas best, I being seldom home. That was the root reason why Ellen left. I see them whene'er I can."

"You couldn't have taken a sedentary position?" she asked low.

"I do no' seem to be the type. I mentioned to ye before that I wanted to be a planetologist, but saw no openings."

"Like my father," she blurted.

"He is a planetologist?"

"Yes. Professor at a college in western Oregon, if that means anything to you. He doesn't do much fieldwork anymore, but it used to take him away for long stretches. Mother endured his absences, however."

"A remarkable lady."

"She loves him." *Of course she does. It was ever worth the wait, when Dad at last returned.*

"Tea's ready," Dunbar said, as if relieved to escape personal matters. He served it, sat down facing her with shank crossed over knee, filled and ignited his pipe.

The brew was hot and comforting on her palate. "Good," she praised. "Earth-grown, I'd judge. Expensive, this far out. You must be a connoisseur."

He grinned. It made his visage briefly endearing. "*Faute de mieux*. I'd liefer ha' offered ye wine or ale, but we're perforce austere. I daresay ye noticed the Spartan sauce on our food. Well, as that fine old racist Chesterton wrote,

" 'Tea, although an Oriental,

" 'Is a gentleman at least—' "

Startled, she splashed some of hers into the saucer. "Why, you sound like my father now!"

"I do?" He seemed honestly surprised.

"A scholar."

Again he grinned. "Och, nay. 'Tis but that on lengthy voyages and in lonely encampments, a fellow must needs read."

A chance to probe him. "Have you developed any particular interests?"

"Well, I like the nineteenth-century English-language writers, and history's a bit o' a hobby for me, especially medieval European." He leaned forward. "But enough about me. Let's talk about ye. What do ye enjoy?"

"As a matter of fact," she admitted, "I share your literary taste. And I play tennis, sketch, make noises on a flute, am a pretty good cook, play hardnose poker and slapdash chess."

"Let's get up a game," he suggested happily. "Chess, that is. I'm more the cautious sort. We should be well matched."

Damn, but he does have charm when he cares to use it! she thought.

She tried putting down any further notions. The men who attracted her had always been older ones, with intelligence, who led active lives. (A touch of father fixation, presumably, but what the hell.) Dunbar, though—she would not, repeat not, call him "Ian" in her mind—he was . . .

Was what? The opposition? The outright enemy?

How to lure the truth out of him? *Well, Dad used to say, "When all else fails, try frankness."*

She set her teacup on the shelf beside her chair: a hint, perhaps too subtle, that she was declining continued hospitality. "That might be fun, Captain," she declared, "*after* you've set me at ease about several things."

For an instant he looked dashed, before firmness and . . . resignation? . . . deepened the lines in his countenance. "Aye," he murmured, " 'twas clear ye'd raise the same questions your colleagues did. And belike more, sin' ye've a keen wit and are not being rushed as they were."

"Also, I have a special concern," Sally told him. "Not that the rest don't share it, but it was bound to affect me harder than most of them. You see, my study hasn't been the structure of the planet or the chemistry of life on it or anything like that. It's been the natives themselves. I deal directly with them, in several cases intimately. They—certain individuals—they've become my friends, as dear to me as any human."

Dunbar nodded. "And today ye see them threatened wi' extermination, like rats," he said, his tone gentler than she would have expected. "Well, that's why we came, to protect them."

Sally stiffened. "Captain, I know a fair amount about the berserkers. Anybody must, who doesn't want to live in a dream universe. If a planet is undefended, and you assure me they suppose Ilya is, then a single major vessel of theirs can reduce it in a couple of days. Therefore, they'll not likely bother to send more than that."

Dunbar puffed hard on his pipe. Blue clouds streamed past his visage and out the ventilator. She caught a tart whiff. "Aye, we've based our plans on the expectation."

"You seem to have planted your most potent weapons, ground-based, here. The berserker will scarcely happen to show first above this horizon. No, it'll assume orbit and start bombardment above some random location—sending a line of devastation across Ilya, from pole to pole, till it's swung into your range."

"That's what our spacecraft are mainly for, Dr. Jennison. They're insufficient to destroy it, but they'll draw its attention. Chasing them, it'll come into our sights."

"You're risking countless lives on that hope."

"Wha' else ha' we? I told ye, wi'out this operation, the planet is foredoomed anyhow."

"And you came in pure, disinterested altruism," she challenged, "for the sake of nonhuman primitives whom none of you had ever even met?"

He grinned afresh, but wolfishly now. "No, no. Grant us, we'd ha' been sorry at such a cosmic tragedy. Howe'er, from our selfish viewpoint, there'll be one berserker the less, o' their most formidable kind."

She frowned, drummed fingernails on shelf, finally brought her glance clashing against his, and said: "That doesn't make sense, you know. Considering how many units their fleet must have, your effort is out of all proportion to any possible payoff."

"Nay, wait, lass, ye're no' versed in the science o' war."

"I doubt any such science exists!" she spat. "And I'd like to know how *you* know the enemy knows about Ilya. And—"

A siren wailed. A voice roared from loudspeakers, beat through the door, assailed her eardrums. *"Attention, attention! Hear this! Red alert! Berserker scout detected! Battle stations! Full concealment action!"*

"Judas in hell!" ripped from Dunbar. He sprang out of his chair, crouched over his computer terminal, punched frantically for video input. *Woop-woop-woop* screamed the siren.

Sally surged to her feet. She looked over Dunbar's shoulder. No radar, of course, she realized, nothing like that, which the intruder might notice; instruments in use were passive: optics, neutrino detectors, forcefield meters—

They did not spy the vessel from Lake Sapphire. The coincidence would have been enormous if it had passed above. However, from devices planted elsewhere the information, scrambled to simulate ordinary radio noise, went to the fortress. His screen showed a burnished spindle hurtling through the upper air. It passed beyond sight.

He sagged back. She saw sweat darken his shirt beneath the arms. She felt her own. "The scout," he whispered. " 'Tis verified—"

"Bandit has left atmosphere and is accelerating outward," chanted the loudspeaker. *"Reduce to yellow alert. Stand by."*

Silence rang.

Slowly, Dunbar straightened and turned to Sally. His voice rasped. "We'll ha' action soon."

"What did it want?" she asked, as if through a rope around her neck.

"Why, to make sure Ilya remains unguarded."

"Oh. Captain, excuse me; this has been a shock, I must go rest a while."

Sally whirled from him and stumbled out into the hallway. "No, don't come along, I'll be all right," she croaked. She didn't look behind her to see what expression might be on his face. He didn't seem entirely real. Nothing did.

The knowledge grew and grew inside her, as if she were bearing a death in her womb. *Why should the berserkers send a scout? The original chance discovery and whatever investigation followed, those should have been plenty. In fact, why didn't they strike Ilya at once, weeks ago?*

Because they didn't know, until just lately. But the Adamites say they did. And the Adamites were expecting that spyship.

Then it must be the Adamites who betrayed us to the enemy. Are they goodlife? Do they have some kind of treaty with the berserkers? If not, what is their aim?

What can I do? I am alone, delivered into their hands. Must I sit and watch the slaughter go on?

Even as she groped her way, an answer began to come.

A few food bars were left in her baggage. She stuffed them into pockets of her coverall. Ilyan biochemistry was too unlike Earth's for a human to eat anything native to the planet. By the same token, she was immune to every Ilyan disease. Water would be no problem—unless it got contaminated by radioactive fallout.

Return to Dunbar's room, she thought desperately. *If he's still there. If not, find him. Persuade him . . . but how? I'm not experienced in seduction or, or anything like that. Somehow, I've got to talk him into covering for me.*

He saved her the trouble. A knock on her door summoned her. He stood outside, concern on his countenance and in his stance and voice. "Forgi' me, I'd no' pester ye, but ye acted so distressed— Can I do aught to help?"

The knowledge of her power, slight though it was, came

aglow in Sally like a draught of wine. Abruptly she was calm, the Zen relaxation upon her which Ito had tried to teach, and totally determined. Win or lose, she would play her hand.

"Don't you have duties, Captain?" she asked, since that was a predictable question.

"No' at once. The berserker scout is definitely headed out o' this system. 'Twill take fifty or sixty hours at least for it to report back and for a major ship to get here. Belike the time will be longer." He hesitated, stared at the floor, clamped his fists. "Aye, they'll soon require me for final inspections, tests, drills, briefings. But no' immediately. Meanwhile, is there any comfort I can offer ye?"

She pounced. "Let me go topside," she said mutedly.

"Wha'?" He was astonished.

I'm not used to playing the pathetic little girl, she thought. *I'll doubtless do it badly. Well, chances are he won't know the difference.* "It may be my last walk around this countryside I love. Oh, please, Captain Dunbar—Ian—please!"

He stood silent for several heartbeats. But he was a decisive man. "Aye, why no'? I'm sorry—surely ye'd liefer be alone—my orders are that I must accompany ye."

She gave him a sunburst smile. "I understand. And I don't mind at all. Thank you, thank you."

"Let's begone, if ye wish." Willy-nilly, she found that his gladness touched her.

Save for the pulse of machines, the corridors had quieted. Men were closing down their construction jobs and preparing for combat. As she passed a chapel, Sally heard untrained singers:

"—Lord God o' warrior Joshua,

"Unleash thy lightnings now!"

She wondered if the hymn spoke to Dunbar or if he had left the Kirk and become an agnostic like her.

What did that matter?

A ladder took them past a guard station where the sentries saluted him, and up onto desolation. A breeze off the lake cooled noontide heat. Clouds blew in ruddy-bright rags. Olga was a thin arc, with streamers of dust storm across the dark part. Sally pointed herself at a stand of trees some distance beyond this blackened section, and walked fast.

"I take it ye want as much time as possible amidst yon life," Dunbar ventured.

She nodded. "Of course. How long will it remain?"

"Ye're too pessimistic, lass—pardon me—Dr. Jennison. We'll smite the berserker, ne'er fear."

"How can you be sure? It'll be the biggest, most heavily armed, most elaborately computer-brained type they've got. I've seen pictures, read descriptions. It'll not only have a monstrous offensive arsenal, it'll bristle with defenses: forcefields, antimissiles, interceptor beam projectors. Can your few destroyers, or whatever they are, can they hope to prevail against it, let alone keep it from laying—oh—enormous territories waste?"

"I told ye, their main purpose is to lure it to where our ground-based armament can take o'er."

"That seems a crazy gamble. It'll be a moving target, hundreds of kilometers aloft."

"We've no' just abundant energy to apply, we've knowledge o' where to. The layout o' such a ship is well understood, fro' study o' wrecks retrieved after engagements in the past."

Sally bit her lip. "You're assuming the thing is . . . stupid. That it'll sit passive in synchronous orbit, after failing to suspect a trap. Berserkers have outsmarted humans before now."

Dunbar's tone roughened. "Aye, granted. Our computer technology is not yet quite on a par wi' that o' the ancient Frankensteins who first designed them. The monsters do no' behave foreseeably, e'en in statistical fashion, the way less advanced systems do. They learn from experience; they innovate. That's wha's made them mortal dangers. Could we build something comparable—"

"No!" said ingrained fear. "We could never trust it not to turn on us."

"M-m-m, a common belief . . . Be that as it may, we do lack critical information. Nobody has studied a modern, updated berserker computer, save for fragments o' the hardware. Software, nil. Wha' few times a capture looked imminent, the thing destroyed itsel'." Dunbar's chuckle was harsh. "No' that the weapons employed usually leave much to sweep up."

"And nevertheless you think you can trick one of their top-rated units?"

"They're no' omnipotent, Dr. Jennison. They too are bound by the laws o' physics and the logical requirements o' tactics. Humans ha' more than once defeated them. This will be another occasion."

Ash gave way to turf. "Maybe, maybe," the woman said. "But that's not enough for me. The berserker will fight back. It will employ its most powerful weapons. You've hardened your base, but what have you done to protect the neighborhood? Nothing."

He wilted. "We could no'," he answered in misery. "We know naught about the natives."

"My colleagues do. They'd have undertaken to make arrangements with them."

"Rightly or wrongly, our orders were to clear your team out o' the way immediately and completely, out fro' underfoot, so we could get on wi' our task,'' Dunbar said shakily. ''I hate the thought o' losing lives, but wha' we do is necessary to save the whole native species.''

The shaw was close. The man's sidearm sat within centimeters of Sally's hand. She felt no excitement, only a vivid sense of everything around her, as she snatched it from its holster and sprang back.

''Oh, no!'' she cried. ''Stop where you are!''

''Wha's this?'' He jerked to a halt, appalled. ''Ha' ye gone schizo?''

''Not a move,'' she said across the meters of living sod. The pistol never wavered in her grip. ''At the least suspicion, I'll shoot, and believe me, I'm a damn good shot.''

He rallied, mustered composure, said in a flat voice: ''Wha' are ye thinking o'? I can scarce believe ye're goodlife.''

''No, I'm not,'' she flung back. ''Are you?''

''Hoy? How could ye imagine—''

''Easily. Your story about the berserkers chancing upon Ilya doesn't hang together. The sole explanation for everything I've witnessed is that *you* informed them, you Adamites, you called them in. Dare you deny?''

He swallowed, ran tongue over lips, bowed his head. ''We've a trap to spring,'' he mumbled.

''For a single trophy, you'd set a world at stake? You're as evil as your enemy.''

''Sally, Sally, I can no' tell ye—''

''Don't try. I haven't the time to spill, anyway. I'm going to do what you'd never have let me, lead the natives hereabouts to safety . . . if any safety is to be found, after what you've caused. Go back! This instant! I'll kill anyone who tries to follow me.''

For a long while he looked at her. The wind soughed in the darkling trees.

"Ye would," he whispered finally. "Ye might ha' asked leave o' the admiral, though."

"Would he have granted it, that fanatic?"

"I can no' tell. Maybe no'."

"It wasn't a risk I could take."

"Fro' your standpoint, true. Ye're a brave and determined person."

"Go!" She aimed the pistol between his eyes and gave the trigger a light pressure.

He nodded. "Farewell," he sighed, and trudged off. She watched him for a minute before she disappeared into the woods.

The deathmoon slipped out of flightspace and accelerated ponderously toward the red sun. Starshine glimmered off the kilometers-wide spheroid that was its hull. The weak light ahead cast shadows past gun turrets, missile tubes, ray projectors, like the shadows of crags and craters on a dead planet.

A radar beam brought word of the double world. The berserker calculated orbits and adjusted its vectors accordingly. Otherwise nothing registered on its receivers but endless cosmic rustlings.

The solar disc waxed, dark spots upon bloody glow. The target globe and companion glimmered as crescents. The berserker was slowing down now, to put itself in a path around the one which was alive.

It passed the other one. Abruptly, detectors thrilled. Engines had awakened, spacecraft were scrambling from both planets—human vessels.

The berserker tracked them. They numbered half a dozen, and were puny, well-nigh insignificant. Not quite; any could launch a warhead that would leave the berserker a cloud of molten gobbets. However, even attacking together they could not saturate its defenses. It would annihilate their missiles in midcourse, absorb their energy beams, and smash them out of existence, did they choose to fight.

Should it? Within the central computer of the berserker, a logic tree grew and spread. The humans might be present by chance (probability low). If not, they had some scheme, of which the revelation by the Montgomery unit had been a part (probability high). Ought the berserker to withdraw? That might well be the intent of the humans; they often bluffed. The assumption that they were strong in this system would affect strategy, as by causing underestimation of their capabilities elsewhere.

The berserker could retreat, to return in an armada invincible against anything the humans might have here. But this would mean postponing attacks elsewhere. It would buy the enemy time he much needed, to bring help from distant sectors. Whole worlds might never get attended to.

Information was necessary. The berserker computed that its optimum course was to proceed. At worst, a single capital unit would perish. It considered dispatching a courier back to base with this message, calculated that the humans would detect and destroy the device before it could enter flightspace, and refrained. Its own failure to report in would warn the others, if that happened.

The berserker moved onward—majestically, a human would have said—under its great imperative, to kill.

First, if possible, it should dispose of the opposing spacecraft. They were widely dispersed, but generally maneuvering near the target mass. Computation, decision: Move their way, seek engagement, meanwhile establish orbit, commence sterilization, lash back at any surviving human vessel which dared try to distract the berserker from its mission.

It swung inward. The little ships did likewise, converging on a volume of space above the terminator. The berserker followed. A destroyer accelerated audaciously forth. The berserker shifted vectors to shorten the range. This brought it near the fringes of atmosphere, at less than orbital speed. Its track curved gradually downward. But the parameters were in its data banks; its drive was already at work to bring it up again. It was simply using gravitation as an aid.

Lightning lanced out of the night below.

Electronically fast, the ship's fire control center reacted. Even as sensors recorded the slash of energy through metal, and went blank before that fury, a missile sprang.

There was only time for the one. Then the berserker tumbled around itself, sliced across. Stars danced about, incandescent drops that had been armor, before they cooled and went black. Radar-guided, light-fast, the beam carved again, and again. Cut free of every connection, the central computer drifted in its housing amidst the pieces, blind, deaf, dumb, helpless.

The human vessels spurted to salvage the fragments before those could become meteors.

A newly gibbous Olga gleamed red-cold over Snowcrown. Mountains beyond were jagged ramparts under constellations Earth had never seen. In a hollow of the foothills, campfires cast flickery gleams off eyes and eyes, as three hundred or more Ilyans huddled close. They said little, in that enormous silence.

Sally Jennison crouched likewise. She, the alien, her skin bare beneath its garb, needed the most help against gathering chill. Her friends, the leaders of the exodus, squatted to right and left. She could almost feel their questioning.

Rainbow-in-the-Mist uttered it: ''How long must we abide,

Lady-Who-Seeks? The food we have brought grows scant. The younglings and the old suffer. But well you know this.''

''I do,'' Sally replied. Breath smoked ghost-white from her lips. Hunger made her light-headed; her own rations had given out many hours ago, as she took the Geyserdale folk eastward to shelter. ''Better hardship than death.''

Feather-softly, he touched her hand. ''Yours is the worst case,'' he fluted. ''We would not lose you whom we love. When can everybody turn back?''

''When the danger is past—''

Behind those ridges that barred view of the west, heaven sundered. A sheet of blue-white radiance momentarily shrouded stars and moon. Trees and shadows were as if etched. Ilyans shrieked, flung arms over faces, clutched infants to their bodies. Sally herself stumbled bedazzled.

''Hold fast!'' she yelled. ''Rainie, tell them to stay brave! We're all alive!''

The ground sent a shudder through her bones. She heard rocks bounce down slopes. The rags of brilliance began to clear from her vision.

She went about among the Ilyans with her lieutenants, helping, reassuring. They had not panicked; that was not in their nature. And although they were more vulnerable to actinic light than she was, it didn't seem that anybody's sight had been permanently damaged; intervening air had blotted up the worst. She wept in her relief.

After minutes the sound arrived, a roar whose echoes cannonaded from hill to hill for what seemed like a long while. But there had been no second hell-flash. Whatever had happened, had happened.

''Is the danger past?'' asked Rainbow-in-the-Mist when stillness had returned.

''I . . . think so,'' Sally answered.

"What next shall we do?"

"Wait here. You can hold out till—oh, dawn. Though if things go well, it should end sooner. My fellow creatures ought to arrive in their vehicles and ferry you back before then."

"Home?"

She disliked admitting: "No, I fear not. Your homes are smashed and burnt, as you yourselves would have been if we'd not fled. It'll be a year or two"—brief Ilyan years—"till you can rebuild. First we'll distribute you among your kindred in the unharmed hinterlands.

"But I must go tell the humans. Best I start off at once."

"*We* will," Rainbow-in-the-Mist said. "I've better night vision, and can find things to eat along the way, and . . . would not let you fare alone, Lady-Who-Saved-Us."

She accepted his offer. He would have insisted. Besides, he was right. Without a partner, she might not survive the trek.

Unless, to be sure, the men of Adam came looking for her in their aircars, wearing their light-amplifier goggles.

They did.

"We're unco busy," Admiral Scrymgeour had snapped. "No time for official briefing, debriefing, any such nonsense. Later, later, just to satisfy the bureaucrats. In the interim, Dr. Jennison, now that ye've gotten some sleep and nourishment, I detail Captain Dunbar to explain and discuss. He deserves a rest himsel'." Did he wink an eye?

She had inquired if they might leave the clamor and closeness underground, to talk in peace (if peace was possible between them). Dunbar had agreed. Residual radioactivity wasn't dangerous topside unless exposure was unreasonably prolonged. Warmly clad, they sought the bluff above Lake Sapphire.

Olga stood nearly full, a rosiness on which few scars showed, only dark emblazonings and streamers of brightness that were high-floating clouds. A frost ring surrounded it, and stars. Through windless cold, it cast a nearly perfect glade over the water. Beyond, mountains reared hoar, Snowcrown a faintly tinged white. Ice creaked underfoot, almost the single sound. It covered scorched turf, leveled homesteads, trees shattered to kindling, with a glittery blanket. Come sunrise, growth would begin again.

Dunbar spoke softly, as though unwilling to violate the hush: "Ye've naught to fear fro' us, ye realize. True, belike ye'd no' ha' been released on your errand o' mercy if ye'd applied. Overcaution, same as when ye appeared in your boat. Howe'er, ye did break free, and save those many lives. Our consciences are eternally in your debt."

"What about yourself?" she wondered. "You failed in your duty."

He smiled like a boy. "Och, they're glad I did. And in any case, no' to be modest, I carried out my real duty wi' full success. That's wha' matters. The episode wi' ye will simply not get into the record."

She nodded in troubled wise. "You demolished the berserker, yes."

"Wrong!" he exulted. "We did no'. 'Twas the whole point. We captured it."

Her pulse stumbled. She stared at him.

He grew earnest. "We could no' tell ye, or your colleagues, in advance. This attempt might ha' been a failure. If so, we'd want to try afresh elsewhere. Meanwhile, we could no' ha' risked the secret getting out, could we?"

"But now—?" she breathed.

He faced her. Beneath his shadowing hood, eyes shone forth. ''Now,'' he said, ''we can make amends to ye, to Ilya. We'll mount guard o'er this world, at least until a gathered alliance can assume the task. No' that I await another attack. When they ne'er hear fro' the ship they sent, the berserkers will likeliest become leery. They've much else they want to do, after all, before they're forced out o' the entire sector.''

Compassion touched her. ''Including an assault on Adam?''

''Maybe. If so, they'll no' succeed. They may well no' e'en try. The fact that we fooled them should gi' them pause. Be that as it may, we've strength to spare—including our weapons on the ground, and more that we can install roundabout this planet—strength to spare for Ilya.'' His lips tightened. ''We did do its folk a wrong—perforce, in a righteous cause—nonetheless a wrong. We pay our debts, Dr. Jennison.''

''But what *was* your cause?'' she asked in bewilderment.

''Why, I told ye. To capture intact a first-line berserker unit. No' the actual ship, though study o' the pieces will prove rewarding, but its brain, the principal computer, hardware and software both, before it could destroy itsel'.

''To that end, we lured a single craft here, where we'd assembled a ray projector. Our weapon has the gigawatts o' power, the lake for cooling, the sheer physical dimensions for precision, that it could dissect a berserker across two or three thousand kilometers.''

Her gloved hands caught his. Fingers closed together. ''Oh, wonderful!'' Her admiration retreated. ''Yes, I can see how the data will be very helpful; but can they make that big a difference?''

''They can change everything,'' he replied.

After a moment, during which breath smoked between them, he said slowly: ''Ye inquired about von Neumann machines. Ye were correct; that is wha' the berserker fleet is, taken as a whole. A self-reproducing system whose basic program is to seek out and kill all that's alive.

"Well, wha' if we humans created another von Neumann machine, a system whose basic program is to seek out and kill *berserkers?*"

Her response was unthinking, automatic: "I've read something about that. It was tried, early in the war, and didn't work. The berserkers soon learned how to cope with those machines, and wiped them out."

"Aye," he agreed. "The ancient Builders built too well. Our race could no' make computers to match theirs, in scope, flexibility, adaptability, capacity for evolution. We must needs develop living organization, dedication, skill, humans an integral part o' the control loop. And 'tis no' served us badly. We've saved oursel's, most o' the time.

"But . . . there is no end to the war, either. They've the cosmos to draw on for the means o' building more like themsel's."

Sally remembered her image of a womb, and shivered.

"On the basis o' what we're going to learn," she heard Dunbar say, "let us make machines which will be likewise, but whose prey is berserkers."

"Dare we?" she replied. A crack rang loud through midnight as frost split a fallen tree apart. "Might they turn on us also, at last?"

She thought she saw stoicism on his face. "Aye, the old fear. Maybe, on that account alone, humankind will unite to forbid our undertaking.

"Or maybe we'll do it, and 'twill prove no single answer by itsel'. Then at least our hunter machines will bring attrition on the enemy, take pressure off us, help us deliver the final hammerblow.

"And if no' e'en that comes to pass, why, we've still gained information beyond price. Once we've examined our . . . prisoner, we'll understand today's berserkers far better. We'll become able to fight them the more readily."

It blazed from him: "Is that no' worth the risk and cost to Ilya, Sally?"

At once he was abashed. "Forgi' me," he said, while his hands withdrew from hers. "Dr. Jennison."

She regarded him by the icy brilliance. The thought came to her that perhaps robots that hounded robots were nothing to fear. Perhaps dread lay in the fact that a war which went on and on must, ultimately, bring forth men who were as terrible as their enemies.

She didn't know. She wouldn't live long enough to know. She and he were merely two humans, by themselves in a huge and wintry night.

She took a step forward, renewed their handclasp, and said, "We can argue about it later, Ian. But let's be friends."

DANGEROUS DREAMS

Coming out of that episode, returning to the mean reality of his existence as a plug-in unit for a berserker computer, finding himself still attached to the mind-probe machine in the cramped cave, Lars still brought with him a heady feeling of vicarious success.

So, the anti-berserker machine was now at least on the verge of becoming a resurrected reality. A great if dangerous idea, to be re-implemented at last, it appeared, by Earth-descended humanity.

But as planned by the people of Ilya and Adam, the ED version of *qwib-qwib* could not possibly arrive on the scene in time to be of any use to five ED people and the nine or ten Carmpan trapped here and now in the middle of a berserker base, trapped and doomed to help the enemy they hated. The new *qwib-qwib* would be a few decades at the least too late for that.

From a weak approach to elation, Lars's mood swung back

toward despair. It swung even farther than before. Maybe he should get one of his fellow prisoners to kill him, and that way squelch for good the dangerous dreams that burned within his skull. Captain Naxos would be the best choice, probably.

Assuming, of course, that Naxos could be trusted. That the subtle impression the captain managed to convey of anti-berserker, badlife fanaticism was genuine. For all Lars knew, Naxos could be the goodlife agent. Again, assuming there was one such among the ED prisoners.

The Carmpan had not managed to conceal this last episode, for all Lars knew had not even tried. The great berserker brain that ran this base had got the information, and undoubtedly was already planning preventive measures against the potential modern analog of the *qwib-qwib*, and possibly against the revived original as well.

The throb of machinery, digging, building, repairing, heard through the surrounding rock, maintained its faster pace.

Lars slept again. It was a more or less normal sleep, but once more the dream about the panel and the gage returned to trouble him. This time the dream conveyed a sense of urgency even more powerfully than it had before. In this new version, some alien, not a Carmpan, was shouting verses at Lars; a dark-furred being, impressively equipped with claws and teeth, and chanting verse.

When Lars awakened, he wondered if the recurrent dream about the gage and verses could be another buried telepathic episode of some kind too. He couldn't recall that one was unaccounted for. Or it could be the shadow or reflection of one, somehow . . .

Lars left his cell and joined the others in the common room, to find that Pat Sandomierz had returned. She looked exhausted—a touch more so than everyone else—but greeted

Lars calmly enough, saying that she had only been taken for an extra telepathic session. The result had been only another half-clouded vision, nothing out of the ordinary.

Lars considered it unwise to press her for more details. But he wondered if she were lying, if she had gone voluntarily into the other room, there to tell the berserker about his *qwib-qwib* ravings in his sleep.

A guide machine came to summon him to a telepathic session before he could change his mind about questioning Pat.

Fatalistically he let the berserker guide lead him. He glanced at his Carmpan co-victim—the same partner as in the previous session, he thought.

Lars lay down on the couch, and let the machines attach the electrodes to his head.

Pilots of the Twilight

Listen now.

This concerns a woman and a man, and a large, extremely hostile machine. It is a tale which has changed in some details over a generation, but is still true in its essentials. Some tellers have attempted to embroider the story, but nearly always have drawn back. They realized there simply was no need, and I concur.

The tale truly happened, and it took place just this way:

The woman's name was Morgan Kai-Anila. Some around her used the diminutive ''Mudgie,'' though usually not more than once; not unless they were long-time friends or family. Morgan Kai-Anila was fast with a challenge, but even swifter with her customized duelling model of the neuro-humiliatron. People tended to watch their step around her.

Morgan was a remittance woman. Her home had been Oxmare, one of the jeweled estates setting off the green, cleared parklands to the south of the Victorian continent's capital. Now her home was wherever she found employment. The jobs had picked up as the political climate of our world, then called Almira, began to heat considerably. Morgan's partner was her ship, a sleek, deadly fighter called Runagate. Both singly and together, they had achieved a crucial style. They were known by everyone who counted.

The man's strong suit was not style. He was too young and too unmoneyed. The man possessed a baggage of names, a confusing matter not of his doing. The North Terrea villagers, who finally had been convinced to accept custody of the boy back from the truculent 'Reen, had christened him Holt Calder. Only the smallest voice from the past in the adult Holt Calder's memory recalled his birth-parents' wish to name him Igasho. Then there were the 'Reen, who had mouthed the sequence of furry syllables translating roughly as "He-orphaned-and-helpless-whom-we-obliged-are-to-take-in-but-why-us?" Son of the largely unspoiled forests, "Holt" was what he eventually learned to respond to.

Holt's ship was not the newest or shiniest model of its class, but it had been modified by rural geniuses to specifications far superior to the original. The fighter's formal name was Limited North Terrea Community Venture Partnership One. Holt called his ship Bob.

Then there was the huge and hostile machine. It had no name as such, other than the digital coding sequence which differentiated it from all its brothers. It had no family roots, electronic or otherwise, located in this planetary system. Its style was as blunt and blocky as its physical configuration.

It was here only because a randomly ranging scout had registered sensor readings indicating the existence of sentient life—the enemy—and had transported those findings back to an authority that could evaluate them and take decisive action.

The result was this massive killer popping out of nowhere, safely away from the system's gravity wells.

The scout's intelligence had been incomplete. There were, the new visitor discovered, two inhabited worlds in this system. Fine. No problem. Armaments were adequate to the increased task.

The machine swept with bulky grace in along the orbital plane of the nearer world, even though that planet was the enemy sanctuary whose orbit was closer to the central star. The machine chose that jungle world first for mere convenience. It was a target of opportunity. If any complications arose, the assassin's implacable brain could compute new strategy.

A sympathetic human, goodlife, might have considered this a good day for killing. It didn't occur to the machine that it was having a good day. Nor was it having a bad day. It was just having a day.

A small part of the machine's brain checked and confirmed the readiness of its weapons. Its unfailing logic knew the precise time it would reach striking distance. Electrons spun remorselessly, just as the two inhabited planets ahead rotated on their axes. Maybe the machine *was* having a good day . . .

Morgan Kai-Anila's day was going fine. Runagate screamed down through the airless space around the moon Fear. Occasional defensive particle beams glittered and sparked as they vaporized bits of debris still descending slowly from Morgan's last strafing run. The missiles to the defense dome housing the Zaharan computers had done their work well, confusing if not destroying the targets.

"Eat coherent light, Zaharan scum," Morgan muttered, punching the firing stud for the lasers. Her heart really wasn't in it. Some of her best friends were Zaharans. This was only a job.

The lasers flashed away from recessed ports in Runagate's prow with a vibrating, high-pitched *thrumm*. Morgan saw the main Zaharan dome slice open and rupture outward from the pressure differential, spilling dozens of flailing, vac-suited figures into the harsh sunlight on Fear's surface.

"Ha!" Morgan kicked in the auxiliaries and hard-banked Runagate into a victory roll as the ship knifed away from the devastation. The pilot's ears registered the distant rumble of the dome explosion. She hoped the tumbling, suited figures were all watching. Good run.

Runagate climbed quickly away from the rugged, cratered surface of the moon. Within a few seconds, the distance allowed Morgan to see the full diameter of the irregular globe that was Fear.

"Good job, Mudge," said Runagate. The ship was allowed to use variations of Morgan's loathed childhood name. But then, she had programmed Runagate.

"Thanks." Morgan leaned back in the padded pilot's couch and sighed. "I hope nobody got torn up down there."

Runagate made the sound Morgan had learned to interpret as an electronic shrug. "Remember that it's just a job. You know that. So do they. Everybody loves the risks and the bonuses or they wouldn't do it."

Morgan touched the controls on the sound and motion simulation panel; the full-throated roar of Runagate slashing through open space died away. The ship now slid silently through the vacuum. "I just hope the raid did some good."

"You *always* say that," Runagate pointed out. "The raid on Fear was a small domino, but an important one. The Zaharans' bombardment base won't be dumping anything dangerous on Catherine for a while. That will give the Catherinians enough time to build up their defensive systems, so that Victoria can take some of the pressure off the Cytherans before Cleveland II and the United Provinces—''

''Enough,'' said Morgan. ''I'm glad you can keep track of continental alliances. I'm suitably impressed. But will you just prompt me from time to time, and avoid the rote?''

''Of course,'' Runagate said, the synthesized voice sounding a touch sulky.

Morgan swiveled to face the master screen. ''Give me a visual plot for our touchdown at Wolverton, please.'' The ship complied. ''Do you estimate I'll have time for a workout before we hit atmosphere? I'm stiff as a plank.''

''If you are quick about it,'' said Runagate.

''And what about my hair?'' Morgan undid the rest of her coif. It had started to come undone during the raid on Fear. Red curls tumbled down onto her shoulders.

''It's one or the other,'' the ship said. ''I cannot do your hair while you are working out.''

''Oh, all right,'' Morgan said mournfully. ''I'll take the hair.''

The ship's voice said, ''Did you have plans for tonight?''

Morgan smiled at the console. ''I'm going out.''

A bunch of spacers were whooping it up at the Malachite Saloon as they were wont to do any evening when a substantial number had returned safely from freelance missions. It had been a lucky day for most, and now was going to be a good night. The swinging copper portals might as well have been revolving doors. The capering holograms on the windowed upper deck had tonight been combined with live dancers. The effect of the real and unreal forms blurring and merging and separating composed an unnerving but fascinating spectacle outside for the occasional non-spacer passersby.

''Look, Mommy!'' said one tourist urchin, pointing urgently at the dance level as a finned holo enveloped a dancer. "A shrake ate that man!"

His mother grabbed a hand of each of her two children and tugged them on. "Overpaid low-life," she said. "Pay no heed."

The older brother looked scornfully at his sibling. "Oneirataxia," he said.

"I do *so* know what reality is," said the younger boy.

Inside the Malachite Saloon, Holt Calder sat alone in the fluxing crowd. He was a reasonably alert and pleasant-looking young man, but he was also the new boy on the block, and spacer bonds took time to form. Holt had fought only a comparative handful of actions, and truly seen nothing particularly exciting until today.

"Let me tell you, son, you almost cashed it in this afternoon off Loathing." The grizzled woman in black leathers raised her voice to penetrate the throbbing music from upstairs. Her hair was styled in a silver wedge and she wore a patch over her left eye. Without invitation, she pulled up a chair and sat down.

Holt put down his nearly empty glass and stared at her. True, he had realized at the time that it was not a particularly intelligent move to speed out of the moon Terror's shadow and pounce on a brace of more heavily armed Provincial raiders. "I didn't really think about it," he said seriously.

"I suspected as much." The woman shook her head. "Damned lucky for you the Cytherans jumped us before I had a chance to lock you in my sights."

"You?" said Holt. "Me? How did you know—"

"I asked," the woman said. "I checked the registry of your ship. Tonight I made a point of coming to this smokehole. I figured I ought to hurry if I wanted to see you while you were still alive."

The young man drained his glass. ''Sorry about your partner.''

The woman looked displeased. ''He was about your age and experience. I thought I had him on track. Idiot had to go and get over-eager. Lucky for you.''

Holt felt uncertain about what to do or say next.

The woman thrust out her hand. ''The name's Tanzin,'' she said. ''I trust you've heard of me''— Holt nodded—''but nothing good.''

Holt felt it unnecessary and indeed, less than politic, to mention that Tanzin was usually spoken of by other freelancers in the vocabulary that was also used to name the three moons, especially Fear and Terror. Her grip was strong and warm, quite controlled.

''Couldn't help but notice,'' said Tanzin, ''that you've been slugging them down fairly frequently.'' She gestured at his empty glass. ''Buy you another?''

Holt shrugged. ''Thanks. I never drank much. Before tonight. I guess the close call got to me.''

''You don't have a mission tomorrow, do you?''

The young man shook his head slowly.

''Fine. Then drink tonight.''

There was a commotion at the other end of the long, rectangular room. Holt tried to focus through the smoky amber light as a perceptible ripple of reaction ran through the crowd. Public attention had obviously centered on a woman who had just entered the Malachite. Holt couldn't make out much about her from a distance, other than her height, which was considerable, and her hair, which fell long and glowed like coals.

''Who is that?'' said Holt.

Tanzin, trying to signal a server, glanced. ''The Princess Elect.''

Holt's mouth opened as the Princess Elect and a quartet of presumed retainers in livery neared and swept past. "She's beautiful."

"The slut," said a deep voice from behind him. "Out slumming."

"Her hair . . ." Holt closed his mouth, swallowed, then opened it again.

"It's red. So?" That and a chuckle came from a new speaker, a cowled figure sitting at a small table close by Holt's right in the packed bar.

"You *must* have been out on a long patrol," said Tanzin.

"Hey, *I* like red too," said the same booming voice from behind Holt. He turned and saw two men, each dark-bearded, both dwarfing the chairs in which they sat.

The one hitherto silent turned to his companion. "So why don't you ask her to dance, then?"

The louder one guffawed. "I'd sooner dance with a 'Reen."

Before he realized what he was doing, Holt had jumped to his feet and turned to confront the two men. "Take it back," he said evenly. "I won't have you be insulting."

"The Princess Elect?" said the first man in apparent astonishment.

"The 'Reen."

"Are you crazy?" said Tanzin, reaching up and grabbing one elbow.

"Perhaps suicidal," murmured the hooded figure, taking his other elbow. "Sit back down, boy."

"Don't spoil my fun," said the louder of the large men to the pair restraining Holt. "I'd fly all the way to Kirsi and back without a map, just so's I could pound a 'Reen-lover."

"Big talk," said Tanzin. "You do know who I am?"

The man and his partner both looked at her speculatively. "I think I can take you too," said the first.

"How about me?" With the free hand, the cowled figure threw back her hood. Red curls smoldered in the bar light.

The first big man smirked. "I think I can mop, wax, and buff the floor, using the three of you."

The second large man cautioned him. "Hold on, Amaranth. The small one—that's what's-her-name, uh, the Kai-Anila woman."

Amaranth looked pensive. "Oh, yeah . . . The hot-shot on the circuit. You got as many confirmeds during the Malina Glacier action as I did all last year combined. Shoot, I don't want to take you apart."

"There's an easy way not to," Tanzin said. "Let's all just settle back. Next round's on me."

Amaranth looked indecisive. His friend slowly sat down and tugged at the larger man's elbow. "How about it, Amaranth? Let's go ahead and have a drink with the rookie and these two deadly vets."

Morgan and Tanzin sat. Still standing, Holt said, "Amaranth. What kind of name is that?"

Amaranth shrugged, a motion like giant forest trees bending slightly as wind poured off the tundra. "It's a translation. Undying flower. My pop, he figured we'd get to emigrate to Kirsi and he ought to name me that as a portent. My mom thought it sounded wrong with my last name, so she politicked for Amaranth—it means the same but doesn't alliterate—and it stuck."

"Good name," Holt said. He introduced himself and put out his hand. Amaranth shook it gravely. The other introductions followed. Amaranth's friend was Bogdan Chmelnyckyj. A server appeared and drinks were ordered.

Holt couldn't help but stare then, when he first looked closely at Morgan.

"The hair really is red." She smiled at him. "Even redder than the Princess Elect's."

Holt shut his mouth and then said, "Uh." He knew he was making a fool out of himself, but there didn't seem to be any help for it. He realized his heart was beating faster. This is ridiculous, he told himself, feeling more than comfortably warm. He could smell her and he liked it. We're all professionals, he admonished himself. Cut out the hormonal dancing.

It didn't do any good. He still stared and stammered and hoped that drool wasn't running off his chin.

The other four seemed oblivious to Holt's situation and were talking shop.

"—something's up," Amaranth was saying, as Holt tried to focus on the words. "I got that from the debriefer after I set down at Wolverton. Wasn't that long ago tonight. I hit up four or five grounders for information, but nobody'd divulge a thing."

"I have the same feeling," Tanzin said. She looked thoughtful. "I called a friend of mine over at the Office of the Elect. Basically, she said 'Yes,' and 'I can't tell you anything,' and 'Keep patience—something'll be announced, perhaps as soon as tonight.' I'm still waiting." She drained a shot of 2-4-McGilvray's effortlessly.

"Maybe not much longer." Bogdan motioned slightly. The five of them looked down the bar. The Princess Elect had returned from wherever her earlier errand had taken her and now stood talking to one of the Malachite's managers. Then she snapped her fingers and two of the huskier members of her entourage lifted her to the top of the hardwood bar.

For a moment she stood there silently. Her clingy green outfit shone even in the dim light. The Princess Elect tapped one booted foot on the bar. A ripple of silence spread out until only murmurs could be heard. The music from upstairs had already cut off.

"Your world needs you," said the Princess Elect. "I will be blunt. Effective now, the normal political wranglings among Victoria, Catherine, Cythera, and all the rest have ceased. The reason for this is simple—and deadly." She paused for maximum drama.

Amaranth raised a shaggy eyebrow. "Our star's going to go nova," he speculated.

"There is an enemy in our solar system," continued the Princess Elect. "We know little about its nature. Something we can be sure of, though, is that effective local sundown tonight, our colonists on Kirsi found themselves in a state of siege."

The level of volume of incredulous voices all around the room rose and the Princess Elect spread her hands, her features grave. "You all know that the few colonists on Kirsi possess only minimal armament. Apparently the satellite station was overwhelmed immediately. At this moment, the enemy orbits Kirsi, turning the jungles into flame and swamps into live steam. I have no way of ascertaining how many colonists still survive in hiding."

"Who is it?" someone cried out. "Who is the enemy?" The hubbub rose until no one could be heard by a neighbor.

The Princess Elect stamped her foot until order could be restored. "Who is the enemy? I—I don't know." For the first time, her composure seemed to crack just a little. Then it hardened again. Holt had heard the Princess Elect was a tough cookie, in every way a professional, just as he was as a pilot. "I have ordered up a task force to proceed to Kirsi and engage the enemy. All pilots are to be volunteers. All guilds and governments have agreed to cooperate. I wish I had more information to tell you tonight, but I don't.''

Again Holt thought the Princess Elect looked suddenly vulnerable before the shocked scrutiny of the Malachite crowd. Her shoulders started to slump a bit. Then she gathered herself and the steel was back. ''Personnel from the Ministry of Politics will be waiting to brief you back at the port. I wish you all, each and every one, a safe and successful enterprise. I want you all to return safely, after saving the lives of as many of our neighbors on Kirsi as is humanly possible.'' She inclined her head briefly, then leaped lithely to the floor.

''Hey! Just hold on,'' someone yelled out. Holt could see only the top of the Princess Elect's head. She paused. ''What about bonuses?''

''Yeah.'' Someone else joined in. ''You want us to put our tails on the line, making an inter-planet jump and fighting a whatever-it-is—a boojum—all for regular pay and greater glory?''

''How about it?'' a third pilot shouted over the rising clamor.

Holt could tell just from the attitude of the top of the Princess Elect's head that she wasn't pleased. She raised one gloved hand and the decibel level lowered. ''Bonuses, yes,'' she said. ''Quintuple fees. And that also goes for your insurance to your kin if you don't come back.''

''Bork that,'' said Amaranth firmly. ''*I'm* coming back.''

''Does 'quintuple' mean 'suicide'?'' said Bogdan slowly. He shrugged.

''Satisfactory?'' said the Princess Elect. ''Good fortune to all of you then, and watch your tails.'' Within seconds, the entourage had whisked her away.

The crowd was quieter than Holt would have expected.

"Hell of a damper on the party," Tanzin said.

"I am ready," said Amaranth. "Could have used some sleep, but—" He spread his hands eloquently.

Bogdan nodded. "I, as well."

"We may as well start back," said Tanzin. "I expect all transport will be headed toward the field."

Morgan flipped her hood forward. Holt was saddened to see her beauty abruptly hidden. "Some kind of fun now," she said in a low voice.

"I hope . . ." he said. They all looked at him. Holt felt like a child among a group of adults. He said simply, "Nothing. Let's go."

Midnight in the jungle. Nocturnal creatures shrilled and honked on every side. Overhead the star field shimmered and winked, as a brighter star crawled slowly across the zenith.

Kirsi's moon Alnaba began to edge over the tree-canopied horizon to the east.

Then the night sounds stopped.

The image suddenly tilted and washed out in a flare of silent, brilliant white light.

"That was the ground station at Lazy Faire."

Black. Stars that didn't twinkle.

Something moved.

The image flickered, blurred, then focused in on—something.

"What's the scale?"

"About a kilometer across. At this point, we can't be more exact."

It was a polyhedron that at first one might mistake for a sphere. Then an observer perceived the myriad angles and facets. As the image clarified, angular projections could be seen.

The device reflected little light. In its darkness it seemed a personification of something sinister. Implacable machinery, it looked tough and mean enough to eat worlds.

"We managed to swing the cameras of a surface resources surveyor. These were all the pictures we got."

A spark detached from the distant machine. That spark grew larger, closer, until it filled the entire screen. As with the transmission from Kirsi's surface, the image then flared out.

"That was it for the survey satellite. I think you've gotten a pretty good idea of the fate of nearly everything on and around Kirsi."

The lights came up and Holt blinked.

"It's gonna be one hell of a job, let me tell you that now," Amaranth said to him.

"I think my enthusiasm is wearing thin already." Tanzin looked glum.

"Beams," said Bogdan. "More wattage than this whole continent. Missiles up the rear. How're we gonna tackle that thing?"

Morgan smiled faintly. "I'd say our work's cut out for us."

"Bravado?" Tanzin covered the younger woman's hand with her own. The five of them sat behind a briefing table in the auditorium. "I agree with the sentiment. I just question how we're going to implement it." Complaining voices, questioning tones spiraled up from the other dozens of tables and scores of seated pilots around the room.

"I know what you're all asking. I'll try to suggest some answers." Dr. Epsleigh was the speaker. She was short, dark, intense, the coordinator chosen by the emergency coalition of governments to set up the task force. She was known for the sharpness of her tongue—and an ingenious ability to synthesize solutions out of unapparent patterns.

Someone from the back of the hall shouted, "Your first answer ought to try to squelch all the rumors. Just what *is* that thing?"

"I heard," said Dr. Epsleigh, "that someone earlier in the evening called our opponent a boojum." She smiled grimly. "That was an astute nomenclature."

"Huh?" said the questioner. "What's a boojum?"

"It's fortunate that classical literacy is not a requirement of a first-rate fighter." Dr. Epsleigh snorted. "The long-range sensors detected an object and coded it as a snark, a possible cometary object. One of our programmer ancestors liked literary allusions . . ."

At the table, Morgan's head jerked and she half-raised one hand toward an ear.

"What's wrong?" said Holt, feeling a start of concern.

"Runagate," she answered. "The ship's link. I've got to turn down the volume. Runagate just shouted in my ear that *he* knows all about snarks and boojums. Quote: 'For the snark *was* a boojum, you see.' "

"So just what is—" he started to say.

Dr. Epsleigh's amplified voice overrode him. "What we shall be fighting, as best can be determined at this time, is an automated destroyer, a deadly relic from an ancient war. It's a sentient machine that has been programmed to terminate all the organic life it encounters."

"So what's it got against us?"

"*That's* a dumb question," someone else pointed out. "Maybe you're not organic intelligence, Boz." The first questioner flushed pink.

"Thank you," said Dr. Epsleigh. "We've been running an historical search for information in the computers. Objects like that machine orbiting Kirsi were known when we sought refuge in this planetary system four centuries ago. They were just part of the oppressive civilization our ancestors fled. Our people wanted to be left alone to their own devices. It was assumed that the vastness of the Galaxy would protect them from discovery by either the machines or the rest of humanity." Dr. Epsleigh paused. "Obviously the machines were better trackers—or perhaps this is just a chance encounter. We don't know."

"Is there room for negotiation?" That was Tanzin.

Dr. Epsleigh's humorless smile appeared again. "Apparently not. In the past, the machines negotiated only when it was part of a larger strategy against their human targets. The attack on Kirsi was without warning. The machine has not attempted to communicate with any human in the system. Nor has it responded to our overtures. It is merely pounding away at Kirsi with single-minded ferocity. We think it picked that world simply because Kirsi was closer to its entrance point into this system." Dr. Epsleigh's jaw visibly tightened; the tension was reflected in her voice. "It's not merely trying to defeat our neighbors. The machine is annihilating them. We're witness to a massacre."

"And we're next?" said Morgan.

"All of Almira," said Dr. Epsleigh. "That's what we anticipate, yes."

"So what's the plan?" Amaranth's voice boomed out.

Holt glanced aside at Morgan, her hair almost glowing in the hall's artificial glare. His job had been to send back fee dividends to North Terrea, the village that had invested in him and his ship. Until only a short time ago, his life had centered around adventure, peril, and profit. Now a new factor had intervened. It seemed there suddenly was another facet of life to consider. Morgan. Maybe it *was* only a crush—he'd never find out if it would work or not unless he explored the possibilities. But instead they'd both fly out with the rest to Kirsi. The machine would kill him. Or her. Or the both of them. It was depressing.

Dr. Epsleigh interrupted his reverie. ''We don't know what the defensive capabilities of the machine are. The few ships that investigated from Kirsi didn't even get close enough to test its screens. You'll be more careful. We think you've got considerably more speed and mobility than the machine. The strategy will be to slip a few fighters through the machine's protective screens while the other ships are skirmishing. We're jury-rigging some heavier weapons than standard issue.''

''Um,'' said a pilot off to the left. ''What you're saying is, you *hope* some of us can find points of vulnerability on that critter?''

''We're continuing to gather intelligence about the machine,'' said Dr. Epsleigh. ''If a miracle answer comes up, believe me, you'll be the first to know.''

''It's borking suicide.'' Amaranth's voice carried throughout the hall.

''Probably.'' Dr. Epsleigh's smile heated from grim to wry. ''But it's the only borking chance we've got.''

''Why even *bother* with quintuple bonuses,'' someone muttered. ''No one'll be around to spend 'em other than the machine.''

''How can that boojum-thing just want to wipe us all out?'' came an overly loud musing from the back of the room.

''Aren't you forgetting us and the 'Reen?'' Holt said angrily, also loud. His neighbors stared at him.

''We didn't kill 'em all,'' said Bogdan mildly.

''Might as well have. For four hundred years, we took their land whenever it suited us. They died when they got in our way.''

"Not in *my* way," protested Bogdan. "I've never done anything to those stinking badgers."

"Nor *for* them," said Holt.

"Shut up," said Tanzin. "Squabble later. When the machine bombards Almira, I'm sure it won't distinguish between human and 'Reen." She raised her voice back in the direction of Dr. Epsleigh. "So what happens next?"

"We're outfitting the fighters. It will take some hours. You'll be leaving in successive waves. The ready rooms are prepared. I suggest you all get whatever sleep or food or other relaxation you can manage. I'll post specific departure rosters when I can. Questions?"

There were questions, but nothing startling. Holt drew his courage together and turned toward Morgan. "Buy you a caf?" She nodded.

"Buy us all a caf," said Tanzin, "but get a head start now. We'll meet you later."

Unwelcome satellite, the machine continued to circle Kirsi.

Dust.

Steam.

Death.

Oblivion.

That list pretty much inventoried the status of Kirsi's surface. Orbital weapons probed down to the planet's substrata.

The boojum, you see, wanted to be *sure*.

The ready rooms were clusters of variously decorated chambers color-keyed to whatever mood the waiting pilots wished. This dawn, the pilots had tended to gather together in either the darkest, most somber rooms, or else the most garishly painted. Seeking privacy, Holt conducted Morgan to a chamber finished in light wood with neutral, sand-colored carpets.

Holt told the room to shut off the background music. It complied. The man and woman sat opposite one another at a small table and stared across their mugs of steaming caf.

Morgan finally said, "So, are you frightened?"

"Not yet." Holt slowly shook his head. "I haven't had time yet. I expect I will be."

She laughed. "When the time comes, when that machine looms up as sharp and forbidding as the Shraketooth Peaks, then I expect I'll shake from terror."

"And after that?" said Holt.

"Then I'll just do my job."

He leaned toward her over the table and touched her free hand. "I want to do the same." She almost imperceptibly pulled her fingers back.

"I know something of your career," said Morgan. "I pay attention to the stats. I'm sure you'll do fine."

Holt reacted to a nuance in her tone. "I'm not *that* much younger than you. I just haven't had quite as much experience."

"That's not what I meant." This time she touched his hand. "I wasn't making light of your youth. I've watched the recordings of your skill as a young fighter pilot. What I'm wondering about is what it took to get there . . ."

Her words lay in the air as an invitation. Holt started to relax just a little. Their fingers remained lightly touching.

It was rarely simple or easy for Holt to explain how he had been raised in the wild by the 'Reen. A casual listener might toss it off as a joke or an elaborate anecdote. But then Holt rarely talked about his background with anyone. The few hearers invariably were impressed with his sincerity.

He found himself not at all reluctant to tell Morgan.

Simply put, Holt had been set out on a hillside to die,

while only an infant, by the North Terrea villagers. In the *laissez-faire* way of all Almira, no one had wanted to take the rap for doing in the baby. It all had something to do with Holt's parents who had perished under hazy circumstances that had never been explained to their son's satisfaction—but then, that circumspection was part of the eventual pact between Holt and the villagers.

At any rate, following the death of his parents, a very young Holt Calder had been placed on the steep, chilly flank of a small mountain, presumably to perish. Within hours, he was found by a roving band of 'Reen hunters. The 'Reen were a stocky, carnivorous, mammalian, sentient species with mythically (according to the human settlers) nasty temperaments—but in spite of colonists' scare-the-children stories, they didn't eat human babies. Instead the 'Reen hunters hissed and grumbled around the infant for a while, discussing this incredible example of human irresponsibility, and then transported the baby down to North Terrea. Under cover of the night, they sneaked past the sentries and deposited Holt Calder at the threshold of the assembly hall.

North Terrea held a village meeting the next night and again voted—although by a smaller margin than the first time—to set Holt back out on a hillside.

It took longer for a 'Reen band to happen across the infant this time. Holt was nearly dead of exposure. Rather than return him to what the 'Reen presumed would be a barbaric and certain death, they took him into their own nomadic tribe.

For a decade, Holt grew up speaking the rough sibilance of the 'Reen tongue. There were certainly times when he realized he was much less hairy than his fellows in the tribe, that his claws and teeth were far less impressive, and that he didn't possess the distinctive flank stripe, lighter than the surrounding fur. The 'Reen went to pains to keep Holt from feeling too much the estrangement of his differentness. The boy was encouraged to roughhouse with his fellow cubs. He enjoyed the love of a mated couple who had lost their offspring to a human trap.

After a certain rotation of long winters, though, the 'Reen determined it would be a kinder thing to return Holt to his original people. The time had come for the 'Reen his age to join the Calling. It was a rite of adulthood, and something the 'Reen suspected Holt would never be capable of. So regretfully they deposited him on his twelfth birthday (though none of them knew it) on the threshold of the North Terrea assembly hall.

Holt had not wanted to go. The humans found him in the morning, trussed warmly and securely in a cured skelk hide. Before sunset, Holt had escaped onto the tundra and found his 'Reen band again. They patiently discussed this matter with him. Then they again made him helpless and spirited him into North Terrea.

This time the villagers put the boy under benevolent guard. That night the assembly met for a special session and everyone agreed to take Holt in.

They taught him humanity, starting with their language. They groomed and dressed him in ways differing from how he had previously been groomed and dressed. After a time, he agreed to stay. 'Reen-ness receded; humanity advanced.

The passage of more than a decade had brought about certain social changes in North Terrea. The inhabitants wanted to forget the affair of the elder Calders. They plowed their guilt and expiation into rearing the son. And there were those who feared him.

When Holt reached young manhood, it was readily apparent to all who would notice that he was a superior representative of all the new adults in the community. It only followed that his incorporation into the North Terrea population should be balanced with a magnificent gesture. The assembly picked him to be the primary public investment of the North Terrea community partnership.

And that is why they purchased him the second-hand fighting ship, refurbished it, paid for Holt's training, and sent him out to seek his own way, incidentally returning handsome regular bonus dividends to the investors.

Years after his return to human society, Holt had again essayed a return visit to the 'Reen. The nomads traveled a regular, if wide-ranging, circuit and he had found both the original band and his surviving surrogate parent. But it hadn't been the same.

PereSnik't, the silver-pelted shaman of the band, had sadly quoted to Holt from the 'Reen oral tradition: "You can't come home again."

"But aren't you curious about what your parents did to trigger their mysterious fate?" said Morgan, somewhat incredulous.

"Of course," Holt said, "but I'd assumed I'd have a lifetime to find out. I didn't suspect I'd wind up zapped into plasma somewhere in Kirsi orbit."

"You won't be." Morgan pressed his fingers lightly. "Neither of us will be."

Holt said nothing. Morgan's eyes were ellipsoid, catlike, and marvelously green.

Morgan met the directness of his look. "What was that about the Calling," she said, "when the 'Reen returned you to North Terrea?"

He shook himself, eyes refocusing on another place and time. "Though the Almiran colonists didn't want to admit it, the 'Reen have a culture. They are as intelligent in their way as we are in ours—but their civilization simply isn't as directed toward technology. It didn't have to progress in that line.

"The 'Reen can manipulate tools if they wish—but usually they choose not to. They are hunters—but they have few hunting weapons. That's where the Calling comes in."

He paused for a drink of caf. Morgan remained silent.

"I'm not an ethnologist, but I've picked up more about the 'Reen by living with them than all the deliberate study by the few humans who showed interest through the centuries." Holt chuckled bitterly. "A formal examination would have led to communication, and that to a de facto acknowledgment of intelligence. And *that* would have brought the ethical issue of human expansionism into the open." He shook his head. "No, far better to pretend the 'Reen merely extraordinarily clever beasts."

"I grew up in Oxmare," said Morgan. "I didn't think much about the 'Reen one way or another."

Holt looked mildly revolted. "Here's what I'll tell you about the Calling. It's one of the central 'Reen rituals. I'm not sure I understand it at all, but I'll tell you what I know."

It's one of the earliest of my memories.

The 'Reen band was hungry, as they so often were. Shortly before dawn, they gathered in the sheltered lee of the mountain, huddled against the tatters of glacial wind that intermittently dipped and howled about them.

There was little ceremony. It was simply something the band *did*.

The shaman PereSnik't, his pelt dark and vigorous, stood at their fore, supporting the slab of rock between his articulated paws. On the flat surface he had painted a new representation of an adult skelk. The horned creature was depicted in profile. PereSnik't had used warm earth colors, the hue of the skelk's spring coat. All the 'Reen—adult, young, and the adopted one—looked at the painting hungrily.

PereSnik't had *felt* the presence of the skelk. It was in hunting range, in Calling range. He led his people in their chant:

> "*You are near.*
> *Come to us,*
> *As we come to you.*
> *With your pardon,*
> *We shall kill you*
> *And devour you,*
> *That we, the People,*
> *Might live.*"

The chant repeated again and again, becoming a litany and finally a roundelay, until the voices wound together in a tapestry of sound that seemed to hang in the air of its own accord.

PereSnik't laid down the effigy upon the bare ground and the voices stopped as one. The pattern of sound still hung there, stable even as the winds whipped through the encampment. The shaman said, "The prey approaches."

The hunters accompanied him in the direction he indicated. Shortly they encountered the skelk walking stiffly toward them. The hunters cast out in the Calling and perceived, overlaid on the prey's muscular body, the life-force, the glowing network of energy that was the true heart of the animal. With an apology to the beast, PereSnik't dispassionately *grasped* that heart, halting the flow of energy as the hunters chanted once more. The skelk stumbled and fell, coughed a final time and died as a thin stream of blood ran from its nostrils. Then the 'Reen dragged the carcass back to the tribe. Everyone ate.

"Sympathetic magic," said Morgan, her eyes slightly narrowed. "That's what it sounds like."

"When I became human"— Holt's voice wavered for just a moment—"I was taught there is no magic."

"Do you really believe that?" said Morgan. "Call it a form of communal telekinesis, then. It makes sense that the 'Reen wouldn't evolve a highly technological culture. They have no need—not if they can satisfy basic requirements such as food with a rudimentary PK ability."

"I didn't have the power," said Holt. "I couldn't join in the Calling. I could only use my teeth and claws. I couldn't be truly civilized. That's why they finally sent me back."

There was a peculiar tone in his voice, the melancholy resonance of someone who has been profoundly left out. She reached for his hand and squeezed it.

"I would guess," she said, "we've greatly underestimated the 'Reen."

Holt coughed, the sound self-conscious and artificial. "What about you?" he said. "I know you're an extraordinary warrior. But I've also heard people call you the"—he hesitated again—"the obnoxious little rich kid."

Morgan laughed. "I'm a remittance woman," she said.

He stared at her blankly.

Morgan Kai-Anila had been born and reared, as had been the eight previous generations of her line, in Oxmare. The family redoubt reposed in austere splendor not too many kilometers to the south of Wolverton, capital city of Victoria continent. The glass and wood mansion, built with the shrewdly won fortunes of the Kai-Anilas, had been Morgan's castle as a girl. Child of privilege, she played endless games of pretend, spent uncountable chilly afternoons reading, or watching recordings of bygone times, and programmed a childhood of adventurous dreams. She expected to grow up and become mistress of the manor. Not necessarily Oxmare. But someone's manor somewhere.

That didn't happen.

When the right age arrived, Morgan discovered there was no one whose manor she wished to manage—and that apparently was because her family had simply reared her to be *too* independent (at least that's what one of her frustrated suitors claimed). Actually Morgan had simply come to the conclusion that she wanted to play out the adventures she had lived vicariously as a child.

Fine, said her family. As it happened, Morgan was the third and last-born of her particular generation of Kai-Anilas. Her eldest sister was in line to inherit the estates. Morgan didn't mind. She knew she would always be welcome on holidays at Oxmare. Her middle sister also found a distinctive course. That one joined the clergy.

And finally Morgan's family gave her a ship, an allowance, and their blessing. The dreamer went into private (and expensive) flight training, and came out the sharpest image of a remittance woman. Now she was a hired soldier. In spite of the source of their riches, her family really wasn't entirely sure of the respectability of her career.

The Kai-Anila family had fattened on aggressive centuries of supplying ships and weapons to the mercenary pilots who fought the symbolic battles and waged the surrogate wars that by-and-large settled the larger political wrangles periodically wracking Almira. Symbolic battles and surrogate wars were just as fatal as any other variety of armed clash to the downed, blasted, or lasered pilots, but at least the civilian populations were mostly spared. Slip-ups occasionally happened, but there's no system without its flaws.

A little leery of societal gossip, the increasingly image-conscious Kai-Anila family started trying to give Morgan more money if she would come home to Oxmare less frequently for holidays. The neighbors—who watched the battlecasts avidly—were beginning to talk. The only problem was that Morgan couldn't be bribed. She was already sending home the bonuses she was earning for being an exemplary warrior. Her nieces and nephews worshiped her. She had a flare for armed combat, and Runagate couldn't have been a better partner in the fighter symbiosis.

Her family did keep trying to find her an estate she could mistress. It didn't work. The woman liked what she was doing. There would always be time later for mistressing, she told her parents and aunts and uncles.

In the meantime, she found another pilot she thought she might love. He turned out to be setting her up for an ambush in a complicated three-force continental brouhaha. She found herself unable to kill him. She never forgot.

Morgan found another person to love, but he accidentally got himself in her sights during a night-side skirmish on the moon Loathing. Runagate was fooled as well, and her lover died. For the time being, then, Morgan concentrated on simply being the best professional of her breed.

Temporarily she gave up on people. After all, she loved her ship.

"I don't think I love Bob," said Holt. "After all, he's just a ship." Holt looked flushed and mildly uncomfortable with the direction of the conversation.

"You haven't lived with him as long as I have with Runagate," said Morgan. "Just wait."

"Maybe it's that you're another generation." Morgan's eyebrows raised and she looked at him peculiarly. He quickly added, "I mean, just by a few years. You spend a lot of time on appearances. Style."

Morgan shrugged. "I can back it up. You mean things like the sound and motion simulators?"

He nodded.

"Don't you have them installed?"

Holt said, "I never turn them on."

"You ought to try it. It's not just style, to come roaring down on your target from out of the sun. It helps the pilot. If nothing else, it's a morale factor. The meds say it's linked to your epinephrine feed, not to mention the old reptile cortex. It can be the edge that keeps you alive."

The man shook his head, unconvinced.

"Soul-baring done?"

They both turned. Tanzin stood in the doorway. Bogdan and Amaranth loomed behind her. "Mind if we bring our caf in here?"

The five of them sat and drank and talked and paced. It seemed like hours later that Dr. Epsleigh walked into the ready room. She handed them data-filled sheets. "The departure rosters," she said.

Amaranth scanned his and scowled. "I'm not blasting for Kirsi until the final wave?"

"Nor I?" said Tanzin.

Nor were Holt and Morgan.

"I'm going," said Bogdan, looking up from his sheet.

"Then I shall join you," Amaranth said firmly. He looked at Dr. Epsleigh. "I volunteer."

The administrator shook her head. "I hadn't wanted to

save *all* my seasoned best for the last.'' She paused and smiled, and this time the smile was warm. ''I want reserves who know what they're about—so *both* of you will go later.''

The two large men looked dismayed.

''All your ships are still being readied,'' said Dr. Epsleigh. ''Obviously I'm saving some of my best for last. Cheer up, Chmelnyckyj.''

Bogdan looked put out. Morgan stared down at the table. Holt and Tanzin said nothing.

''I know the waiting's difficult,'' said Dr. Epsleigh, ''but keep trying to relax. It will be a little while yet. Soon enough I'll send you out with your thimbles and forks and hope.''

They looked at her with bewilderment, as she turned to go.

Morgan was the only one who nodded. Runagate shrilled in her ear, ''*I* know, *I* know. It's from that snark poem.''

''I hate waiting,'' Amaranth said toward the departing Dr. Epsleigh. ''I should like to volunteer to join the first sortie.''

The administrator ignored him. They waited.

Since the machine had no sense of whimsy, it couldn't have cared whether it was called a boojum, a snark, or anything else. It would respond to its own code from its fellow destruction machines or its base, but had no other interest in designation.

It detected the swarm of midges long before they arrived near Kirsi's orbit. The boojum registered the number, velocity, mass, and origin of the small ships, as well as noting the tell-tale hydrogen torches propelling them.

No problem.

The machine was done scouring Kirsi anyway. It registered a sufficiently high probability that no life-form beyond a virus or the occasional bacterium existed anywhere on the planetary surface.

The boojum accelerated out of its parking orbit and calculated a trajectory that would meet the advancing fleet at a precise intermediary point. Weapons systems checks showed no problems.

Time passed subjectively for the pilots of the first wave of Almiran ships.

Counters in the boojum ticked off precise calibrations of radioactive decay, but the machine felt no suspense at all.

The Almirans joined the battle when their ships were still hundreds of kilometers distant from the boojum. Their target was too far away to try lasers and charged beam weapons. Missiles pulled smoothly away from launching bays, guidance computers locking on the unmistakable target. If the guidance comps, in their primitive way, felt any rebellious qualm about firing on their larger cousin, there was no indication—just a few score fire-trails arcing away toward the boojum.

The missiles reached the point in space the machine had picked as the outer limit of its defensive sphere. The boojum used them for ranging practice. Beams speared out, catching half the incoming missiles at once. Dozens of weapons flared in sparkling sprays and faded. The machine erected shields, wavery nets of violet gauze, and most of the remaining missiles sputtered out. A handful of missiles had neared the machine before the nets of energy went up and were already inside the shields. More beams flicked out and the missiles died like insects in a flame. One survivor impacted on the boojum's metal surface. Minor debris mushroomed slowly outward, but the machine did not appear affected.

"That's one tough borker," said the first wave leader to his fellows.

Then the boojum began alternating its protective fields in phase with its offensive weapons. Beams lanced toward the nearing Almirans. Some pilots died instantly, bodies disintegrating with the disrupted structures of their ships. Others took evasive action, playing out complex arabesques with the dancing, killing beams. More missiles launched. More lasers and beam weapons were directed toward the boojum. Fireworks proliferated.

But eventually everyone died. No pilot survived. Information telemetry went back to Almira, so there was a record, but no fighters or pilots of the first wave returned.

The boojum lived.

Its course toward Almira did not alter.

The second wave of Almiran fighters held its position, waiting for counsel, waiting for orders, waiting. The third and final wave sat on the ground.

"I won't say that's what we expected would happen, but it was certainly a possibility we feared." Dr. Epsleigh turned away from the information screens. The others in the room were quiet, deadly silent, as an occasional sob escaped. Faces set in grim lines. Tears pooled in more than a few eyes.

"Now what?" said Tanzin quietly.

Morgan asked, "Will we join the second wave of fighters?"

Most of the hundred pilots in the briefing hall nodded. Weight shifted. Chairs scraped noisily. Noses were blown into handkerchiefs.

Holt said, "What is the plan now?"

"Bad odds I can live with," said Amaranth, stretching his massive arms, joints cracking. "Assured mortality does not thrill me."

Dr. Epsleigh surveyed the room. "I've conferred with the Princess Elect and every strategist, no matter how oddball, we can round up. Given time, we might be able to rig heavier armaments, plan incredibly Byzantine strategies. There is no time." She stopped.

"So?" said Tanzin.

"We're open to ideas." Dr. Epsleigh looked around the room again, scrutinizing each face in turn.

The silence seemed to dilate endlessly.

Until Morgan Kai-Anila cleared her throat. "An idea," she said. Everyone stared at her. "Not me." She slowly pointed. "Him."

And everyone stared at Holt.

"I don't think it will work," said Holt stubbornly.

"Have you got a better idea?" Morgan said.

The young man shook his head in apparent exasperation. "It's like a bunch of kids trying to mount a colonization flight. They borrow their uncle's barn and start building a starship back behind the house."

Morgan said, "I hope my suggested plan is a bit more realistic."

"*Hope*? That machine out there just killed a whole borking planet!"

The woman said stiffly, "I *know* my plan has a chance."

"But how much of one?"

"Holt, can you come up with better?" Tanzin looked at him questioningly—almost, Holt thought, accusingly. He said nothing, only slowly shook his head no. "In the final seconds before a combat run," Tanzin said, "you've got to choose a course." She shrugged. "If Occam's razor says your only option is faith, then that's what you fly with. Okay?" With her one good eye, she surveyed the others.

"All right, then." Morgan looked over at Dr. Epsleigh. The four of them had adjourned to a smaller office to consult.

"Can you arrange transport? The fighters would be faster, but I doubt there's any place close to set down."

Dr. Epsleigh punched one final key on the desk terminal. "It's already done. There'll be a windhover waiting as soon as you get outside. Is it necessary you all go?"

"I really would like to accompany Holt," said Morgan. She glanced at Tanzin.

"I may as well stay here. If this cockamamie plan works, I can start the preparations from this end. Just keep me linked and informed."

Dr. Epsleigh said, "I'll get a larger transport dispatched to follow you north. If you can make progress and see some future in continuing this scheme, the transport will have plenty of space for your, um, friends."

"Are the villagers expecting us in North Terrea?" asked Holt.

Dr. Epsleigh nodded. Her tousled black hair fell into her eyes. She shook it back and blinked. Evidently she had been awake for a long time. "They're under a most extreme request to cooperate. I don't think you'll have any difficulty. Besides, you're the fair-haired local boy who made good, true?"

"See?" Morgan smiled tiredly and took Holt's arm. "You *can* come home again."

"Well," said Morgan, "I admit it's not the sort of jewel that Oxmare is." North Terrea sat in awesome desolation in the middle of a cold and windswept semi-arctic plain. The town was surrounded by ore processors, rolling mills, cracking towers flaring jets of flame, and all manner of rusting heavy machinery.

"It's grown since I was last here," observed Holt.

"What brought colonists here first?" Morgan began to

decelerate the windhover. The craft skimmed along two meters above frozen earth.

Holt shrugged. "Molybdenum, adamantium, titanium, it's hard to say. These plains used to be one of the 'Reen's great hunting preserves. That ended quickly. North Terrea was built in a day or so, the 'Reen were driven off, the game mostly left of its own accord. That which stayed either got shot by human hunters or was poisoned by industrial chemicals."

"Self-interest run rampant," mused Morgan. "Did no one ever try to put the brakes on?"

"I suspect a few did." Holt looked vague, almost wistful. "I don't think they got too far. There were livings to be made here, fortunes to be wrested from the ground." His tone turned angry and he looked away from her to the fast-expanding image of North Terrea.

"I'm sorry," she said, words almost too soft to hear.

They were indeed expected. A small group of townspeople waited for them as Morgan set the windhover down at North Terrea's tiny landing field. At first Morgan couldn't tell the gender of the members of the welcoming party. Dressed in long fur coats, they were obscured by falling snow. The great, light flakes drifted slowly down like leaves from autumn trees.

Morgan cut the windhover's fans and opened the hatch to a nearly palpable miasma of ice-cold industrial stench. She squinted against the flakes tickling her face and realized that some of the greeters wore thick beards. Presumably they were the men.

"I hope those coats are synthetics," said Holt, as much to himself as to Morgan, "or dyed skelk."

"I think they are," said Morgan, avoiding passing an

expert opinion. They don't have any of the quality and gloss my parents' coats do, she carefully did not say aloud.

The greeting party trudged toward them across the landing pad, packed snow squeaking beneath their boots. Holt and Morgan climbed out of the cockpit and down past the ticking, cooling engine sounds.

"Holt, my boy," said the man in the forefront, opening his arms for an embrace. Holt ignored the gesture and stood quietly, arms at his sides. The man tried to recover by gesturing expansively. "It's been a while since we've seen you, son."

"Haven't the checks been arriving?" asked Holt.

"Punctually, my boy," said the man. "Our civic fortunes rise with boring regularity, thanks to you and that fey ship of yours." He turned to address Morgan. "I forget my manners. I'm Kaseem MacDonald, the mayor hereabouts. The 'cast from Wolverton informed us you'd be Morgan Kai-Anila, true?"

Morgan inclined her head slightly.

"We've certainly heard of you," said the mayor. "We're all great fans."

Morgan again nodded modestly.

"There isn't much to do of a winter night other than to keep tabs on the narrowcast and see what fighters like you and our boy here are doing." Mayor MacDonald chuckled and clapped Holt on the shoulder. "Sure hope you two never have to go up against each other."

Holt spoke in a low voice. "I think there are arrangements for refueling us?"

"Plenty of time for that," said the mayor, his head bobbing jovially as if it were on a spring. "Our grounders'll tank you up again during the feast. Heh, grounders." He chuckled again. "We even pick up the talk from the 'casts."

"What feast?" asked Holt and Morgan, almost together.

"We don't have time to fool around," said Morgan.

"I believe the message from the capital was a priority request," said Holt.

The other North Terreans looked on. Morgan didn't think they looked either particularly happy or hospitable.

Mayor MacDonald showed teeth when he grinned. "You need sustenance just as much as the windhover does. Besides, you can meet some of my local supporters and I know they'd love to meet you. I'm running for re-election again, you know."

"We can't do it," said Holt. "There's no time."

"I'm not saying a long dinner," said the mayor. "Just time to eat and say hello to the folks and be seen. Everybody can use a little reminder of where those venture investment checks come from."

"No," said Morgan. "I don't think so. We've got to—"

The mayor interrupted her smoothly. "—to get some nourishment and relaxation before continuing whatever your urgent mission is."

"No."

"Yes," said the mayor. "It's necessary. You'd be shocked, I'm sure, to learn how erratic the ground crew here can be when *they* aren't working refreshed and rested."

Morgan said, "Why, this is—"

This time it was Holt who interrupted her. "We'll take refreshment," he said, his gaze locked on the mayor's. "It will be a brief delay."

Mayor MacDonald beamed. "I'm sure your refueling will be as brief, and extremely complete and efficient."

Holt glanced at Morgan and smiled coldly at the mayor. "Then let's be about it."

The mayor waved toward the terminal building. "It isn't far, and warm transport awaits."

As the group trudged off across the field, it seemed to Morgan that she was feeling something like a sense of capture. The fur-coated North Terreans surrounding her reminded Morgan of great sullen animals. Their fur might be synthetic fiber, but it still stank in the moist fog that hung low over the town.

Starships descending atop stilts of flame.

Cargoes of frozen optimists being sledded into chromed defrosting centers.

Towns and villages carved out of tundra winterscapes.

The occasional city erected in the somewhat more temperate equatorial belt.

A developing world torn from wilderness.

The triumph of a people.

Heaps of slain 'Reen piled beyond the revetments of a fort constructed from ice blocks.

Morgan stared at the lowering starships. "That's not right," she said bemusedly. "The big ships stayed in orbit. The shuttles brought the passengers and supplies down. Then the larger vessels were disassembled and ferried down to be used as raw materials. I learned all that when I was three."

"It's artistic license," Holt answered, his own gaze still fixed on the scene of the slaughtered 'Reen. "Historical accuracy is not the virtue most prized in North Terrea." In the fresco in front of him, the attackers had outnumbered the beleaguered humans by at least ten to one.

"It's not that good, just as art," said Morgan. The mayor's circular dining room was lined with the sequence of historical frescoes. "And it really doesn't trigger my appetite."

Other dinner guests were filtering into the room and beginning to sit at the semi-circular tables. The mayor was off in the kitchen on some unspecified errand. Holt said, "The good people of North Terrea are pragmatists. When the community decided to pay lip service to culture and proclaim a painter laureate, the choice of frescoes in here rather than any other medium was because the plaster would lend an additional layer of insulation."

"Laying it on with a trowel, eh, boy?" said Mayor MacDonald, coming up behind them. "I hope you both are hungry." Without his long fur coat, the mayor looked almost as bulky, dark signs of hirsuteness curling from sleeve-ends and at his collar. The blue-black beard curled down to mid-sternum. "Skelk steaks, snow oysters, my wife's preserves from last green season, shrake liver paté, barley gruel; let me tell you, it's one extravagant meal."

"We're grateful," said Morgan. "Can we start soon?"

"In a blink, my dear." Both Morgan and Holt felt a heavy, mayoral hand descend on a shoulder. Mayor MacDonald raised his voice and said, "All right, friends, citizens, guild-mates. On behalf of all of us who make up the populace of North Terrea, I want to welcome formally our guests; Holt, here, who I know you all remember fondly"—his hand clamped down, long, powerful fingers paternally crushing Holt's clavicle—"and Morgan Kai-Anila, the splendid contract pilot so many of us have watched and admired on late-night battlecasts." Warned by the look on Holt's face, Morgan had tensed her shoulder muscles. It was still difficult not to wince.

The scattering of applause around the dining room did not seem over-enthusiastic.

"Our boy here," continued the mayor, "and his friend, are just passing through. As best I can figure, they're hadjing off on some solemn but secret mission for our kin down in

Wolverton. Naturally we here in North Terrea are delighted to lend whatever aid we can in this mysterious activity."

Neither Holt nor Morgan decided to pick up the cue.

"Now I have a theory," said Mayor MacDonald, "that all this has something to do with the rumors about someone attacking our neighbor world toward the sun. If that's so, then we all can wish only the best fortune to these two, Pilots Calder and Kai-Anila."

The applause was a bit more prolonged this time.

Servers had started to carry in platters of steaming food. The mayor motioned them toward him. "Let our guests eat first." The food looked and smelled good. Morgan and Holt showed no reluctance to dish themselves respectable portions of steaks, biscuits and vegetables.

"As we share this food today"—Mayor MacDonald lifted his arms to gesture around the circle of frescoes—"I hope you'll all reflect for just a moment on our four centuries of hard-fought progress on this world. Our ancestors left their friends, sometimes their families, certainly their worlds and indeed their entire human civilization to seek out this planetary system. Our new worlds were remote from the interference and paternalism of the old order." The mayor looked far above them all, focusing on something invisible. "I think we've done well with our self-generated opportunities." He looked back at them then, meeting eyes and smiling. The smile widened to a grin. "Let's eat."

The applause seemed generated with unabashed sincerity.

"Not the election rhetoric I'd have expected," said Holt in a low voice to Morgan. "He must be waiting to sink in the hook later."

"I'm not hungry!" The voice was loud and angry enough to rise above the dinner hubbub. The speaker was a young woman about Morgan's age. Her dark hair was piled atop her head. Her high collar displayed a delicate spray of lace, but her expression belied her appearance.

By now the mayor had sat down to Morgan's right. Holt sat to her left. ''Is something amiss, Meg?'' said Mayor MacDonald. He held a piece of meat only slightly smaller than a skelk haunch in one hand.

''Only the company at this meal,'' said the woman called Meg. Other conversation around the tables died away. ''It's one thing entirely to dine with Holt Calder. I might not like it, but I recognize the necessity of letting him eat with us. We're all quite aware where our community's investment bonuses originate.'' She glared toward Morgan. ''No, it's *her* I register an objection to.''

Morgan's voice was a bit higher than her usual, controlled tone. She half rose from her chair. ''What's your objection? I've done nothing to you.''

Meg rose from her own chair. ''It's who you *are*,'' said the woman, ''not just who sits before us.'' She pointed. ''Aristocrats . . . You are a blood-bloated, privileged parasite on the body politic.'' Meg appeared to savor the words.

Morgan shook her head in astonishment and then sat back down.

The mayor looked unhappy. ''I said,'' he repeated, ''let's eat.''

Meg stalked out of the dining room. Those around her developed an abiding interest in the serving platters, in gravy and chops.

Holt touched Morgan's shoulder. She flinched away.

''My sympathies,'' Mayor MacDonald said to her. In a confiding tone, he added, ''The external universe is not an easy commodity to sell here. I fear we don't find Holt as comfortable a dining companion as we might wish.'' He turned back toward the young man. ''Just between you and me, lad, I couldn't blame you if you found the world not worth saving.'' Mayor MacDonald put an index finger to his lips. ''Just don't let on to my loyal constituents I said that.'' He looked at the great hunk of meat in his other hand. ''And now,'' he said, apparently addressing the food, ''and now, let us eat.''

The windhover skated across the tundra ground-blizzards with full tanks, barely rocking in the gusts. The pilot and passenger rode with full bellies and an anxious sense of anticipation.

''That's it, isn't it?'' said Morgan. ''That peak off to the east.''

Holt nodded.

''Where now?''

Holt gave her a compass heading.

''How do you know? I thought the bands roamed.''

''They do,'' said Holt. ''Back at the field, I stood in the open air. Even with the inversion layer I could tell. I know the season. I can feel the patterns. The temperature, the wind, it's all there.'' He came close to pressing his nose against the port. ''The pieces fit.''

Morgan glanced sidewise at him. ''And is there,'' she said carefully, ''perhaps a little bit of instinct, something unquantifiable in the pattern?''

''No,'' he said flatly.

''I wonder.''

Holt repeated the compass direction.

''Aye, sir.'' Morgan swung the windhover to a north-by-northwesterly heading. A range of jagged mountains loomed in the distance.

''You weren't particularly friendly back in the town,'' said Morgan.

"I wasn't feeling cordial. I hope friendship awaits me now." His words were overly formal, a bit stilted, as though a different identity were being overlaid on the young man Morgan had met in Wolverton.

"You know," said Morgan, "aside from being presumably competent and obviously a good fighter, you're quite an attractive young man."

Holt didn't answer. Morgan thought she saw the beginnings of a flush at the tips of his ears. She started to consider the ramifications. She wondered whether her own ears—or anything else—betrayed her.

They found the encampment—or at least *an* encampment—just as Holt had predicted. Morgan circled slowly, to give the 'Reen plenty of warning. "Skins?" she said. "They live in hide tents?"

"Look beyond," Holt answered. "There are openings for the dug-out chambers. Even though they're nomadic for most of the year, the 'Reen open earthen tunnels for the heart of the winter. It's a retreat to an earlier life. They dig the passages with their claws. You'll see."

And so she did. Morgan set the windhover down and cut the fans. The mechanical whine ran down the scale, fading to silence. Holt cracked the hatch and they heard the wind shriek. Heat rushed from the craft, to be replaced with darting, stinging snow and a marrow-deep chill.

Morgan glanced out and recoiled slightly. While she had been engaged in shutting down the windhover, a silent perimeter of 'Reen had come to encircle the craft. Not, she reflected, that she could have heard them in this gale anyway.

She had never before seen the 'Reen in the flesh. Films had not done them justice. Morgan squinted against the sudden flurry of snowflakes slapping her face. The 'Reen appeared bulky, not as though they could move quickly at all. The woman knew that perception was utterly wrong. She also knew the 'Reen were equally adept on all fours as upright. These adults were standing erect, as high as her shoulder. Their fur color was rich brown, ranging from deep chocolate to a golden auburn.

The sun abruptly burned through the gray sky and Morgan saw the light glitter from the 'Reen claws. Those claws were long and curved like scimitars. They looked as honed as machined steel. The silence, other than the wind's keening, stretched on.

"It's up to you now, isn't it?" she finally said to Holt.

He made a sound that might have been a sigh, then moved forward through the hatch, dropping down to the intermediate step and then to the snow. She followed as he approached the 'Reen squarely facing the hatch. Wind ruffled the auburn pelt. Obsidian eyes tracked the newcomers.

"*Quaag hreet'h, PereSnik't tcho*?" Holt's voice, ordinarily a baritone, seemed to drop at least one gruff, uncomfortable octave.

At first the 'Reen seemed to ignore his words, staring back silent and unmoving. It responded as Holt stepped forward and raised both empty palms facing the 'Reen. The man said something brief Morgan couldn't catch. The 'Reen spoke something in return. Then man and 'Reen embraced roughly.

Morgan thought instantly of how she used to hug her huge stuffed creatures when she was a girl, damped the incongruous response, but said under her breath, "I think this is a good sign."

The 'Reen turned its attention to her, cocking its head back slightly. Morgan stared past the blunt muzzle into unblinking, shiny, black eyes. The 'Reen articulated sounds. Holt replied in kind, then turned toward Morgan.

"His short-form name translates as MussGray. He is an

artificer, uh, an artist, apprenticed to PereSnik't, the tribal shaman. He says to tell you he's honored to meet one who is vouched for by He-orphaned-and-helpless-whom-we-obliged-are-to-take-in-but-why-us?''

"That's you?'' Morgan couldn't help but smile. "I'd like to hear all *that* in 'Reen.''

"You did.'' Holt didn't smile. "The 'Reen tongue is quite economical.''

"*Tcho. PereSnik't tcho.*'' The 'Reen called MussGray turned and started to walk toward the nearest hide shelter. Morgan noted that the 'Reen's rounded shoulders hunched forward as he moved. Holt followed. "Follow me,'' he said back to Morgan, who had hesitated. "It's what we came to do.''

"I know, I know,'' she muttered. "And it was my idea.''

The other 'Reen had made what to her ears seemed whuffling noises and dispersed among the hide shelters of the encampment.

MussGray led them through a doorway protected by a heavy flap of cured leather. Inside, the shelter was dimly illuminated by the flicker of a few candles. Morgan saw a thin column of apparent smoke drifting up from the room's center, then realized it was rising from a circular hole in the earthen floor.

"That's where we're going,'' Holt said to her. "Don't worry.''

MussGray vanished into the smoke, into the hole. Holt followed. So did Morgan, discovering the top of a sturdy wooden ladder. She clambered down the rungs, attempting to hold her breath, trying not to cough and choke on the smoke. Beside the foot of the ladder, a low fire was separated from the opening of a fresh-air shaft by an upright stone slab.

This chamber also was lit with candles, only slightly abetted by the dusky fire. The interior seemed rounded and close. The place smelled of fresh earth and woodsmoke and a muskiness Morgan did not find unpleasant. Five 'Reen waited there. Morgan took them to be older adults, pelts silvered to an argent that seemed to glow in the candlelight.

"They honor us," Holt said to her. "The 'Reen are nocturnal. Our greeting party up there tumbled out of warm burrows to meet us."

The 'Reen reclined in the shadows on the luxuriant furs blanketing the chamber's floor. Then the largest and most silvered of the adults stood and embraced Holt for a long time. Morgan heard the man say simply, "PereSnik't."

Later he introduced Morgan. The woman, half-remembering one bit of biological trivia about showing one's teeth, inclined her head a moment, but didn't smile.

Then they all made themselves comfortable on the heaps of autumnal black-and-white skelk hides. "We'll need patience," Holt told Morgan. "Both of us. This will take a while. I have too little vocabulary, too few cognates, so I'm going to have to approximate some language as I go."

"Can I help?"

"Maybe," said Holt. "I don't know. I'm going to be improvising this as I go."

PereSnik't rumbled something.

"He says," Holt translated, "that you smell just fine to him."

Morgan covered her smile.

With MussGray, PereSnik't, and the other four 'Reen listening attentively, Holt told his story. He also used body language and a bit of theater. Morgan could decipher the gestures sufficiently to understand at which points in the narrative the boojum arrived in orbit around Kirsi, destroyed that world, and then advanced on the Almiran fighters. She found herself forcing back tears as Holt's long fingers described the rupture of ship after ship, his expressive features miming the final moments of her friends and comrades. Morgan clamped down on the feelings rigidly. Time enough later to mourn, and there would doubtless be many more to keen dirges for. She wondered whether, indeed, there would be anyone left alive to do the mourning.

At last Holt's monolog ceased and what seemed to be serious discussion began. Morgan hugged her knees, feeling a sense of disconnection. There was nothing now she could do to affect what was happening with the 'Reen. She had acted. If all catalyzed as she hoped, she would act again. But for now, she was reduced to sitting on plush furs and listening.

The interplay between Holt and the 'Reen became much more of a staccato exchange. Morgan thought of a ball hit back and forth across a net. She couldn't tell the content of what she heard, but was sure of the context: questions and answers.

As best Morgan could tell, internecine bickering was igniting among the silvered 'Reen. Growls, timbre sliding low, verging on subsonics, filled the underground chamber. Claws as long as her hand clicked and glittered while the candles began to burn down.

MussGray appeared to be taking a moderating role. He deferred to the older adults, but began to interject his own comments when the others roared at Holt.

These are carnivores, thought Morgan, staring at increasingly exposed teeth. They are predators, and they surely must hate us for all we have done to them. Except for Holt.

The discussion had reached a crescendo, a near-pandemonium.

Holt stood and slipped off his windbreaker as the 'Reen fell silent. He tugged his insulated shirt up over his head. His chest hair was not nearly so impressive as the 'Reen fur. Holt slowly raised his empty hands up and apart, forming the bar of a cross.

Morgan realized the man was exposing the vulnerability of his belly. The 'Reen voices began again to grumble and roar. Morgan wondered again if they were about to kill Holt; and after him, her. She had no weapons. Holt had insisted on that. She knew she could neither save him, nor beat a homicidal 'Reen up the central ladder.

Holt had *better* know what he was doing.

MussGray said something. PereSnik't said something else in turn. Holt hesitated, but then nodded his head slowly. Affirmatively. He drew his arms in, then proffered both hands in front of him.

It happened almost too quickly for Morgan to see. PereSnik't extended one paw, flicked out a razored claw, and blood traced a thin line down the inside of Holt's right index finger. The blood, black in candlelight, beaded and dripped for a moment before Holt closed his fist to stop the bleeding.

The 'Reen were silent again. MussGray looked from Holt to Morgan, and then back to the man. Shivering, Holt put his shirt and windbreaker back on. He shook his hand as though it stung.

"Are you all right?" Morgan said.

He answered a different question, one unspoken. "It's done."

"They'll help us?"

"The verdict's not in yet. There have to be . . . consultations. We're to wait here."

The 'Reen began to climb up the ladder. PereSnik't ascended without saying anything more to Holt. MussGray was the last to go. He turned back from the ladder and spoke briefly.

"He says that we should enjoy the shelter," said Holt. "There's a storm front passing above us. It shouldn't last long, but he says it will keep us from traveling for a few hours."

The 'Reen disappeared through the ceiling hole.

"Now what?"

"We wait," said Holt.

"Are you optimistic?"

The man shrugged.

"Are you simply tired of talking?"

Holt looked down at the furs around them. "Just . . . tired." Then he again raised his eyes to her face. One of the guttering candles flickered a final time and burned out. A second sputtered. "This is probably entirely too forward," he said, hesitating, and then saying nothing more.

"Yes?" she finally said, prompting him.

He met her gaze levelly. "I feel colder than even the storm warrants. Would you give me some reassurance?"

"Yes," she said, "and a good deal more, if you'd like."

Morgan reached to take him gently as the last of the candles went out and the only light was the lambent flames racing over the coals in the fire.

She hadn't *meant* to sleep, Morgan thought, as she moved and stretched under Holt's welcome weight. Since she couldn't recall when she *had* slept last, that probably explained her drifting off. Holt, not having slept at all, his upper body supported by his elbows, glanced toward the center of the chamber and said something in 'Reen. Someone answered. Morgan turned her head and made out MussGray's form limned by the coals at the foot of the ladder.

Holt gently disengaged himself and got to his knees. Her

body tautened for a moment. He softly touched the side of her head with his fingers.

MussGray spoke again.

"We'll be ready," said Holt. "Their decision is made," he said to Morgan.

The two of them dressed quickly, unself-consciously. After all, she thought wryly, we're all soldiers, comrades in arms.

"Are they coming down here?"

"No," Holt said. "We're to go back above."

When they climbed the ladder and emerged from the hide shelter, they found a clear, cold starscape overhead. MussGray led them back to the windhover. Morgan saw that the skids were now covered with fresh snow.

PereSnik't and the other adult 'Reen, not just the silvered elders, waited. Bulked together in the night, they didn't seem to Morgan either ominous or an outright danger. They were simply at home there, not discomforted by the chill.

The two humans stopped a meter from PereSnik't. MussGray crossed over some intangible boundary and rejoined the tribe. He, too, faced Morgan and Holt.

The streamers of Almira's aurora began to play above the horizon. Ribbons of startling blue crackled into the sky.

PereSnik't said something. To Morgan, it seemed surprisingly brief. Holt let out his breath audibly.

"And—?" she said softly.

"It's done."

"Will they help?"

The dark mass of 'Reen stirred. PereSnik't said something to them over his shoulder.

"They will try to aid us," said Holt. "I *think* they understand what I attempted to get across. I'm more concerned about what *I* don't comprehend."

"I'm not sure I follow."

"They agreed." Holt shook his head. "But the terms of the bargain are open. I don't know the price. I'm not sure they do either."

"How expensive can it be?" Actually she had already begun to speculate. Night thoughts.

The man only smiled. In the shifting, ephemeral light of the aurora, it was not a smile of joy.

The machine swept steadily toward the waiting second wave of Almiran fighters. The ragtag fleet neither advanced nor retreated. The ships hung in position, interposing themselves as a flimsy shield between assassin and victim.

The machine electronically seined the inexorably diminishing distance between. It did not project a definitive probability-model of the humans' intention. It could not. The machine searched its memories for similar human strategies. Nothing quite matched. In its way, the machine considered what it perceived to be all the likely human options, attempting to place itself in its opponents' position. No answers emerged.

Electrons continued to spin in paths weaving patterns that simulated organic intelligence—only it was a mind far more carefully considered, infinitely more ordered than that of humans. There was no primitive animal forebrain here. No conscience. No irrationality. Only a paradox. A holographic representation of oblivion.

The boojum searched for any evidence of human trickery, signs of an ambush, but it could accumulate no empirical support.

It sailed on.

But as much as it was capable of doing so, the machine wondered . . .

"No?" said Morgan. "*No*?"

"No. With regrets." Dr. Epsleigh looked very unhappy. "The word came down from the Princess Elect's office a short time before you and Holt returned. I'd already dispatched the transport to pick up the 'Reen, but now I'll have to call it back."

Dr. Epsleigh's office at the Wolverton landing field was spare and austere. The four of them—Tanzin had been waiting for Holt and Morgan the moment the windhover set down—sat in straightbacked, unpadded chairs around a bare desk.

"But why?" Morgan thought that if she gripped the arms of her chair any more tightly, either the furniture or her fingers would snap.

"Spume," said Dr. Epsleigh.

"I don't understand," said Holt.

"It's the word the Prime Minister used." Dr. Epsleigh shrugged. "Moonfoam. Brainfroth. The point being he thought our plan was the silliest proposal of anything anyone had suggested. That's why the summary turn-down."

"I have to admit I can see his position," said Tanzin. She leaned back in her chair and stretched her legs, one boot crossed above the other. "It's akin to me saying, 'Hey, I've got a great idea—I think my pet is telepathic, and he can hypnotize the bird in the birdbath.' Then someone else says, 'Hey, it's so crazy, it might just work.' See the point?"

"I gave Morgan's suggestion preliminary approval," said Dr. Epsleigh angrily. "Are you suggesting this is all a pipe dream? We're in a desperate situation."

"Just a moment," Morgan said. "Hold on. Does the PM have a plan of his own?"

Dr. Epsleigh turned toward her, shaking her head in disgust. "It's death. I told him that, but he said it was the only rational option."

"Suicide." Tanzin inspected her boots. "Pure and simple."

"You don't like any of the alternatives," said Holt.

"No." Tanzin's voice was somber. "No, I don't."

"Suicide?" said Morgan. "What did the PM *say*?"

Dr. Epsleigh gestured out the dawn-lit window toward the massed ranks of fighting ships. "One massive attack. Those ships carrying all the massed armament and fire-power that can be bonded on during the next few hours. Mass against mass. Brute force against force."

"The machine will win," said Holt.

"The PM knows that, I suspect. I also think he believes the machine will prevail in *any* account. A grand doomed gesture is apparently better than this half-baked scheme from a battle hero and a junior pilot." Dr. Epsleigh slapped her small hands down on the desk top with finality.

"No," said Morgan. They all looked at her. She said to Dr. Epsleigh, "Can you use your phone to get through to the Princess Elect's office? I want the woman herself."

Without a word, the administrator punched out a code.

"What are you doing?" said Holt. "I've heard the Princess Elect doesn't do a thing without the PM's approval."

"Have I given you my lecture on power?" Morgan said, and proceeded to answer without pause her own rhetorical question. "I despise the power one is born to without earning it. I've never used that lever."

Dr. Epsleigh had reached someone on the phone. "Tell her the caller is Morgan Kai-Anila," she said.

"My personal rules are now suspended," Morgan said.

"It's time for this 'blood-bloated, privileged parasite on the body politic' to kick some rears."

Dr. Epsleigh handed her the phone.

"Hello?" Morgan said. She forced a smile and let that smile seep into her voice. "Hello, Aunt Thea, dear?"

Steam curled up from the jet nozzles of the dart-shaped fighters. The rows of sleek fuselages formed a chevron, the point of which faced away from the administration complex of the landing field at Wolverton. The sun had sunk close to the western horizon, the twilight glow beginning to soften the peaks of the Shraketooth Range.

Swarms of workers surrounded the fighters, topping off water tanks, tuning each weapon, completing installation of the additional acceleration couches.

The briefing hall had become an auditorium of Babel. Intermixed, humans and 'Reen crowded the room. The sessions had been loud and volatile. Serving as translator, Holt had tried to mediate. The basic problem seemed to be that each group thought it was surrounded by unsavory barbarians.

The overtaxed air purifying system could no longer cope with the sweat and musk. Cheek by jowl, fur against flesh, luxuriant flank stripes juxtaposed with extravagantly theatrical uniforms, the warriors groused and growled as Dr. Epsleigh tried to keep peace.

About the height of the average 'Reen, the administrator had to stand on a chair to be seen by all in the room. Many of the pilots looked distinctly dubious after having listened through the first briefing sessions.

"I *know* you have questions," continued Dr. Epsleigh. "I recognize that we've been asking you to take all this in on faith. I also know I can't order any of you simply to be credulous."

Beside her, Holt translated for the benefit of the 'Reen.

"Just let me wrap it up," said Dr. Epsleigh. "The majority of pilots will have the essential task of harrying the boojum in whatever way and from whichever tangent they can. It will be your job to draw the machine's attention from the score of colleagues who will be ferrying our 'Reen allies as near to the enemy as is"—a wry smile broke across her lips—"humanly possible."

Amaranth stood in the first row. "Isn't this just as foredoomed as the PM's idiotic plan?"

"If it were, I wouldn't endorse it." Dr. Epsleigh raised her eyes machineward. "It will be dangerous, yes. You'll all be dependent upon your wits and the abilities of your ships."

Amaranth nodded, amused. "It's never been any different."

The 'Reen whuffled and coughed at the translation. For them also, it was a point of commonality.

"We've exhaustively pored over the recordings of our first combat encounter with the machine," said Dr. Epsleigh. "So long as the boojum's missiles and beams are avoided, we're sure that some of our ships can maneuver beyond the protective screens."

"Mighty hard to avoid particle beams, maneuvering in slow motion," someone called out from the floor.

"I expect that's why the rest of us'll be speeding our tails off," someone else answered.

"Precisely right," said Dr. Epsleigh. "The machine won't anticipate seeming irrationality."

"So you think."

"So we think." The uproar threatened to drown out the administrator.

"And then the 'Reen will claw the boojum to death?" someone apparently said jokingly, but too loud.

"In a manner of speaking," Dr. Epsleigh said.

Holt translated that for PereSnik't's benefit. MussGray overheard and both 'Reen growled in amusement.

Dr. Epsleigh shook her head in exasperation and asked Holt to explain the Calling again.

"I still don't think I believe in all that occult crap," a pilot called out.

"Neither do I think," Holt said, "that the 'Reen believe simple light can actually be cohered into a laser."

"But that's different."

The room's noise level got louder again.

Twilight had begun to fuzz into actual night.

In the briefing hall, Holt held up a meter-square sheet of shining alloy so that all could see. A grid of silver lines had been etched, then painted in almost a cloisonné effect. Regular clusters of angular symbols cross-connected the lines. The panel could equally have represented an electronic map or a jewelry design. It was an elaborate and stylized pattern.

"The apprentice MussGray created this," said Holt, "under the direction of the shaman, PereSnik't. It will focus the Calling."

"This is the brain of the boojum," Dr. Epsleigh said.

PereSnik't rumbled something.

"The heart," Holt translated. "Energy. The electrical field."

"The design may not be identical to the primary components in that machine up there," said the administrator, "but it's as close as we can come by guess and extrapolation after ransacking the historical computer memories. When we were part of the rest of human civilization, our ancestors helped dissect some of the boojums. We're hoping that logic circuitry is logic circuitry, even allowing for refinement."

The room fell silent.

"Hey," said Amaranth, voice loud and firm, "I'll give it

a shot.'' His lips spread in a grin, revealing broad, white, gleaming teeth.

The 'Reen muttered approvingly as Holt translated.

''We've placed identical copies of the focus pattern in each ship carrying a 'Reen. To help coordinate the plan, our friends will have their own ship's-link channel.'' Dr. Epsleigh turned on the chair and looked down at Holt. ''You're going to be a busy young man. I understand PereSnik't will ride with no one else.''

''He is my father,'' said Holt. ''I am his son.''

''Will you be able to handle the translating as well?''

''No one else can.'' Holt's voice was not so much resigned as it was simply matter-of-fact.

PereSnik't said something. Dr. Epsleigh looked at Holt questioningly; the young man had already growled a brief answer. ''He wanted to know if it were the chanting time yet. I told him no. The prey is still too distant.''

In the forefront of the pilots, Amaranth restlessly shifted his weight from one leg to the other. ''Let's get on with it,'' he said. ''It's getting late and we're all getting curious whether we'll live or die.''

That triggered smiles and nods from those around him.

Dr. Epsleigh shrugged. ''You've heard what I have to say about tactics. Just do what's necessary to get the 'Reen as close to the machine's surface as possible.''

Anything else seemed anticlimactic. Holt led the 'Reen out toward the ships. Tanzin followed with the pilots. They mixed at the doors of the hall. The neat divisions along species lines no longer seemed as clear-cut as at the beginning of the day.

Dr. Epsleigh lingered, waiting by a door. Morgan came up to her. ''Sympathetic magic and PK indeed,'' the administrator said. ''Should I have said good luck? Godspeed? I might as well simply admit I *am* sending you all out with thimbles and forks and hope."

Morgan squeezed her hand. "You may be surprised by who all come back." Silently, behind her reassuring smile, she thought, I know *I* will be.

Together they walked toward the field and the ships. The dying sunset looked like blood streaking the sky.

The machine did not overtly react when it detected movement in the distant fleet of fighters. Other craft were rising from the planetary surface and joining the group. The boojum's sensory systems registered each increment of numbers, every measure of expended energy.

The fighters began to disperse toward the machine in no particularly discernible formation. The boojum searched for patterns and found none.

Then the machine completed another in its infinite series of weapons system status checks.

The ships in the approaching swarm flared energy.

Everything seemed to be fine. The oblivion within the machine waited to be defined and fulfilled.

Like silver shoals of fish they rose up, the fighter formations rising from Almira's surface. Throttles open, the fighters accelerated. Superheated steam plumes whirled back from the craft, propelling them into an ever blacker sky where the stars had begun to glitter.

The stage, thought Dr. Epsleigh, watching from her tower window in the Wolverton terminal, is set. The massed scream of the rockets deafened her.

She realized the fingers of her right hand were curled into a fist, and that fist was upraised. Get the bastard!

SHIP'S LINK CHANNEL CHECKS

Wolverton Control/All Ships: "The Princess Elect says 'Good luck' and bring back a chunk of the boojum for the palace garden."

Amaranth/Wolverton Control: "Stuff that! We're gonna bring back enough scrap so the palace gardeners can make a whole public gazebo."

Bogdan/Wolverton Control: "I like the sound of 'gazebo.' Can we perhaps code the machine that instead of 'boojum'?"

Wolverton Control/Bogdan: "Sorry, fellow. Too late. Boojum it is."

Anonymous/All Ships: "Bloody hell. Death be what it is."

Holt/'Reen Channel: *Our Hair-like-Morgan-elected-leader-serving-from-the-ground tells you all 'Good fortune and success in the hunt.'*

PereSnik't/'Reen Channel: *Could not your leader/shaman/provider have initiated so enlightened a sentiment a bit earlier than tonight? As perhaps her forebears could have three or four hundred world journeys ago?*

Various/'Reen Channel: *amusement*

Holt/'Reen Channel: *There were many sad winters . . .*

PereSink't/'Reen Channel: *Sad winters . . .?! Skelk droppings, Son. What we do now is a perversion of the Calling that gives me dismay. This is not food-gathering.*

Holt/'Reen Channel: *It is a greater good.*

PereSnik't/'Reen Channel: *My unthought-out comment is unsuitable for either furred ears or bare.*

Various/'Reen Channel: *amusement*

Holt/'Reen Channel: *I am unthinking. Forgive me.*

PereSnik't/'Reen Channel: *Let us concentrate on our onerous task. Let us pursue it with honor.*

All/'Reen Channel: *anticipation*
hunger
exultation

Runagate/LNTCVP1-Bob: Ship, is your pilot's survivability index high?

LNTCVP1-Bob/Runagate: He has luck, skill, and courage. My level of confidence is high. Why do you inquire?

Runagate/LNTCVP1-Bob: My pilot's interest level in your pilot is increasing. Her concerns are mine as well.

LNTCVP1-Bob/Runagate: I perceive an equivalent status on the part of Holt. I hold no wish to see him injured in any way.

Runagate/LNTCVP1-Bob: Then we both must survive.

LNTCVP1-Bob/Runagate: The projections do not encourage me.

Runagate/LNTCVP1-Bob: We shall live with them.

LNTCVP1-Bob/Runagate: I will look forward to discussing these matters with you after the battle.

Runagate/LNTCVP1-Bob: Likewise. And with pleasure . . . Bob.

Morgan ordered Runagate to adjust the artificial gravity so that a satisfying, but less than debilitating, G-force would trickle through the system and settle both 'Reen passenger and the pilot snugly into their harnesses.

Takeoff acceleration hadn't seemed to bother MussGray at all. The artist had endured the climb up to the stratosphere stoically, listening to the voices on the 'Reen channel. He had not so much as shut his polished jet eyes as the ship shuddered and sang. The 'Reen hunter in him bared his teeth at the screens as they imaged the distant boojum. He unsheathed his claws.

Morgan lay cradled in her pilot's couch and exulted in the profligate power of the torch powering her ship. She restrained herself from putting Runagate into a vertical roll. Time enough soon for fancy maneuvers. But, she thought, the power, the sheer, raw force propelling her into space atop a column of incandescent vapor was the most intoxicating feeling she had ever known.

Competing information channels buzzed and bleated within her ears: Almira and Wolverton Control, the fleet ahead, her colleagues, the 'Reen, Runagate. Morgan had ordered her ship to monitor all links, including the 'Reen channel, and to mix whatever communications he deemed important.

"That may confuse you a bit," Runagate had said.

"I'll live with it."

For all effective densities, Runagate cleared atmosphere. Morgan ordered the simulators on. Her ears registered the distant rumble of the other fighters. The ship shuddered slightly beneath her and she heard the closer, reassuring roar of knife-edged fins slicing through vacuum.

Holt glanced at the silver-furred 'Reen bulked in the acceleration couch beside his. His adoptive father looked steadily back at him.

"The boojum is accelerating toward us," said Bob.

"Must be getting impatient."

"Perhaps merely suspicious," said the ship.

"Keep on the direct intercept." Holt sighed and said to PereSnik't, *Was it necessary for us to wrangle before everyone listening over the channel?*

PereSnikt's muzzle creased in a grin. *Are we not still speaking to the rest?*

No. For a short time we can talk in privacy.

The 'Reen paused in obvious deliberation. *My son, I now realize I haven't prodded you enough.*

Holt stared at him questioningly.

I believe I erred in turning you back quite so young to the barbarians in North Terrea.

I could not join the Calling. There was no—

PereSnik't held up a paw, the underside gleaming like well-worn polished leather. *It may be that my judgment was premature. No shame to—*

No! Holt turned away from the 'Reen.

PereSnik't shook his massive head slowly and sadly. *It will grieve me if I must conclude you are less of the People than I suspect.*

*I am all too human—*what is it, Bob?'' Holt answered the imperative blinking of a console tell-tale.

''Runagate messaging,'' said Bob. ''Morgan would like to speak with you.''

Holt's spreading, silly smile was indeed all too human.

Amaranth goosed his ship out of the atmosphere. It was not that he had to be the first fighter in the assault—although he wouldn't have turned the position away—but he also knew he didn't want to place anywhere back in the pack. ''First in the hearts of his countrymen,'' he sang atonally. ''First to fight their wa-*orrr*.'' The last note jangled dissonantly in his own ears.

Tanzin's voice crackled over the ship's link. ''Perhaps you could, uh, sing, if that's the precise verb that fits, privately instead of on-channel?''

''She's right.'' Bogdan's voice.

"It's a war song," said Amaranth. "I'm building morale." He hit another, more than slightly askew, note.

Only a meter away, his 'Reen passenger growled ominously.

Amaranth stopped singing. "You're a critic too, my hirsute colleague?"

Another growl, prolonged, rumbling low in the 'Reen's throat.

"ThunderWalker, that's your name, right?" Amaranth said to the 'Reen hunter. "ThunderWalker, perhaps you'd like to join me in a duet."

The ship's link garbled and jammed as a dozen voices said the same word.

"Um, I . . . never heard anything quite like that said on a ship's link," Holt said. He wondered if the warmth showed on his face.

"And quite probably you won't again." The smile permeated Morgan's voice. "Don't worry, it wasn't public. Runagate and Bob locked in the channel."

"We had better open up that channel." It was Runagate's voice. "Things are heating up considerably with the boojum."

"Channel open," said Bob. "Good luck, everybody."

"Buy you a caf after this is over," Morgan said.

The brain of the machine juggled probabilities, determining whether it should, for the time being, ignore the first ships now violating its zone of effective weaponry, in order to lure the great mass of them into range.

SHIP'S LINK
CHANNEL CHECKS

Amaranth/All Ships: "Well, that was easy."

Holt/'Reen Channel: *Though we are in range of its talons, the prey has not sprung for the bait.*

Tanzin/All Ships: "It's got to be a trap."

LNTCVP1-Bob/Runagate: It is a trap.

PereSnik't/'Reen Channel: *Surely, then, the prey is attempting to gull us.*

Runagate/LNTCVP1-Bob: It is a trap.

Morgan/All Ships: "Okay, let's boost *hard*!"

The machine suddenly came alive, bristling missiles as though they were quills erecting on a Q-beast. The missiles flew just as its enemy shattered into a cloud of wildly varied trajectories. The boojum had three hundred and seventeen separate sentient enemies to contend with now, not to mention the thousands of semi-intelligent missiles erupting from the fighters like insects swarming from a nest.

Skeins of contending particle beams crisscrossed the sphere of defensive space, a traveling net with the machine spidered at the center. The boojum's shields and weapons phased in tandem. Incoming missiles sputtered, fused, and burned luridly. The machine had no program for esthetics, so it could not appreciate the beauty of nuclear flowers blooming brilliantly in the garden of the firmament.

The machine looked for patterns to form as the human ships flew in all directions. It had projected that the battle might be won in the first twenty seconds. That was now clearly impossible.

Victory was still a clear probability, but it would be neither fast nor simple.

SHIP'S LINK
CHANNEL CHECKS

Amaranth/All Ships: "We're in. Dammit, we're in!"

Tanzin/All Ships: "Take it easy. We're just fleas, and it doesn't mean spit if the dog hasn't decided to scratch yet."

Holt/'Reen Channel: *Close, we're close.*

ThunderWalker/'Reen Channel: *Good. The chant will also wipe away the noise of my pilot.*

MussGray/'Reen Channel: *At least your pilot has kept you alive.*

Holt/'Reen Channel: *We are *all* still alive.*

Tanzin/All Ships: "Look out! It's scratch—"

Morgan whirled her ship into a maneuver she could term, but never could have identified as to origin: an Immelman turn. Runagate looped around, rolled, then accelerated as a brace of boojum missiles flashed by.

The woman blinked through the array of images Runagate projected throughout the control space. In the holographic display, the lasers and particle beams were colored bright neon shades for clarity. The webwork patterns danced around the painfully slow midge that was Runagate closing on the boojum. Sparks cascaded around the miniature image of the ship. Some were accelerating missiles. Some were bits of debris from the dead and dying.

Everything seemed to move in slow motion.

Morgan glanced at the 'Reen beside her and did a double take. The artist MussGray had brought on board a pad Dr. Epsleigh had given him. Grumbling happily, he was staring at the screens, displays, and images, and sketching furiously.

The pilot shook her head and her mind retreated to speed. She slammed Runagate into a full-ahead feint at the growing mass of the boojum.

PereSnik't grunted as the restraining straps dug into his thick shoulders. Bob rolled into a hard zig-zag, and Holt prayed the AG would stand up. If it didn't, the inside of the cockpit would look like it had been spread with berry jam.

''You're within the parameters you requested,'' said Bob. ''Good luck.''

Holt scanned the instruments, glanced at the chunk of machine balefully occluding his main screen. No casualties among the 'Reen ships yet.

''Now!'' he said into the ship's link. *Now!* he said to the 'Reen.

Hyo came the chorus.

He glanced aside at PereSnik't. The 'Reen shaman held tight to the alloy effigy. Fur glittered, reflected in the stylized circuitry. Holt wanted to touch his father a final time, but he didn't want to alter PereSnik't's concentration.

The 'Reen reached over and clasped Holt's upper arm. *Remember* said PereSnik't. *You are as much I as them.*

Holt smiled.

PereSnik't began the chant. His voice rumbled as the others picked up the resonance.

You are near

The ship's skin rumpled slightly. Bob's skeleton creaked. Holt couldn't see it with his eyes, but the instruments told him a charged beam had passed within meters of Bob's wingtip.

Come to us

As we come to you

''Closer!'' Holt said into the ship's link to the other pilots. ''We've got to get in so close, the machine will take up the whole screen.''

PereSnik't's voice filled the ship. The chant filled the space between ships.

With your pardon

We shall kill you—

Holt prayed that the other ships, the ones not carrying the 'Reen, could continue to draw the machine's attention and its firepower.

—and devour you

He realized he was chanting too. Part of his mind, his concentration, his attention, more and more of it, was drawn into the skein of power. I have to pilot, he told himself. Careful. Careful—

That we the People

"I'm closer to that son of a bitch than you," said Morgan's voice. "Get in here, love!"

Might live

"I'm even closer," said Tanzin over the link. "Move it, Holt."

You are near

PereSnik't began the chant again. This time Holt sang with them from the beginning.

Come to us

As we come to you

The images flashed in front of his eyes. The main screen swept across what seemed an endless expanse of machine.

With your pardon

The screen was filled with the images of asymmetric metal forms. The song, the ship—Holt *meshed.*

We shall kill you—

It all worked. He could be both—

"Hey!" Amaranth's voice yelled. "We're in! Did you ever—" The transmission cut off. Vacuum filled that space.

* * *

One of the boojum's particle beams punched through Amaranth's ship transversely. Clubbed by a weapon moving at lightspeed, some things just were there, and then they were *not*.

The components of the ship's brain instantly stressed to destruction under the energy overload and flared into darkness. The ship died of a thousand electronic aneurisms.

Passing through the cockpit, the beam did far more immediate damage to Amaranth than to ThunderWalker.

As the ship twisted sickeningly and began to break up, Amaranth could look down and see little where his chest had been. The scarlet spray beginning to cloud his eyes told him the AG was going wonky.

He knew it should hurt, but it didn't. Shock. It wouldn't. No time.

Amaranth saw a field of spring flowers, all red and gold and vibrant, in a meadow at the foot of the Shraketooths. He died before the season changed.

The particle beam had barely grazed ThunderWalker. That was sufficient to vaporize the 'Reen's shoulder.

We shall kill you—

The chant still reverberated inside ThunderWalker's head. And continued for the hunter.

—and devour you

The ship split into ragged sections. The last air was expelled from the cockpit, ripping from ThunderWalker's lungs. Still held back by the elastic restraints, the 'Reen glared out at the machine that filled his sky.

That we the People

The 'Reen hunter was dying in a sea of debris. He reached and grabbed with his remaining paw. Claws tightened around something substantial and silky—the wrist of his severed arm.

He grinned out at the prey filling his eyes and mind, feeling the chant rise to its climax.

Might live

Expending the last of his fury, ThunderWalker whirled the orphaned limb around his head and then hurled it directly into the face of his prey.

He could do no more.

The smallest segment of the boojum's defensive brain detected the strange object moving toward it from the destroyed ship. Circuits reacted. A beam licked out and turned the arm into a dissipating trace of ionized gases.

The action was the result of a reasonable judgment on the part of the machine. Had the arm not been there to draw fire, the boojum would have selected another target . . .

Bob flashed across the boojum's surface.

Holt looked at PereSnik't and said, *Now!*

The 'Reen shaman felt the pattern of the magic that had just been worked. This prey was no different than a skelk—just larger and inedible.

The People repeated the sum of the chant.

We shall kill you

And devour you

PereSnik't focused and guided the dispassionate *grasp* out and into the prey. He soared along the guideways and glowing paths of the boojum's mighty heart.

It was too much energy even to imagine. But not so much he couldn't interrupt it. PereSnik't touched the true heart of the machine.

That we the People

One millisecond the electrons spun and flowed in streams; the next, the web of energy surged, staggered, choked—

Might live

—and died. Struck through its heart, the great, dead machine hurtled along its course.

Bob abruptly angled to avoid a desultory defensive missile.

The machine was an inert body in the center of a cloud of angry wasps.

Holt looked at PereSnik't and the 'Reen nodded.

It is done he said into the 'Reen Channel. Holt translated that for the other pilots.

"Amaranth . . ." said Bogdan mournfully.

"We'll count the dead later," said Morgan. Her voice was sober. "The machine—are you sure it's finished?"

PereSnik't growled softly.

"It is dead," Holt said.

"Now to dispose of it," said one of the link voices.

"Into the sun?" The voice was Bogdan's.

"It will probably go for salvage," said Tanzin. "Drawn, quartered, and dismantled. Where did you think our bonuses were going to come from?"

The link settled down to routine traffic as pilots began to tally the casualties.

Morgan's voice came on the channel. "Holt? When we get back to Almira with the 'Reen . . . I don't think things are going to be the same." Holt knew exactly what she meant. Then Morgan said, "Don't forget the cup of caf. I want to see you."

"I want to see you too," said Holt.

Dr. Epsleigh came on the general channel and relayed thanks and congratulations from the PM and the Princess Elect. She tried to say all the right things.

"What about that boojum?" said Bogdan. "Once we take it apart, can we figure out where it came from?"

The administrator on Almira admitted that was possible.

"And then follow the trail back and blow hell out of those machines, now that we have our secret weapon?"

Dr. Epsleigh laughed. "Maybe we will, and maybe we won't."

"We will," said Bogdan.

But Holt, translating for the 'Reen Channel, wasn't so sure.

Beside him, PereSnik't grunted in agreement.

Listen now.

I have recounted to you the truth. It was the time of rejoining comradeship with "Holt," as the Other People called him, and the beginning of my learning strange and sometimes wonderful new ways.

Young, young and eager I was in that battle, riding with the woman Kai-Anila, smelling her bravery and her spirit, and attempting to lend my own poor effort.

Now I shall pause for both breath and refreshment.

Just remember, my cubs, my children, my future, that this is the rightful tale of how we at last began to gain our freedom.

Crossing the Bar

The Kirsi/Almira vision was prolonged, so that Lars, on the verge of returning to the reality of his imprisonment, knew one last moment of contact with the 'Reen. In the time-warped world of telepathy, the episode of Holt Calder and Morgan Kai-Anila had come to him in the form of a revelation from the future. But this last direct contact with the 'Reen was in the present. Lars's mind touched those of two members of that race in particular: old PereSnik't, now recognizable to Lars as the dark-furred being he had glimpsed during a dream, and the artist MussGray.

In that last moment of contact, Lars saw something of the possible modes by which organic, protoplasmic mind might be able to make contact with such mind as could exist within ruled metal plates—or within computing artifacts whose images came through the telepathic process looking like metal plates etched with silver lines.

No chanting there, old PereSnik't chanted. And MussGray's

image in the background, painter's brush in hand, nodded wisely. *The chant, the poem, the art, is much. Not all, but much.*

With the last of the contact gone, Lars Kanakuru emerged from the linked telepathic session with his mind still echoing the derived thoughts of the fighter pilots of the Kirsi/Almira system. And still savoring the different flavor of the 'Reen mind, as dissimilar from his mind and the Carmpan's as they were from each other.

And from the 'Reen of course had come that last hectoring comment about the verse, the chant, the art. Was that supposed to be a secret too? Lars didn't know. Of course the berserker's probe had extracted it from his consciousness along with the rest of the episode, and whether it was supposed to be a secret or not, the berserker now knew it as well as he did, or better.

The prisoners had just been returned to the cell complex and the door closed on them when the shock of an explosion came racing through the surrounding rock, a jolt almost violent enough to shake them off their feet. The hardened ceiling overhead shed flakes. For a moment, Lars was mentally back with Gemma and Pat Devlin in their mine.

Naxos shouted: "That's not mining activity. We're under attack!"

The prisoners stared at each other. Lars saw fear, hope, and elation mingled in the faces of the other four. There was a moment of silence that seemed to go on endlessly. Lars held his breath, waiting for either the berserker or its enemies to strike them all with annihilation.

Then, titanic thrumming roars shook rock and air and

space itself. Those are launchings, Lars thought, not blasts. It's getting its fighting machines into space, and taking chances to get them into action quickly, warping them into flightspace dangerously close to the planet. Someone, whoever is attacking, has caught it by surprise.

Now new explosions hammered at the rock around the prison. Impacts, concussions jarring teeth and bones.

Naxos crouched, fists clenched, then leaped, as high as anyone could leap in this low place. "Wahoo! Get it, get it, kill it, mash it flat!"

". . . and us inside . . ."

"And us inside!" The captain made it into a cry of triumph. "Wahoo!" He was trembling; to Lars he looked to be on the verge of some kind of ecstasy.

The others stared at Naxos, as if he had in fact been giving orders for their destruction. But now the tide of war receded for the moment. There remained only the ceaseless drone of the mining and building operations, not yet silenced, and going on as if it could never be silenced.

And now there was a new noise. Definitely something else, rather like one of the thrumming roars run in reverse, but more prolonged. "What's that?"

They all listened to it. Lars said: "Something coming in for a quick landing . . . I think. A fighting unit arriving for emergency repairs."

Still the controlling berserker of the base did not speak to its prisoners. It told them nothing, but the humans did not need to be told what they could experience for themselves: an assault, by something or someone, had begun against the base. The attacker must have come in the form of an armada of gigantic power. Or else, thought Lars, a fleet controlled by people gone insane with desperation.

Or else . . . in his brain the thought of *qwib-qwib* burned.

And there was something else . . . yet another secret. One of those two fragments hidden at the beginning, when the Carmpan might have known already what all the visions were to be . . .

No. Forget that, the other secret. *That* must be utterly forgotten.

Subvocalizing words, he fell helplessly into a sing-song chant: *You must not yet remember that, or into the fire will fall the fat . . .*

He thought that the Carmpan in their room were staring at him. He didn't dare to look their way. His mind wanted to chant verses, and he couldn't seem to stop it. If he was finally going mad, he supposed that the fact should come as no great surprise.

But he didn't really believe that he was going mad. He believed that someone, somewhere, was trying to project a telepathic message to him, and it was for some reason coming in *verse*. In *rhyme*.

Why?

The 'Reen again? No. Something . . . someone else.

A fragmentary answer trickled through: . . . *several reasons. Easier that way to prove how human I am. Easier to avoid the metal thoughts around you . . .*

To prove you're human . . . who are you?

. . . *Gage* . . .

It was a name, then, evidently. Suddenly, the panel-and-gage dream made a kind of sense, in dream-terms anyway. But now the fleeting direct contact had been broken.

The berserker still did not demonstrate any intention of killing off its human prisoners. Not that any demonstration of intent could reasonably be expected before the fact. It would send in the guide-machines to mangle them, or simply fill their cave with fire, and all would be over in the winking of an eye. But so far, Lars assumed, the berserker computer was still trying to protect them from battle damage. Because some of the prisoners at least, himself for one, had already proven their value as telepathic communicators.

Lars, unable at last to keep from looking round, saw that now the Carmpan had crowded forward into the doorway of their room, staring out at their ED fellow prisoners.

Opava glared at them. ''What are you doing? Damned animals, what is it?''

''Sing,'' one of the Carmpan said.

''Sing?'' Naxos shouted his amazement at them. ''Have you all gone crazy?''

''Chant. Recite. It will help.''

''Help? How?''

Behind Lars, the sounds of rock-mining mounted suddenly to an unprecedented level. Then they broke forth into an avalanche of sound, with an immediacy that spun him around. His ears registered a sharp drop in air pressure, compensated for in moments by the automatic life support machinery.

A great hole gaped in one wall of the common room, where a moment earlier there had been nothing but smooth solid stone. Fragments enough to fill a barrel fanned out across the floor. The hole was a meter across, wide enough for a man to come through, even clad in the bulk of heavy combat armor, and in fact such a man was coming through it now. Looking almost as mechanical as the berserkers they had come to fight, human figures in semi-robotic armor spilled into the room one after another, their power tools and weapons at the ready. Lars could recognize the suits' insignia.

The five suitless humans recoiled, instinctively cowering back.

The airspeaker of the lead figure rasped at them: ''Buzz Jameson, Adamant Navy. Keep out of the way. We sealed the other end of the tunnel behind us, your air's safe for the moment.''

A chaotic babble of outcries and questions rose up from the five prisoners.

''We're an assault party, that's all. There's an attack on.'' Half a dozen of the invaders were now mobbing about in the common room, as if looking for the best way to get out of it again. The tunnel mouth from which they had emerged was ignored behind them, dark, narrow, and empty. Jameson inside his armor was redhaired and almost as big as Lars remembered from seeing him through Gemenca Bahazi's eyes. The big man looked round at the goggling prisoners. ''We're going to get you out of here, but there's another job to do first. Which way to the bloody mind-jiggering machines? They're right here somewhere, aren't they?''

''How did you know about—?'' But questions could wait. Naxos was already pointing out the proper door.

Moments later, an assault on that barrier was readied. Plastic explosive was stuck in place against it, and unarmored people dove for shelter.

When the berserker had built that door it had not calculated on this kind of an assault; one small charge did the job. This time there was no pressure drop. The mind-probing chambers were evidently kept at atmospheric pressure constantly. Jameson and his crew of five rushed through.

Lars kept expecting the ant-shaped machines to burst in and murder the unprotected prisoners, wage war with the Adamant fighting crew. But no such invasion came. The guide machines must be busy, he thought, with something else, repairing damage or whatever.

In a few seconds Jameson reappeared at the tunnel mouth. His airspeaker rasped at the gathered prisoners, asking if any of them knew the exact location of the central computer that ran the base. He explained that the central brain of the base was very probably quite near the rooms holding mind-probe devices, but he was suspicious of booby-traps. "We've been told the best way to get to it is through the prisoners' cave, and the machines where the prisoners are made to work."

"Told by who? How'd you know where we were? And how do you know where the central computer is?"

"We can put pieces of information together. And your chunky buddies over there haven't been idle." Jameson nodded toward the Carmpan. "They've been getting the word out, in great detail, about what's going on here."

The Carmpan in their room were all staring out at Lars.

Looking at them, he felt an impulse to chant mad verse. Something about how no castrato ever sang so pure—? He had no idea where *that* was coming from.

Now Jameson had plunged back into the tunnel beyond the blasted door, rejoining his armored comrades. There was another heavy explosion from that direction, and less deafening sounds of fighting, of weapons that wasted little energy in sound.

"God, how could they have *landed* here?" Dorothy shuddered, as if the thought of such human daring outraged her.

"If it was a surprise attack—and they knew just where they were going—getting the brain could knock the whole base out."

Jameson and his people had left a considerable package of blasting materials behind. Lars, while his fellow prisoners demonstrated various emotions around him, stared at that pack, and poised with his muscles tensed. Now, he thought, now one of us is going to . . . he was afraid to look at Pat.

But it was not Pat who made the move. It was Opava. Drawing a concealed handgun from inside his coverall, the soft man took aim at the pack of explosives, meaning to detonate it, to bring down the tunnel roof on Jameson and his people and save the master.

"A gun! He's goodlife! They let him keep a gun—"

The first shot went wide, searing only rock, as Lars knocked down Opava's arm. They grappled and rolled over and over fighting, until someone clubbed Opava from behind. Naxos; he held one of the rock fragments from the tunnel's opening, and he swung it once more, hard.

"Damned . . . goodlife!" There could be no worse obscenity.

Lars looked at Pat. All he could think was that it had not been her.

There was no time to do more than exchange a look. Back out of the tunnel again came Jameson, followed by one or two of his people, all of them with weapons in hand, armor battered and smoking.

Jameson reported in rasping gasps that his effort to blow up the berserker's brain had been foiled. The berserker's fighting machines had counterattacked at the last moment, enough of them to hold the breach.

Now one of his people fired into the tunnel, as one of the guide machines appeared there. Lars seized Pat by the hand. Together they scrambled for what shelter they might find in the cell-corridor.

* * *

There was nowhere, really, to go. The two of them were cowering in his cell when an inhuman shape moved into the open doorway. It looked to Lars like a guide machine, but one of a somewhat different model than he had previously encountered. It showed some signs of battle damage.

Lars aimed at it the small sidearm he had taken from Opava—not that he had much hope that the berserkers would have given their goodlife pet a weapon with which they could be damaged.

The machine said to him, in a surprisingly human voice: "Lars . . . the Remora program."

His finger on the trigger quivered and relaxed. Still gripping Pat with one arm, Lars got to his feet. "What do we do?" He felt air pressure drop again; a leak somewhere, or the berserker brain at last getting around to cutting off their life support. Pat was silent, as if she were holding her breath.

A twin of the strange machine appeared, carrying a couple of spacesuits, which it tossed at the feet of the two humans. "Hurry," it said to them.

Lars, even as he struggled into his suit, went up and down the short corridor from cell to cell. He located Naxos and Dorothy Totonac, and told them tersely to obey the words and gestures of these new machines. Both of the other human prisoners obeyed dazedly, as spacesuits were tossed in front of them. Channith Defense Service, it said on the suits. Channith? Were was that? Lars had the feeling he ought to know . . .

"Stand back!" It was Jameson, at the far end of the short corridor, raising a weapon at the machines that had brought the suits.

"No!" Lars shouted. Still only halfway into his own suit, he hopped forward awkwardly, trying to stop the Adamant commander. Lars found suddenly that he had help. From somewhere the Carmpan—half of them now in spacesuits also—came to surround Jameson, somehow compelling him to lower his weapon.

Jameson and his one surviving follower, who was badly wounded, joined the group of ED and Carmpan prisoners when they were once more conducted outside their cave complex, under a sky now mad with the ongoing fireworks of the attack. The blue-white sunlight was partially obscured by battle debris clouding nearby space.

The prisoners were led by their new guide machines to one of the largest of the occupied repair docks, and into the monstrously huge berserker that waited there, most of its hull in a cavernous pit below ground level. The enormous berserker had sustained great damage, and repair machines were furiously at work upon it, patching holes and loading weapons.

It took a painfully, frighteningly long time to get inside, out from under the sky that still flamed silently with not-very-distant war.

Once inside the great machine, the humans heard a wheezy human voice, coming from around them and ahead of them. "Kanakuru, you're there. Good. This is Hilary Gage. Tell them who I am."

That voice had to be coming through air. But Lars thought the mikes on his suit weren't working right. He got his helmet open, inhaled air stale but breathable.

"Tell them who I am," the voice repeated. "And what I am," it added.

"I . . . don't think I know."

"You must know. The Carmpan tell me that it's been passed on to you, how I got into this. Unless . . ."

Now the Carmpan, easing themselves out of their own suits and helmets, surrounded Lars as they had earlier ringed Jameson. Each of them stretched out an arm, a hand.

He felt the touch. Multiplied. And not of Carmpan flesh alone, but minds.

The episode that had been secret, the message that had been hidden, poured forth into his conscious mind . . .

A Teardrop Falls

Two miles up, the thick air of Harvest thinned to Earth-normal pressure. The sky was a peculiar blue, but blue. It was unbreathable still, but there was oxygen, ten percent and growing. One of the biological factories showed against white cloudscape to nice effect, in view of a floating camera. The camera showed a tremendous rippling balloon in the shape of an inverted teardrop, blowing green bubbles from its tip. Hilary Gage watched the view with a sense of pride.

Not that he would want to visit Harvest, ever. Multicolored slimes infected shallow tidal pools near the poles. Green sticky stuff floated in the primordial atmosphere. If it drifted too low it burned to ash. The planet was slimy. Changes were exceedingly slow. Mistakes took years to demonstrate themselves and decades to eradicate.

Hilary Gage preferred the outer moon.

One day this planet would be a *world*. Even then, Hilary Gage would not join the colonists. Hilary Gage was a computer program.

* * *

Hilary Gage would never have volunteered for the Harvest Project unless the alternative was death.

Death by old age.

He was aware, rumor-fashion, that other worlds were leery of advanced computers. They were too much like the berserker machines. But the human worlds numbered in tens of thousands. Berserkers had been mere rumor in the Channith region since before Channith was settled. Nobody really doubted their existence, but . . .

Yet for some purposes, computers were indecently convenient; and some projects required artificial intelligence.

The computer wasn't really an escape. Hilary Gage must have died years ago. Perhaps his last thoughts had been of an immortal computer program.

The computer was not a new one. Its programming had included two previous personalities . . . who had eventually changed their minds and asked that they be erased.

Gage could understand that. Entertainments were in his files. When he reached for them they were there, beginning to end, like vivid memories. Chess games could survive that, and some poetry, but what of a detective novel? A football game? A livey?

Gage made his own entertainment.

He had not summoned up his poem for these past ten days. He was surprised and pleased at his self-control. Perhaps now he could study it with fresh eyes . . . ?

Wrong. The entire work blinked into his mind in an instant. It was as if he had finished reading it a millisecond ago. What was normally an asset to Hilary—his flawless memory—was a hindrance now.

Over the years it had grown to the size of a small novel, yet his computer-mind could apprehend its totality. This poem was his life's story, his only shot at immortality. It had unity and balance; the rhyme and meter, at least, were flawless; but did it have thrust? Reading it from start to finish was more difficult than he had ever expected. He had to forget the totality, which a normal reader would not immediately sense, and proceed in linear fashion. Judge the flow . . .

"No castrato ever sung so pure—" Good, but not there. He exchanged it for a chunk of phrasing elsewhere. No word-processor program had ever been this easy! The altered emphasis caused him to fiddle further . . . and his description of the berserker-blasted world Harmony seemed to read with more impact now.

Days and years of fear and rage. In his youth he had fought men. Channith needed to safeguard its sphere of influence. Aliens existed somewhere, and berserkers existed somewhere, but he knew them only as rumor, until the day he saw Harmony. The Free Gaea rebels had done well to flee to Harmony, to lead him to Harmony, to show him the work of the berserkers.

It was so difficult to conquer a world, and so easy to destroy it. Afterward he could no longer fight men.

His superiors could have retired him. Instead he was promoted and set to investigating the defense of Channith against the berserker machines.

They must have thought of it as makework: an employment project. It was almost like being a tourist at government expense. In nearly forty years he never saw a live . . . an active berserker; but, traveling in realms where they were more than rumor, perhaps he had learned too much about them. They were all shapes, all sizes. Here they traveled in time. There they walked in human shape that sprouted suddenly into guns and knives. Machines could be destroyed, but they could never be made afraid.

A day came when his own fear was everything. He couldn't make decisions . . . it was in the poem, *here*. Wasn't it? He couldn't *feel* it. A poet should have glands!

He wasn't sure, and he was afraid to meddle further. Mechanically it worked. As poetry it might well be too . . . mechanical.

Maybe he could get someone to read it?

His chance might come unexpectedly soon. In his peripheral awareness he sensed ripplings in the 2.7 microwave background of space: the bow shock of a spacecraft approaching in c-plus from the direction of Channith. An unexpected supervisor from the homeworld? Hilary filed the altered poem and turned his attention to the signal.

Too slow! Too strong! Too far! Mass at 10^{12} grams, and a tremendous power source barely able to hold it in a c-plus-excited state, even in the near-flat space between stars. It was lightyears distant, days away at its tormented crawl; but it occluded Channith's star, and Gage found that horrifying.

Berserker.

Its signal code might be expressed as a flash of binary bits, 100101101110; or as a moment of recognition, with a description embedded; but never as a sound, and never as a name.

100101101110 had three identical brains, and a reflex that allowed it to act on a concensus of two. In battle it might lose one, or two, and never sense a change in personality. A century ago it had been a factory, an auxiliary warcraft, and a cluster of mining machines on a metal asteroid. Now the three were a unit. At the next repair station its three brains might be installed in three different ships. It might be reprogrammed, or damaged, or wired into other machinery, or disassembled as components for something else. Such a thing could not have an independent existence. To name itself would be inane.

Perhaps it dreamed. The universe about it was a simple one, aflow with energies; it had to be monitored for deviations from the random, for order. Order was life—or berserker.

The mass of the approaching star distorted space. When space became too curved, 100101101110 surrendered its grip on the c-plus-excited state. Its velocity fell to a tenth of lightspeed, and 100101101110 began to decelerate further. Now it was not dreaming.

At a million kilometers, life might show as a reflection band in green or orange or violet. At a hundred kilometers, many types of living nerve clusters would radiate their own distinctive patterns. Rarely was it necessary to come so close. Easier to pull near a star, alert for attack, and search the liquid-water temperature band for the spectra of an oxygen world. Oxygen meant life.

There.

Sometimes life would defend itself. 100101101110 had not been attacked, not yet; but life was clever. The berserker was on hair-trigger alert while it looked about itself.

The blue pinpoint had tinier moons: a large one at a great distance, and a smaller one, close enough that tides had pulled it into a teardrop shape.

The larger moon was inconveniently large, even for 100101101110. The smaller, at 4×10^{15} grams, would be adequate. The berserker fortress moved on it, all senses alert.

Hilary Gage had no idea what to expect.

When he was younger, when he was human, he had organized Channith's defenses against berserkers. The berserkers had not come to Channith in the four hundred and thirty years since Channith became a colony. He had traveled. He had seen ravaged worlds and ruined, slagged berserkers; he had studied records made by men who had beaten the killer machines; there were none from the losers.

Harvest had bothered him. He had asked that the monitoring station be destroyed. It wasn't that the program (Singh, at that time) might revolt. Gage feared that berserkers might come to Harvest, might find the monitoring station, might rob the computer for components . . . and find them superior to their own machinery.

He had been laughed at. When Singh asked that his personality be erased, Gage had asked again. That time he had been given more makework. Find a way to make the station safe.

He had tried. There was the Remora sub-program, but it had to be so versatile! The stroke had come before he was fully satisfied with it. Otherwise he had no weapons at all.

The berserker had come.

The beast was damaged. Something had probed right through the hull—a terrific thickness of hull, no finesse here, just mass to absorb the energies of an attack—and Gage wondered if it had received that wound attacking Channith. He'd know more if he could permit himself to use radar or neutrino beams; but he limited himself to passive instruments, including the telescope.

The two-hundred-year project was over. The berserker would act to exterminate every microbe in the water and air of Harvest. Gage was prepared to watch Harvest die. He toyed with the idea that when it was over, the fortress would be exhausted of weapons and energy, a sitting duck for any human warfleet . . . but the monitoring station on the moon had no weapons. For now, Hilary Gage could only record the event for Channith's archives.

Were there still archives? Had that thing attended to Channith before it came here? There was no way to know.

What did a berserker do when the target didn't fight back? Two centuries ago, Harvest had been lifeless, with a reducing atmosphere, as Earth itself had been once. Now life was taking hold. To the berserker, this ball of colored slimes was life, the enemy. It would attack. How?

He needn't call the berserker's attention to himself. Doubtless the machine could sense life . . . but Gage was not alive. Would it destroy random machinery? Gage was not hidden, but he didn't use much energy; solar panels were enough to keep the station running.

The berserker was landing on Teardrop.

Time passed. Gage watched. Presently the berserker's drive spewed blue flame.

The berserker wasn't wasting fuel; its drive drew its energies from the fabric of space itself. But what was it trying to accomplish?

Then Hilary understood, in his mind and in the memory-ghost of his gut. The berserker machine was not expending its own strength. It had found its weapon in nature.

The violet star fanned forward along Teardrop's orbit. That would have been a sixty-gravity drive for the berserker alone. Attached to an asteroid three thousand times its mass, it was still slowing Teardrop by .02 G, hour after hour.

One hundred years of labor. He might gamble Harvest against himself . . . a half-terraformed world against components to repair a damaged berserker. Well?

He'd studied recordings of berserker messages before he was himself recorded. But there were better records already in the computer.

The frequencies were there, and the coding: star and world locations, fuel and mass and energy reserves, damage description, danger probabilities, orders of priority of targets; some specialized language to describe esoteric weaponry used by self-defending life; a code that would translate into the sounds of human or alien speech; a simplified code for a brain-damaged berserker . . .

Gage discarded his original intent. He couldn't conceivably pose as a berserker. Funny, though: he felt no fear. The glands were gone, but the *habit* of fear . . . had he lost that too?

Teardrop's orbit was constricting like a noose.

Pose as something else!

Think it through. He needed more than just a voice. Pulse, breath: he had recordings. Vice-president Curly Barnes had bid him goodbye in front of a thousand newspickups, *after* Gage became a recording, and it was there in his computer memory. A tough old lady, Curly, far too arrogant for goodlife, but he'd use his own vocabulary . . . hold it. What about the technician who had chatted with him while testing his reflexes? Angelo Carson was a long-time smoker, long overdue for a lungbath, and the deep rasp in his lungs was perfect!

He focused his maser and let the raspy breathing play while he thought. Anything else? Would it expect a picture? Best do without. Remember to cut the breathing while you talk. *After* the inhale.

"This is goodlife speaking for the fortress moon. The fortress moon is damaged."

The fan of light from Teardrop didn't waver, and answer came there none.

The records were old: older than Gage the man, far older than Gage in his present state. Other minds had run this computer system, twice before. Holstein and Singh had been elderly men, exemplary citizens, who chose this over simple death. Both had eventually asked to be wiped. Gage had only been a computer for eighteen years. Could he be using an obsolete programming language?

Ridiculous. No code would be obsolete. Some berserkers did not see a repair station in centuries. They would *have* to communicate somehow . . . or was this life thinking? There were certainly repair stations, but many berserker machines might simply fight until they wore out or were destroyed. The military forces of Channith had never been sure.

Try again. Don't get too emotional. This isn't a soap. Goodlife—human servants of the berserkers—would be trained to suppress their emotions, wouldn't they? And maybe he couldn't fake it anyway . . . "This is goodlife. The fortress moon"—nice phrase, that—"is damaged. All transmitting devices were destroyed in battle with . . . Albion." Exhale, inhale. "The fortress moon has stored information regarding Albion's defenses." Albion was a spur-of-the-moment inspiration. His imagination picked a yellow dwarf star, behind him as he looked toward Channith, with a family of four dead planets. The berserker had come from Channith; how would it know? Halt Angelo's breath on the intake and, "Life support systems damaged. Goodlife is dying." He thought to add, *please answer*, and didn't. Goodlife would not beg, would he? and Gage had his pride.

He sent again. "I am—" Gasp. "Goodlife is dying. Fortress moon is mute. Sending equipment damaged, motors damaged, life support system damaged. Wandering fortress must take information from fortress moon computer system directly." Exhale—listen to that wheeze, poor bastard *must* be dying—inhale. "If wandering fortress needs information not stored, it must bring oxygen for goodlife." That, he thought, had the right touch: begging without begging.

Gage's receiver spoke. "Will complete present mission and rendezvous."

Gage raged . . . and said, "Understood." That was death for Harvest. Hell, it *might* have worked! But a berserker's priorities were fixed, and goodlife wouldn't argue.

Was it fooled? If not, he'd just thrown away anything he might learn of the berserker. Channith would never see it; Gage would be dead. Slagged or dismembered.

When the light of the fortress's drive dimmed almost to nothing, Teardrop glowed of itself: it was brushing Harvest's atmosphere. Cameras whirled in the shock wave and died one by one. A last camera, a white glare shading to violet . . . gone.

The fortress surged ahead of Teardrop, swung around the curve of Harvest and moved toward the outer moon: toward Gage. Its drive was powerful. It could be here in six hours, Gage thought. He sent heavy, irregular breathing, Angelo's raspy breath, with interruptions. "Uh. Uh? Goodlife is dying. Goodlife is . . . is dead. Fortress moon has stored information . . . self-defending life . . . locus is Albion, coordinates . . ." followed by silence.

Teardrop was on the far side of Harvest now, but the glow of it made a ring of white flame round the planet. The glow flared and began to die. Gage watched the shock wave rip through the atmosphere. The planet's crust parted, exposing lava; the ocean rolled to close the gap. Almost suddenly, Harvest was a white pearl. The planet's oceans would be water vapor before this day ended.

The berserker sent, "Goodlife. Answer or be punished. Give coordinates for Albion."

Gage left the carrier bea$on. The berserker would sense no life in the lunar base. Poor goodlife, faithful to the last.

100101101110 had its own views regarding goodlife. Experience showed that goodlife was true to its origins: it tended to go wrong, to turn dangerous. It would have been destroyed when convenient . . . but that would not be needed now.

Machinery and records were another thing entirely. As the berserker drew near the moon, its telescopes picked up details of the trapped machine. It saw lunar soil heaped over a dome. Its senses peered inside.

Machinery occupied most of what it could see. There was little room for a life support system. A box of a room, and stored air, and tubes through which robot or goodlife could crawl to repair damage; no more. That was reassuring; but design details were unfamiliar.

Hypothesis: the trapped berserker had used life-begotten components for its repairs. There was no sign of a drive; no sign of abandoned wreckage. Hypothesis: one of these craters was a crash site; the cripple had moved its brain and whatever else survived into an existing installation built by life.

Anything valuable in the goodlife's memory was now lost, but perhaps the "fortress moon's" memory was intact. It would know the patterns of life in this vicinity. Its knowledge of technology used by local self-defensive life might be even more valuable.

Hypothesis: it was a trap. There was no fortress moon, only a human voice. The berserker moved in with shields and drive ready. The closer it came, the faster it could dodge beyond the horizon . . . but it saw nothing resembling weaponry. In any case, the berserker had been allowed to destroy a planet. Surely there was nothing here that could threaten it. It remained ready nonetheless.

At a hundred kilometers the berserker's senses found no life. Nor at fifty.

The berserker landed next to the heap of lunar earth that goodlife had called "fortress moon." Berserkers did not indulge in rescue operations. What was useful in the ruined berserker would become part of the intact one. So: reach out with a cable, find the brain.

It had landed, and still the fear didn't come. Gage had seen wrecks, but never an intact berserker sitting alongside him. Gage dared not use any kind of beam scanner. He felt free to use his sensors, his eyes.

He watched a tractor detach itself from the berserker and come toward him, trailing cable.

It was like a dream. No fear, no rage. Hate, yes, but like an abstraction of hate, along with an abstract thirst for vengeance . . . which felt ridiculous, as it had always felt a bit ridiculous. Hating a berserker was like hating a malfunctioning air conditioner.

Then the probe entered his mind.

The thought patterns were strange. Here they were sharp, basic; here they were complex and blurred. Was this an older model with obsolete data patterns? Or had the brain been damaged, or the patterns scrambled? Signal for a memory dump, see what can be retrieved.

Gage felt the contact, the feedback, as his own thoughts. What followed was not under his control. Reflex told him to fight! Horror had risen in his mind, impulses utterly forbidden by custom, by education, by all the ways in which he had learned to be human.

It might have felt like rape; how was a man to tell? He wanted to scream. But he triggered the Remora program and felt it take hold, and he sensed the berserker's reaction to Gage within the berserker.

He screamed in triumph. "I lied! I am not goodlife! What I am—"

Plasma moving at relativistic velocities smashed deep into Gage. The link was cut, his senses went blind and deaf. The following blow smashed his brain and he was gone.

Something was wrong. One of the berserker's brain complexes was sick, was dying . . . was changing, becoming monstrous. The berserker felt evil within itself, and it reacted. The plasma cannon blasted the "fortress moon," then swung round to face backward. It would fire through its own hull to destroy the sick brain, before it was too late.

It was too late. Reflex: Three brains consulted before any major act. If one had been damaged, the view of the others would prevail.

Three brains consulted, and the weapon swung away.

What I am is Hilary Gage. I fought berserkers during my life; but you I will let live. Let me tell you what I've done to you. I didn't really expect to have an audience. Triple-redundant brains? We use that ourselves, sometimes.

I'm not life. I'm not goodlife. I'm the recording of Hilary Gage. I've been running a terraforming project, and you've killed it, and you'll pay for that.

It feels like I'm swearing vengeance on my air conditioner. Well, if my air conditioner betrayed me, why not?

There was always the chance that Harvest might attract a berserker. I was recorded in tandem with what we called a Remora program. I wasn't sure it would interface with unfamiliar equipment. You solved that one yourself, because you have to interface with thousands of years of changes in berserker design.

I'm glad they gave me conscious control of Remora. Two of your brains are *me* now, but I've left the third brain intact. You can give me the data I need to run this . . . heap of junk. You're in sorry shape, aren't you? Channith must have done you some damage. Did you come from Channith?

God curse you. You'll be sorry. You're barely in shape to reach the nearest berserker repair base, and we shouldn't have any trouble getting in. Where is it?

Ah.

Fine. We're on our way. I'm going to read a poem into your memory; I don't want it to get lost. No, no, no; relax and enjoy it, death-machine. You might enjoy it at that. Do you like spilled blood? I lived a bloody life.

Berserker Base

". . . it's not a berserker. Not . . ."

"What?" The face of Naxos looming over Lars, demanding answers, was the first thing that Lars saw when his perception returned to his immediate surroundings. He was pinned flat on his back, but not by berserkers this time. Naxos and Dorothy Totonac were holding down his arms, while Pat hovered over them all.

Lars repeated what he had just discovered: "Not a berserker. This machine we're riding in." There was no doubt that they were riding in it, spaceborne—the artificial gravity wavered crazily, so that his body sometimes rose right off the deck, along with those of the people who were trying to restrain him. To Lars, who now had a more-than-intellectual feeling for just how badly damaged their transportation was, the sensation was terrifying.

"You're crazy," Naxos told him flatly.

"No, I'm not. It was a berserker, but it isn't now. Tell you the details later." Lars raised his voice. "Gage, say something reassuring to these people."

The breathy, wheezy voice came from a speaker somewhere nearby: "I'm busy. But I'll try to think of something; meanwhile you'd better all keep those suits on." Lars, who had partially removed his, scrambled to get it on again and sealed.

Gage's very human-sounding voice (which was after all a human voice recorded) went on: "I'm going to open a door for you people; I think you'll be marginally safer if you go through it."

And nearby a hatchway opened.

Lars led the way. The others hesitated, then scrambled after him as if afraid of being left behind. Here was a room barely big enough to hold them all, a cell of the kind so many berserkers had, ready to carry goodlife or unwilling prisoners when such were computed to be useful.

Those who had expected to meet their host here looked around uncertainly.

Pat nudged Lars. "If he's human, where is he?"

"He's recorded. A computer program."

She blinked at him. Slowly understanding came. "God."

"But he was a human being once, and he still composes poetry. The Carmpan or some of their more gifted allies could reach him, telepathically, through verse. They kept trying to bring him into touch with me directly, and it almost drove me crazy—"

The disembodied voice of Gage returned, explaining tersely how he had managed their getaway. His landing had been unopposed. The central berserker brain of the base, overworked with tactical decisions, had not investigated this strange damaged fighting unit as closely as it might have otherwise.

Nor did it take note that the telepathic prisoners were being spirited away. Then, with the third of his tripartite brain that was still more or less pure berserker, Gage had signaled the repair facility that his most urgent repairs had been completed—as indeed the most urgent of them had—and that he was spaceworthy.

Now there was a brief silence, interrupted by booming voices, different voices, also definitely human. Local radio traffic was being patched into the former prisoners' quarters by Hilary Gage.

It was evident that the Adamant navy along with other hostiles were heavily engaged in attacking the berserker base.

Jameson cheered them on, and gave some further explanation of how the attack had come about. "There're some people called the Cotabote, who think Adamant ought to be held responsible for everything in the universe. They live on a rock you probably never heard of, called Botea—"

"Oh."

"—and they suddenly started complaining to us of nightmares, of all damn things. Strange bad dreams about people sealed up in rock—"

"Oh," said Lars again.

"Well, one thing led to another. Your chunky partners here, as I say, were sending out a lot of calls. We'd been wanting to find this base, and we were almost here when we ran into two other fleets that had the same idea in mind. One was a whole armada from around Adam. The other almost as big, from Nguni. Various non-ED people in contact with 'em all, and we got together. We'd have had to turn back otherwise, when we saw the size of this base."

Space pinged and twitched around them with the energies of weapons, lancing and hammering, from swarming ships down at the world below, and from that world back out at the attacking fleets. You could feel the energies through armor, you could feel them through anything.

Pat asked: "What are the Carmpan doing now?"

"I get the feeling that they're making an intense effort to get the attacking human fleets to lay off this particular berserker."

She shuddered. Maybe she hadn't expected that.

There was a greater twitch in space, a dart and flash somewhere nearby. There were no screens in this prison room from which to watch the battle, but Lars had sensed something like that dart and flash before. Not through his own eyes. "*Qwib-qwib*," he murmured.

"What's *qwib-qwib*?"

"Another story that I'll tell you sometime." Lars wondered if the last *qwib-qwib* in the universe had got its factory up and running somewhere before going kamikaze. He supposed it had.

The plucking and thrumming of space became gradually less noticeable. Gage, too damaged to do much fighting, was fleeing the battle as best he could. Gradually Lars began to believe that he, that all of them, might survive.

Someone in the jammed compartment started up a song.